本书出版得到岭南师范学院外国语学院“科研提升计划”资助

锡德尼的诗学建构

Sidney's Poetical Construction

陈尚真　著

WUHAN UNIVERSITY PRESS
武汉大学出版社

图书在版编目(CIP)数据

锡德尼的诗学建构:汉、英/陈尚真著.—武汉:武汉大学出版社,2018.6

ISBN 978-7-307-20322-8

Ⅰ.锡…　Ⅱ.陈…　Ⅲ.诗歌研究—英国—中世纪—汉、英

Ⅳ.I561.072

中国版本图书馆CIP数据核字(2018)第142234号

责任编辑:李　玚　　责任校对:汪欣怡　　版式设计:汪冰滢

出版发行:**武汉大学出版社**　(430072　武昌　珞珈山)

(电子邮件:cbs22@whu.edu.cn 网址:www.wdp.com.cn)

印刷:北京虎彩文化传播有限公司

开本:720×1000　1/16　印张:16.75　字数:231千字　插页:2

版次:2018年6月第1版　2018年6月第1次印刷

ISBN 978-7-307-20322-8　定价:48.00元

献给恩师区铁先生

Preface

This book is my dissertation completed in 2007, a naive try of a PhD candidate who had just received elementarily the academic training. Ten years have passed though, the writing always reminds me of the happy time I spent on the Kang Le Yuan campus of Sun Yat-sen University. I decide to keep this immature form of my writing when I have it published to cherish the memory of the prime of my academic life.

Sidney's anglicization of foreign poetical forms and prosodies, being part of the Elizabethan exploration of the rising lyrics, is an embodiment of his sense of nativeness. The form of poetry, as Sidney observes it, is the way via which the poetic aim realizes. Sidney emphasizes the domination of language over the metre in a line. He explores the poeticality of the English language, drawing poets' attention to the new possibility that the change of language leaves to them in their writing. In seeking the new metre for poetry, Sidney attempts to transplant the Latin quantitative verse into English poetry. His experiments on the English quantitative verse, though not successful, stimulate him to further exploring the musical effects of the quantitative elements in the English pronunciation and the value of the accentual-syllabic verse to the English poetry. Sidney develops the accentual-syllabic verse, establishing two types of the duple-metre lines: the line with rising rhythm, performed mainly by iambus, and the line with falling rhythm, performed mainly by trochees. The latter type is combined with Sidney's revival of the feminine rhyme from the tradition of the Middle English prosody. To make the poetical pattern compatible to language, Sidney adopts some techniques in his design, among which the pause and the substitution are prominent. The pause evolves from the caesura practiced by both the Greco-Roman poets and the vernacular poets of Italian, French and other Roman family, while the substitution might be the creation of the English poets ignited by their apprentice-training on the classical prosody. In weaving lines into a stanza, Sidney employs the rhymes and the enjambment. These techniques in Sidney's poetical construction are generally accepted by his compatriots after his exercise. Sidney has also anglicized many foreign poetical genres, and the influential ones are the elegiacs, the Sapphic stanza, the madrigal-poem and the sonnet.

I would express my deep gratitude to Professor Ou Hong, my supervisor, Mr. J. H. Prynne, my mentor, and Dr. Shen Jie, my trusty friend. Without the insightful guidance of Professor Ou, this book would not have been accomplished. Without the enlightenment on me in the field of Sidney studies by Mr. Prynne and the warm-hearted aids from him, my research would not be based on a sound basis. Without the help of Dr. Shen in improving my writing, this book would be uncultivated.

I thank sincerely Professor Mao Zhuoliang and Professor Yuan Xianjun, my tutors when I was a postgraduate for the degree of M. A., who have set me on the road of academic pilgrimage. Professor Mao has initiated me into Sidney studies. His encouragement had promoted my ten-year preparation for this book.

My special and sweet thanks are due to Guo Lan, my dear wife, and

Chen Jingchang, my beloved son, who always support me with their love.

Now I am very grateful to Wuhan University Press which helps me in publishing this book.

Notes

Ⅰ. The Abbreviations of Sidney's Works Cited in the Book

AS *Astrophil and Stella*

AS 1 Sonnet One from the *Astrophil and Stella*

...

AS i The First Song from the *Astrophil and Stella*

...

CS *Certain Sonnets*

OA *Old Arcadia*

PS *The Psalms of David* (or *Psalms*)

Ⅱ. The Marks Used for Scansion in the Book

|| principal caesura (or pause)

| subordinate caesura (or pause)

/ division between feet

// division between lines

' stressed syllable (stress)

" double stressed syllable (principal stress)

* unstressed syllable

x that the stressed syllable and the unstressed syllable can substitute with each other; or a syllable can be scanned either as the stressed or the unstressed.

- ¯ long syllable
- ˘ short syllable
- \+ that the long syllable and the short syllable can substitute with each other; or a syllable can be scanned either as the long or the short.

Contents

Introduction

Sidney's ideas and practice on poetical form, in essence, are the embodiment of his sense of nativeness. The trace of his literary activities clearly illustrates that transplantation of foreign poetical genres is a progress of anglicization. From 1557 on when he probably had begun the *Old Arcadia* to his death in 1586, Sidney has composed several influential works, including two versions of the *Arcadia*, a group of experimental poems entitled *Certain Sonnets*, a sonnet sequence called *Astrophil and Stella*, an entertainment named *The Lady of May*, some rewritings of *The Psalms of David* (*Psalms*) in verse form, and a critical treatise under the title "The Defence of Poesie" (or "An Apology for Poetry"). ① Many of these works are the first samples of the genres in the English literary history, the new genres of English literature, and the results of Sidney's anglicization of foreign poetical techniques and literary forms. The use of pauses (caesuras), the design of accentual-syllabic verse, the treatment of feminine rhymes and the enjambment in his poems are triumphs of English prosody. The reshaping of the eclogue, the sonnet, and the Sapphic stanza etc., are the victory of English poetical evolution. Sidney naturalizes the foreign poetical forms. This naturalization in his practice is the anglicization, which is guided by his sense of nativeness. He makes all his

---

① Sidney's treatise, when published, was given the title "The Defence of Poesie" by publisher Ponsonby in 1595, and "An Apology for Poetry" by Olney in the same year. The Ponsonby title seems more popular than the Olney one (*Sir Philip Sidney*: *The Major Works* 371).

efforts to improve the new poetry to meet the demand of the development of the English poetry, his native literature.

The fact that Sidney was absorbed in poetical construction might be inspected against the cultural background of the Elizabethan society in the late sixteenth century. The panorama may be illustrated through the following historical events and cultural trends. The distant views are the Great Discovery, the English having defeated the Spanish armada, the religious reform, and the development of science and techniques in the pre-industrial revolution era, which pushed the English nation moving from the margin of Europe to the center, either in economy or in politics. Less distant views are the spread of printing which cultivated the fashion of writers to publish their works, the dissemination of Renaissance which spurred the bloom of European arts and literature of that time, and the rise of vernaculars which promoted the emergence and rapid growth of modern European nations and their cultures. But the nearer views are the contrast—the English felt dwarfed when facing the brilliant achievements of the Italian and French people in their native cultures. Therefore, the views in front of the reader are the busy learning of the English elites from the European continental countries. In literature, the first thing they did is to import and digest the new genres. Lyrical poetry, suitable to express the personal feelings, became the highlight of the importation. They tried to use the foreign poetical forms to express their own feelings. They had to contemplate the compatibleness of foreign genres with the English language. The discussion on the forms of these newly appeared English lyrics is the main and heated topic among poets and critics during the Elizabethan era. Sidney's ideas and practice on the poetical construction is only one part of this cultural movement.

And, when the subject is concentrated on Sidney's poetical construction, some related concepts have to be defined. The meanings of "poetical" should be clarified; the extension of "language structures" should be limited; the distinction of "prosody" from "versification" should be made; and the implication of "sense of nativeness" should be explained.

The words "poetic" and "poetical" share almost identical meanings in English dictionaries. However, in the mind of a critic, "poetic" (or "poetics") is often used to refer to "the part of literary criticism that deals with poetry" (Trumble and Stevenson 2259), while "poetical" is not. "Poetical" "now used chiefly in reference to form", whereas "poetic" "refers to the basic qualities of poetry" (Webster's Dictionary of the English Language 1388). In the subject on Sidney's poetical construction, the word "poetical" consistently refers to the form of poetry, suggesting both the prosodic and the linguistic aspects.

An appropriate implication of "language structures" is helpful in analyzing the form of poetry. The form of poetry contains two groups of things: the sheer prosodic ones, such as metre, enjambment, caesura/pause, or different stanzaic structures, and the linguistic ones, such as phonetics and phonology, grammar (including morphology and syntax), and semantics (the forming of meaning). Different people may have different taxonomy when dealing with the "language structures" (Crystal 82-83), however, one catalogue that "language structures" consist of phonetics, phonology, grammar (morphology and syntax) and semantics seems more convenient for poetical analysis. The first three aspects will be frequently mentioned in the discussion of Sidney's poetical construction.

Although people incline to mix the terms "prosody" and "versification" when they use them, it is necessary to differentiate between them here. Compared with "versification" which often reminds people of the practice of composing verse (Trumble and Stevenson 3525), "prosody" refers to not only the practice, but also the theory of composing verse and "the branch of knowledge that deals with the forms of metrical composition" (2374). The word "prosody" is also linked with the musicality of poetry, for, in history, it has been used to describe the pronunciation of words in the composition of verse (2374). So "prosody" will be used in the following discussion of Sidney's poetical construction, either in ideas or in practice.

"Sense of nativeness" is a concept put forward by Professor Ou Hong, a Chinese scholar, in the study of cultural communication between nations. Professor Ou thinks that the essence of the sense of nativeness is the sense of national culture, which expresses, in different time and/or on different individuals, as the sense of a time and/or the sense of an individual, including the sense of a class (general) reflected through the sense of an individual (particular) (*Dangdai Wentan Bao* (*Contemporary Literary World*) 1). The "sense of nativeness" may suggest the feelings and attitudes a cultural individual holds in the evaluation of culture(s) when facing the foreign culture(s). This cultural individual may be a social person or a nation. The evaluation may be towards the alien culture(s) or the culture of this individual. The standard or measure applied to the evaluation is the ideal culture based on native culture of the individual. Sidney has his "sense of nativeness" as he comments on the English poetry and the foreign ones. His sense of nativeness is also reflected in his poetical construction in which he combines the English poetical tradition with the anglicized foreign prosodies.

Sidney's works began circulating among the small circle of his close friends and producing influence from about 1570s. However, in the Sidney studies, he was regarded as a literary man and his works are examined as literary products begin only in the late 19th century, and reach a constant bloom during the 20th century with many valuable research results published. Such an explanation does not mean that the existence of Sir Philip Sidney and his works throughout nearly three hundred years can be neglected. But one awkward situation about the recognition of Sir Philip Sidney is that both he himself and his works have been regarded as an emblem of the national patriotism, or of an ideal morality, which was strengthened by the story of water bottle in Zutphen. The main stream of Sidney studies of these three hundred years concerns roughly to the moral themes of his works with only a few anabranches discussing the rhetorical achievements Sidney reaches in his works, especially in his *Arcadia*, and the disadvantages of his verbose romance which is thought only suitable for a lady spending her leisure time①. In the eyes of some people, Sidney himself is more poetic than his poetry. Yet, two things which relate to the topic of Sidney's poetical construction of this period should be mentioned: one is the publication of Sidney's works and references (such as his biography), the other is George Puttenham's analysis of Sidney's poetry in his *The Arte of English Poesie*.

Puttenham's case may be explained in a few words first. In Book Three of *The Arte of English Poesie*, there is one chapter (Chapter 19) with a title "Of Figures sententious, otherwise called Rhetoricall", in which Puttenham quotes Sidney's poems or lines of poems to illustrate figures of "Prosonomasia, or the Nicknamer" (203), "Epithonema, or the Surclose" (217), "Epimone, or Loveburden" (225), and "Icon, or Resemblance by imagerie" (244). Puttenham might be among the first people who cite Sidney's works to a certain amount and analyze them with a poetical purpose.

Sidney's works have been mainly circulated inside his circle without being printed during his life time. There are only three or four poems published. However, after his death, with people's eulogizing his idealized personality, his works are published one after another. During the last decade of the 16th century, almost all of Sidney's works have been published, of which

---

① Walpole and Hazlitt severely attacked Sidney's style (Garrett "The Introduction").

Katherine Duncan-Jones, a scholar of Sidney studies, illustrates clearly with a brief chronology (Duncan-Jones xxi). The first group of publications provides examples of imitation for literary people of the next century and targets which are attacked or praised from the people of the century following the next. They are: the first publication of *Astrophil and Stella*, in a poor text, with a preface by Thomas Nashe in 1591; publication of "New" *Arcadia* with Book 3-5 of the "Old" appended in 1593; the publication of *Defence of Poesie* in 1595; the first *Complete Sidney* published in 1598; the publication of Sidney's translation of *Psalms* under the supervision of his sister, *the Countess of Pembroke* in 1599 (Duncan-Jones xxiii). (And there are ten further editions in the 17th century).

Although Sidney's works have been re-edited and published in new editions before the last decades of the 19th century, it seemed that there is no distinct progress in Sidney studies, except the publication of Sidney's biographies which include Fulke Greville's famous eulogy *Life of Sir Philip Sidney* (1652) and, the translations of Sidney's works published in other countries.

The last decades of the 19th century witness a turning point of Sidney studies which have gained several substantial achievements in the first decades of the 20th century.

It is convenient to examine the results of Sidney studies appeared in the 20th century as a whole. Professor Donald Stump from Saint Louis University has listed 98 publications of Sidney's works, on which Dr. Gavin Alexander has added 33 items. There is a slight overlapping of their lists, and their lists have not covered all the publications in the whole century, yet, their statistic results show that the amount of the publication of Sidney's works in the whole 20th century had already surpassed in the amount the previous 300 years after Sidney died. And the academic value of the later publications is also uncompetitive. The publications of Sidney studies, according to Professor Stump's statistics, are 637 in the 20th century, compared with 151 from the end of 16th century to the end of the 19th century. And there appear some monumental achievements in the 20th century.

The first achievement is that *The Complete Works of Sir Philip Sidney*, being edited by Albert Feuillerat, appeared between 1912 and 1926 in four volumes. This is the first nearly complete edition of Sidney's works. And during this period, Malcolm W. Wallace publishes his *Life of Sir Philip Sidney* (1915), which remains as the standard biography.

The second achievement is Professor C. S. Lewis's *English Literature in the Sixteenth Century: Excluding Drama*, first published in 1954. In this extraordinary book, Professor Lewis gives a considerable space to a careful judgment of Sidney and his works, which becomes the authoritative opinion in Sidney studies, cited by many scholars. Professor Lewis is also among the first who scrutinize Sidney's poems and dig out some poetical merits from Sidney's efforts.

The third achievement is *The Poems of Sir Philip Sidney*, edited by William A. Ringler, Jr., published in 1962①. Ringler provides in his book not only the rich collation materials, but also the valuable introduction, commentary, and editorial matter, in which Ringler expresses his influential analysis of Sidney's poems one by one, both in themes and in poetical techniques. After exploring all the poems of Sidney, Ringler gives a summary of Sidney's prosody, listed as a "Table of Verse Forms"—an extremely valuable contribution to Sidney studies.

---

① Alexander B. Grosart edited *The Complete Poems of Sir Philip Sidney* in three volumes during the second half of the 19th century and published them in 1877. In this edition, Grosart added a memorial introduction and made the notes to the poems. Yet, there are mistakes the editor could not avoid, especially in the textual research. Grosart's edition becomes an important reference for Ringler's work.

The fourth achievement is *Sir Philip Sidney: the Major Works*, edited by Katherine Duncan-Jones, published in 1989. As a more authorized edition of the abridged collection, this book presents more exact texts of Sidney's representative works to the reader. The introduction and the editorial matter offered by Duncan-Jones are beneficial to both beginners and experienced scholars.

These four achievements are only four representatives among those monumental endeavours which cause a notable change in Sidney studies. Accompanying these four achievements there arises a long time ardour of Sidney studies from the early twentieth century on. For example, in biographies about Sidney, besides Wallace's work, there are also John Addington Symonds's *Sir Philip Sidney* (1909), Mona Wilson's *Sir Philip Sidney* (1931), and Katherine Duncan-Jones's *Sir Philip Sidney: Courtier Poet* (1991), etc.; in the studies concerning Sidney and his works, there are John Thompson's *The Founding of English Metre* (1961), Derek Attridge's *Well-weighed Syllables* (1974), Junior O. B. Hardison's *Prosody and Purpose in the English Renaissance* (1989), and Lisa M. Klein's *The Exemplary Sidney and the Elizabethan Sonneteer* (1998), etc.; in the monographic studies on Sidney and his works, there are Kenneth Orne Myrick's *Sir Philip Sidney as a Literary Craftsman* (1935), John Buxton's *Sir Philip Sidney and the English Renaissance* (1964), David Kalstone's *Sidney's Poetry: Contexts and Interpretations* (1965), Neil L. Rudenstine's *Sidney's Poetical Development* (1967), Junior Sherod M. Cooper's *The Sonnets of Astrophil and Stella: A Stylistic Study* (1968), and Dorothy Connell's *Sir Philip Sidney: The Maker's Mind* (1977), etc. There are also numerous periodical articles and increasingly added collections of papers on Sidney and his works. Dr. Gavin Alexander might be one of the most active scholars in Sidney studies today, who is writing a book about the response to Sir Philip

Sidney. There are also two websites worthy of mentioning in particular. One is named "Sir Philip Sidney, On Line" sponsored by the Department of English & Center for Medieval & Renaissance Studies of Saint Louis University under the direction of Professor Donald Stump (Project Director), C. Stuart Hunter and Jerome S. Dees. The other is the website of the International Sidney Society sponsored by Cambridge English Renaissance Electronic Service and Faculty of English, Cambridge. The Sidney Society also published a journal—*Sidney Journal.* These two websites furnish online electronic texts of Sidney's works and rich information of Sidney studies.

Today, Sidney studies have been producing abundant outcomes in almost every aspect on Sidney and his works. However, a systematic study of Sidney's poetical construction against a wide cultural background appeals for being strengthened so that the ideas like "delightful moving" which is closely connected with Sidney's consideration about the form of a literary work (in his time, mainly poetry) can be understood in a clearer and more profound way.

Sidney studies are rather weak in China, though his poetical ideas are important for China's New Poetry development at present. Only a few works have been done by Chinese scholars who are majoring in the study of English Literature. Qian Xuexi has translated Sidney's "Defence of Poetry" (1963) and attaches to the translation with detailed annotations. Professor Liang Shiqiu, in his *The History of English Literature* (1985) and *Selected Works of English Literature* (1985), discusses a few words of Sidney and translates a few pieces of Sidney's works. Professor Wang Zuoliang gives several places to Sidney and his works in *The Literary History of the English Renaissance* (1996), focusing on distinguishing Sidney by his literary achievements. Dr. Liu Jianhua introduces the latest view of the international Sidney studies in a very summarized way (Li 236-239). "The Defence of Poetry" and one or two poems from *Astrophil and Stella* are also taught in some university lectures.

Comprehensive Sidney studies in China still need to be carried out even today.

The ideas and the practice that Sidney anglicizes the foreign poetical forms are some kind of cultural activity. And the sense of nativeness, maybe unconscious, sits in the heart of Sidney and controls him. Because of this, Sidney's sense of nativeness will be hidden in the account of his poetical construction; and his efforts in the anglicization of foreign poetical forms will be made clear through analyzing his poetical experiments.

It is necessary to sketch Sidney's poetical construction at the beginning of this research. The observation of Sidney's poetical construction will be reported in six parts: his ideas on poetical form, his discussion on the poeticality of English language, his experiments on English quantitative verse, his design of accentual-syllabic verse, his arrangement of stanzaic forms, and his transplantation of foreign poetical genres.

Sidney's ideas on poetical form relate to the poeticality of the English language and the functional roles of the form. On these two points, Sidney surpasses his predecessors. The aim of Sidney's poetical construction is forging "delightful form" which serves for the "delightful moving". Sidney takes the latter as the aim of poetry. To reach the aim, two groups of relations which reflect Sidney's attitude have to be analyzed: language and metre, and foreign prosody and native tradition. Most of Sidney's contemporary poets tend to tame the language with metre in their composition. George Gascoigne is a representative of this tendency. The result is that language becomes twisted and rigid in their poems. Sidney advocates the compatibleness of language and metre. He tries to balance these two elements in his poems. And when these two elements do conflict, Sidney will reconstruct the metre within the permitted limit so as to give way to the naturalness of language. As for the relation between foreign prosody and native tradition, Sidney always endeavours to bring the foreign prosodies into the system of English native conventions. His endeavours are explained by his poems of innovative forms. They are unities of foreign influences within the English poetical conventions.

It is important to highlight on Sidney's discussion of the poeticality of English language. Sidney's own ideas on English prosody are based on his understanding of the poeticality of English language. The recognition of the poeticality of a language makes it possible for a poet using the language in a conscious way in his composition. Sidney's recognition is farseeing, for at a time when "English did not become the primary literary language of England until the second half of the sixteenth century. ... English was still being formed" (Jensen 349), the poeticality of it is often neglected. But the study of the poeticality is important to the development of poetry, especially when the poetry in its infancy. In his "Defence of Poesie", Sidney analyzes three aspects (of the grammatical, lexical, and phonetic) of the swiftly changing English of his time, pointing out that English can serve any purpose of poetry. Sidney's idea reflects people's desire to improve English when the nation was in her rising era. It expresses the urgent necessity to the study of language at almost the very beginning of composing new poetry. His "Defence of Poesie" provided the theoretical support and guidance to the poetical construction of his contemporaries and poets from the coming decades. People who study Sidney's poetry are frustrated when trying to dig out the greatness of the themes embedded in his works. All of Sidney's poetic endeavours seem to prove the expressiveness of the English language. People may neglect, or largely neglect, the decisiveness of Sidney's ideas on language to his poetical construction.

Sidney's experiment on English quantitative verse is an attempt to introduce the Latin prosody into English. The reason for him doing this might be that Sidney takes it as a cultural task for English elite of his time. The rise of modern European nations paves the way for the growth of vernacular literature. Compared with Latin literature, these vernacular ones are underdeveloped. Cultivating the national literature becomes a trend, in which Italian and Frenchmen having been achieving brilliant achievements. English people are far behind. Sidney is eager to catch up with the foreign competitors. However, he fails in introducing Latin prosody into English poetry, because English and Latin are two different kinds of languages. The forming of rhythm, which is the essence of a verse, of English line depends on the isochronously appeared stresses; however, the forming of rhythm in a Latin line relies on the regularly arranged long syllables. Sidney thinks that the Latin verse composed with the same principle of music, hence, possessing stronger musical effect than an English line. The experiment makes Sidney be aware of the quantitative elements existed in his mother tongue, leading him to the design of accentual-syllabic verse, which is delightful for its sweet musicality.

The English accentual-syllabic verse is a combination of foreign prosodies and English poetical tradition. In Sidney's practice, the stress-timed and syllable-counted rules are exactly but flexibly observed. The syllable-count is the prosodic practice followed by poets who write in languages of Roman family, like French and Italian. Sidney is not the first poet who learns to use it in English poems, but he is among those influential innovators. In designing the accentual-syllabic verse, Sidney naturalizes "an entirely new rhythm, the accentual trochaic" and brings it to perfection in the songs of *Astrophil and Stella* (Ringler lv). He also triumphantly converts Latin caesura (as well as the caesura in the French Alexandrine) into English pause, invigorating it through liberating it from the fixed positions. To avoid the conflict of language and metre, Sidney makes the inversion of initial foot of the line and substitution of feet within the line normalized. In these respects, Sidney promotes the new prosodic conventions established before the bloom of

English Renaissance poetry.

Sidney knits his stanzaic forms mainly with the enjambment and the rhymes. These devices appear very common in metrical poems today, however, having been tamed not easily by Elizabethan poets, including Sidney. The models Sidney can learn from abroad. With the enjambment, Sidney makes the grammatical structure of a sentence covering two or more lines so as to guarantee the meaning expressed completely and the feelings flows unhindered. The metrical structure of separate lines is stretched with enjambment. The rhyme in Sidney's poems is a method both of emphasis and linkage. Sometimes it serves as the assistor in expressing the meaning and feelings too. One of Sidney's noted contributions to English poetry is that he revives the feminine rhymes and makes it "a formal structural element in the shaping of his stanzas" (lvi). The kinds of rhymes Sidney uses in his poems are from internal rhymes to end rhymes, from feminine rhymes to masculine rhymes.

In constructing his poetical forms, Sidney introduces a large number of verse forms. "His 286 poems contain 143 different line and stanza patterns... Most of these were entirely new to English" (lviii). Among these new stanzas, the Sapphic stanza, madrigal and sonnet are worthy of research, for Sidney influences the English poetry with the anglicization of them. Sidney sets down the standard form for English Sapphic stanza, which is basically followed by poets of the later generations. His proposition of madrigal encourages the fashion of the Elizabethan vocal music. His assiduous exploration of the sonnet form, though he is not the first who introduces it into English poetry, is decisive in the evolution of English sonnet.

Sidney has not reached the height in poetry that Spenser and Shakespeare have reached though; he has influenced much in the shape of Elizabethan poetry through his unremitting poetical construction. In the starry sky of the

Elizabethan literature, Sidney is that Polaris, not very bright, but very central, and no one will neglect that if he does not want to be lost when watching that dazzling galaxy.

Chapter 1 Sidney's Ideas on Poetical Form

Poetical form is the major concern of the composition and criticism of Elizabeth poetry. Perfection of form seemed to be the initial task in the poetical construction at that time. There are some reasons for this literary phenomenon: the growth of English language, the emergence of the new lyric in English poetry and the poetic tenets from Aristotle. The growth of English offers the new poeticality in language for poets to explore; the emergence of the new lyric in English poetry urges the poets to master the poetical forms; and the Aristotelian principles emphasizing on questions of form ("Theories of Literary Kinds") lead the poets to the concentration of the poetical form. In the minds of these people, the poetical form itself, being the carrier of meanings and feelings a poet expresses, must be in accordance with his aesthetic demand, must meet the reader's aesthetic expectation, and must be amusing—harmonious in cadence, symmetric in structure and natural in language. Sidney expresses the similar idea in his "Defence of Poesie". He advocates that poetry should be delightful so as to "holdeth children from play, and olde men from the Chimney corner"; and that a poem should have a delightful form, "with words set in delightful proportion" (Feuillerat 20). Sidney's idea in this respect comes directly or indirectly from some influential writers from Pythagoras, Plato and Aristotle to Scaliger, Castelvetro and Gascoigne. Many people might take it for granted that Sidney only summarizes the poetic ideas from his precursors and his contemporaries from the European continents, but he has his own thoughts too. Sidney recognizes the importance of the poeticality of language to poetry. Sidney recognizes the functional roles the poetical form plays in conveying the theme. These two recognitions make him ahead of his time in literary criticism. His ideas on poetical form contain the aim of poetical construction, the argument of the relation between language and metre and that between foreign prosodies and native tradition, and the prosodic principles he applies in his composition.

1.1 The Aim of Poetical Construction

After the revival of Platonism and Aristotelianism in the fifteenth century, the philosophical theories of those ancient Greco-Roman scholars spread influentially throughout the Renaissance countries in Europe. The ideas of form or forms by those from Pythagoras to Aristotle are powerful in the intellectual life of literate people. Pythagorean concept of form says that form means limit, which is understandable especially in numerical terms. All things *are* numbers. "Number, then represents the application of limit (form) to the unlimited (matter)" (Stumpf 12). The harmonious numbers form the order of universe, which presents the beauty of nature. Sidney repeatedly mentions the concept "proportion" in his works, for examples, "exquisite observing of number and measure in words" (Feuillerat 6), and "peasing each sillable of eache word by just proportion, according to the dignitie of the suject" (Feuillerat 11). The debate on versification between Dicus and Lalus, two shepherds in the Old Arcadia, and "What length of verse can serve brave Mopsa's good to show" (Ringler 12), etc., and even the carefully designed romance and sonnet sequence, all imply such an idea.

Aristotle considers that "'nature' means two things, the matter and the form" (Adams and Searle 50), that "everything that exists is some concrete individual thing and everything is a unity of matter and form" , and that people never find matter without form or form without matter in nature (Stumpf 91). "Form thus may be some thing that is simply perceived, but it may also depend heavily on conventions and a system of presentation that has a history (Townsend 58)." The Elizabethan people generally accepted the dichotomy of "content versus form" which they called the matter and form. To a poem, the matter is the subject and theme the poem conveys, or the meaning expressed through the language which is turned into lines and stanzas of poetry. This recognition looks quite naive to a modern formalist or structuralist (Wellek and Warren 140-141)①. However, people must not measure the Elizabethan efforts by later experience (Smith xii). Francis Bacon's narration of form might be a representative of Elizabethan time. He answers that form itself is physical, and "of a given nature to discover the form ... is the work and aim of human knowledge", and "The forms are, as it were, the alphabet of nature" (Sorley 27-28). Therefore, knowing the form is the just way of knowing the world.

The Elizabethan aesthetic appetite of form is symmetry, harmony and proportion, which answer the Plotinus that "the beautiful thing is essentially symmetrical, patterned" (Adams and Searle 128). This idea is applied to the poetical form by Sidney and many poets which are also critics of that time. As Giambattista Giraldi puts it that

---

① René Wellek and Austin Warren have summarized the idea of a modernist on the content and form: "In a successful work of art, the materials are completely assimilated into the form: what was 'world' has become 'language'. The 'materials' of a literary work of art are, on one level, words, on another level, human behaviour experience, and on another, human ideas and attitudes. All of these, including language, exist outside the work of art, in other modes; but in a successful poem or novel they are pulled into polyphonic relations by the dynamics of aesthetic purpose (Wellek & Warren 241)."

> ... the poet ought to consider not only the whole body but each particular part, so that each may be set with beautiful order in its place, with admirable grace, and with the proper proportion and so that the whole, with that beauty and grace, will be to each of them proper and fitting (Leitch 274).

In Sidney's opinion, the form of a poem refers to that "words to expresse the matter" (Feuillerat 37). "For there being two principall parts, Matter to be expressed by words, and words to expresse the matter (37)." The expression contains two aspects, the language and the use of language. In what language a poem is composed? Sidney prefers the formal and elegant English spoken by those literate people at Queen Elizabeth's court, "the language of everyday polite conversation" (Ringler lii). Then the use of the language in a poem suggests the suitableness of language to the subject it expresses and the compatibility of language and the prosodic rules. To the former, Sidney raises an idea of "energia" to emphasize the forcefulness of a poet's handling the language (Feuillerat 41).

Sidney's idea on the aims of poetry seems only an echo among the responses to Horace's words that "the aim of the poet is to inform or delight, or to combine together, in what he says, both pleasure and applicability to life" (Adams and Searle 83), or to Strabo's that poetry "introduces us to the art of life and instructs us, with pleasure to ourselves, in character, emotions, and actions" (Adams and Searle 87). During the Renaissance, Horace's thought spread over and conquered the continental countries in Europe. Julius Caesar Scaliger accepts the Horatian doctrine, saying that the end of poetry is "the giving of instruction in pleasurable form", for "poetry bends all its energies to these two ends, to teach and to please" (Adams and Searle 174). Lodovico Castelvetro, in his interpretation of Aristotle's *Poetics*, following

Horace, utters that a poem should be both to delight and to teach (Adams and Searle 178). It is from these people that Sidney touches the ancient criticism and gets the foreign influences. Of course Sidney is not alone among the English in answering the Horatian chorus. But most of his countrymen are in "degrees of adaptation—from the absolute 'scissors-and-paste' method ...to the happily disguised borrowings of the 'Apologie for poetrie'" (Smith xxi). William Webbe, Thomas Nash and George Puttenham are their representatives. Webbe affirms that the poems are "the sweete allurements to vertues" (Smith 252). Nash announces that "delight doth prick men forward to attaining of knowledge, and that true things are rather admired if they be included in some witty fiction" (Smith 329). Puttenham says that poetry, being "the common solace of mankind in all his trauails and cares of this transitorie life", instructs the moral doctrine (24). Sidney is among the first Englishmen who give the complete interpretation of the Horatian idea. In "Defence of Poesie", Sidney narrates his understanding of the aim of poetry: a poet in his imitation of the world creates his better imagined art world; he imitates "both to delight & teach, and delight to move men to take that goodnesse in hand, which without delight they would flie as from a stranger; and teach to make them know that goodnesse whereunto they are moved" (Feuillerat 10). He also points out the way of reaching the poetic aims, that is, delightful moving (11). Sidney regards the delightful moving as the way via which a poet reaches his poetic aim, to teach, whereas a delightful form is the concretisation of such a way. The metaphors in "Defence of Poesie" illustrate the idea, such as the journey through a faire vineyard:

> "hee commeth to you with words set in delightfull proportion, either accompanied with, or prepared for the well enchanting skill of *Musicke*, and with a tale forsooth he commeth unto you, with a tale, which

> holdeth chldren from play, and olde from the Chimney corner; and pretending no more, doth intend the winning of the minde from wichedness to vertue;" (20)

The words in proportion, the words with musicality, all these descriptions refer to the form of poetry, in which the popular ideas about form during the English Renaissance are echoed. There is an aesthetic taste in the description as well. The form should be in discipline, otherwise it will spread disorderly and cannot reflect the theme and feelings well. The form should be delightful, so as to draw the attention of the audience. The form should be with musicality in order to achieve the higher aesthetic achievement. Proportion suggests the aesthetic elements like symmetry and harmony.

And from this "delightful proportion", Sidney sets up his ideas on poetical construction: that "everie word having his natural seat" (27), that words "carrying even in themselves a Harmonie, without perchance number, measure, order, propotion" (27), that a poet "peasing each sillable of eache word by just proportion, according to the dignitie of the suject" (11) and fitting "speech for music" (27), thus making people

> having their hard dull wittes softened and sharpened with the sweete delights of Poetrie, for untill they finde a pleasure in the exercise of the minde, great promises of much knowledge, wil little persuade them that know not the frutes of knowledge (5-6).

1.2 Two Arguments on Metrical Design

Sidney has two arguments, which can be treated as the guidelines of the application of his poetical aim, implied in designing the poetry form. One is about the dominancy of language and metre, two basic factors in the composition of metrical poems. In this respect, Sidney's idea, which emphasizes the priority of language, contrast clearly with that of George Gascoigne who prefers that language rigidly obeys to metre. The other reflects Sidney's attitude towards foreign prosodies. His intention is to reform the foreign prosodies through anglicization and makes them adapt to the English poetry. Sidney advocates the amalgamation of foreign prosodies and native tradition. The argument of Sidney on language and metre will be clarified in comparing the idea of Sidney with that of Gascoigne. The argument of Sidney on foreign prosodies and native tradition will be analyzed by revealing Sidney's inheritance of English prosody from the history.

1. 2. 1 Language and Metre

George Gascoigne, in his "Certayne Notes of Instruction", puts forward his own opinion on language and metre, two essential elements of poetical form. As for the language of poetry, Gascoigne advocates observing on natural English word-order and following natural English pronunciation, "to place all wordes in their naturall or most common and vsuall pronunciation," and "to frame all sentences in their mother phrase and proper *Idióma*", not "after the maner of other languages" (Smith 53). It is obvious that Gascoigne emphasizes the Englishness of the language in poetry, which is pertinent to his disagreement to the Latinized usage of English in some people's composition. On this point, he further explains that

> the most auncient English wordes are of one sillable, so that the more monasyllables that you vse, the truer Englishman you shall seeme, and the lesse you shall smell of the Inkehorne (51).

And "woordes of one syllable will more easily fall to be shorte or long as occasion requireth, or wilbe adapted to become circumflexe or of an indifferent sounde" (51). On the contrary, "it not amisse to forewarne you that you thrust as few wordes of many sillables into your verse as may be", because "wordes of many syllables do cloye a verse and make it vnpleasant" (51).

As for metre of poetry, Gascoigne insists that poets should "remember to holde the same measure wherwith you begin, whether it be in a verse of sixe syllables, eight, ten, twelue, etc." (49) And this same measure is the iambic without slight variation①. This insistence might be a result of Gascoigne's observation of his contemporaries' writings. One merit of the strict iambic verse may be that each syllable of a polysyllabic word can get enough weight and value in recitation. But it causes difficulties in the practice of composition. If a line consists of sheer monosyllable words, it can be scanned, to some degree, as the iambic. And this result may not always be satisfactory. For example, in "Next that, he shot to be a man of lawe" ("Up the theme: Magnum vectigal parcimonia"), the whole verse is in the metre of iambic pentameter, whereas the beginning part, "Next that", can be scanned as an iambic foot, or a spondee, or a trochee, according to the reader's understanding. If a verse is formed with some disyllable words or even trisyllable words or "words of many syllables", it is not easy arranged into an iambic line:

① Gascoigne explains that he feels lamentable "that commonly now a dayes in English rimes (for I dare not cal them English verse) we vse none other order but a foot of two sillables, whereof the first is depressed or made short, and the second is eleuate or made long; and that sound or scanning cintinueth throughout the verse." He repeats his insistence at least three times in two adjacent paragraphs. (Smith 50-51).

\ / \ /\ /\ / \ /

Your meaning I vnderstand by your eye. ①

Gascoigne points out that it is "neither true nor pleasant" (51); the fault is that the word "vnderstand" has been placed in a wrong place so that the stress falls on the weak syllable "der" (/də/), " which is contrarie to the naturall or vsual pronunciation, for we say

\ \ / \ / \

vnderstand, not vnderstand" (51).

Gascoigne presents two essential demands for a verse: the language being natural with its words in the natural order and pronunciation according to the common use; the metre being "simple and rigid", "consisting of two degrees of stress in alternation, and nothing in it can be changed" (Thompson 73). When these two elements are considered separately, they are reasonable and instructive in making a verse. When they come together in a line, complexity arises. If language and metre coincide exactly, the verse looks natural and regular and in harmonious beauty. If they do not coincide, Gascoigne decides that the metrical pattern rules the verse and the language is subject to the metre. Then the above case (the treatment to "vnderstand") happens. In answering the question which is decisive in forming the rhythm of a verse, language or metre, Gascoigne loses his way. Still, he has noticed one important issue of English prosody which attracts the later generations to probe

---

① This is an example Gascoigne raises in his treatise *Certayne Notes of Instruction*. The marks he uses are, " \ " for weak syllable (the light accent as Gascoigne calls it), "/" for stressed syllable ("the graue accent" in Gascoigne's terminology). Gascoigne was among the first English who recognized that the prominent phonetic charcteristic of the English syllable is stress.

into. Among the explorers is Sir Philip Sidney.

Sidney does not neglect Gascoigne's "Certayne Notes of Instruction", "the first prosodic treatise in English" (Ward and Waller 298), which outlines a vague picture in making verses. Being both in the attendance of Kenilworth entertainments in 1575, Sidney should have known quite much of Gascoigne, an active poet performer at the festival and a leading court poet at a short time in the kingdom thereafter (Duncan-Jones 138). The influence of Gascoigne on Sidney may exist in the latter's determination to surpass the former in every aspect of poetry. People should have noticed that after Gascoigne presented an "echo" poem with "drab" poulter's measure on the Kenilworth ceremony, Sidney provided a much better one with "far more exacting classical hexameters" (98):

Gascoigne:

... And who gave all these gifts, 6①
I pray thee, Echo, say? +6
Was it not he who but of late 8
this building here did lay? +6
Echo: Dudley. 2
O Dudley, so methought; 6
he gave himself and all, +6
A worthy gift to be received, 8
and so I trust it shall. +6
Echo: It shall (98). 2

---

① The figure added to the end of each line labels the numbers of syllables in the line, thus be convenient for scansion.

Sidney:

Philisides:

But if he know not his harms what guides hath he whil'st he be blind?

Echo:

Blind.

Philisides:

What blind guides can he have that leanes to a fancy?

Echo:

A fancy (OA 31).

Gascoigne adopts poulter's measure①, one popular poetical form of his time, in his "echo" poem, and varies the couplet into a quatrain by dividing hexameter and heptameter lines with caesuras according his own theory②. Duncan-Jones criticizes the poem is lumpish and not witty (98). It is true. The small letters at the initial position of the even lines tell the reader that these lines should be treated as the second parts which immediately follow the first parts just above. Even if these lines with small letters at the beginning are

① Poulter's measure is a staple metre of the 1560s and 1570s in the Renaissance England. It is a heterometric rhymed couplet consisting of one line of twelve syllables followed by one of fourteen (iambic hexameter and heptameter). The term seems to be a quaint moniker coined by George Gascoigne, who alleges a proverbial practice among poultrymen of giving twelve eggs for the first dozen and fourteen for the second (Preminger and Brogan 972). Gascoigne, in his "Certayne Notes of Instruction", says, "And the commonest sort of verse which we vse now adayes (*viz.* the long verse of twelue and fourtene sillalbes) I know not certainly howe to name it, vnlesse I should say that it doth consist of Poulters measure, which giueth xii. for one dozen and xiij. for another" (Smith 56). In poets practice, the couplet often be varied into a quatrain of short measure, i. e. a form having lines of three, three, four and three stresses, a metre of English hymns (Baldick 176).

② In his "Certayne Notes of Instruction", Gascoigne puts forward his idea of the application of caesura in a line of twelve syllables and a line of fourteen syllables, "in the verses of twelue in the firste and fouretene in the seconde wee place the pause commonly in the midst of the first, and at the ende of the first eight sillables in the second" (Smith 54).

treated as independent verses and the poulter's measure varied into a short measure, still, the poem lacks harmony of rhythm. Some people will not agree with that the lines like "And who gave all these gifts", "Was it not he who but of late" and "this building here did lay" have followed strictly the iambic metre. And that strict iambic metre is just what Gascoigne determines to observe in his writing. It's hard to say that Gascoigne has adjusted his lyre to a cadence. The "echo" poem,① in which the echo's reply to a question raised in the line it follows is often commentary, contrastive, punning or ironic, is rich of witty and of unexpected amusement (Preminger and Brogan 317). Gascoigne fails on this point. The echo's answer to "Was it not he who but of late this building here did lay?" should be "lay" or "did lay" or "here did lay" but not "Dudley", for the change is not natural. The natural echo cannot answer a question. Gascoigne has to make a false echo to solve the problem. Unfortunately he is not cunning enough to make the false echo more interesting, because in his poem the "Echo's response is often absurdly predictable, being anticipated by Sylvanus (Duncan-Jones 98)". So, just as Katherine Duncan-Jones points out, "Though Gascoigne's is probably the earliest 'echo' poem in English, it left plenty of room for improvement (98)".

Sidney's poem shows the improvement of the genre Gascoigne first set in English. Instead of the poulter's measures, Sidney adopts the classical hexameters in his lines. Compared with Gascoigne's disharmonious lines, Sidney's verses are much better though they are still metrically imperfect as samples of his quantitative verse experiments. A line like "But if he know not his harms what guides hath he whil'st he be blind?" sounds more melodious than "Was it not he who but of late this building here did lay?", for the poet

---

① Echo poem is named "echo verse" by T. V. F. Brogan and Laurence Perrine (Preminger and Brogan 317).

has calculated the natural language rhythm of the sentence, both in syllable stress and in syllable length. And the echo's answers in Sidney's verses have been inosculated with the questions. A man is not aware of the dangers ahead, then what guides him in his walking? Does he walk blindly? And "What blind guides can he have that leanes to a fancy?" It is only a fancy. Sidney's echo answers naturally, jocularly and brilliantly.

Gascoigne was one of the leading poets in the 1560s and 1570s, and Sidney was active as a poet leader in the 1570s and 1580s. They both have contributed much to the English poetry with their innovative experiments on and practice of the English prosody construction, and both have left their critical ideas on English language and on language and metre of poetry. Both Gascoigne's "Certayne Notes of Instruction" and Sidney's "The Defence of Poesie" have dealt with these motifs. Sidney also has the especial discussion of these in his *Old Arcadia* (363-364). Further comparative study of their poems will explain more clearly the evolution trace of the idea about language and metre of poetry from Gascoigne to Sidney.

Gascoigne's poetry explains and clarifies his prosodic purpose. His verses are regular in terms of syllable count and syllable accent, noting that he is wedded to "mother phrase and proper *Idióma* (Smith 53; Hardison 112)" and "the same measure" of the "playne foote" "wherof the first is depressed or made short, and the second is eleuate or made long; and that sound or scanning continueth throughout the verse" (Smith 49-50). He uses "the englishe phrase", avoiding complex syntax and "straunge" polysyllable words and unnatural word order from Latin (52-53). His metrical pattern is simple and regular, away from inversion and the blend of different feet. He even rejects the complex rhetorical devices in his writing. Of course, the conflict between language and metre is obvious as well:

> Fie, pleasure, fie! thou cloyest me with delight;
> Thou fill'st my mouth with sweetmeats overmuch;
> I wallow still in joy both day and night:
> I deem, I dream, I do, I taste, I touch
> No thing but that smells of perfect bliss,
> Fie, pleasure, fie! I cannot like of this (Ault 68).

Monosyllable words which manifest Gascoigne's tenet of "truer Englishman" are in majority, and many of these words are of the English origin and of common use, organized with simple grammatical structures. Lines as "I deem, I dream, I do, I taste, I touch // No thing but that smells of perfect bliss" intensify a very strong tension with the help of terse rhetorical devices, here the parallelism. The alliteration, an ancient English metre which has become one solid part of the tradition of English versification, arranged neatly and densely, achieves the effects that Caesar reached in his well-known dispatch to the senate after a victory, *Vēnī, vīdī, vīcī.* However, the metrical pattern of the lines leaves room for improvement. For example, "Thou fill'st my mouth with sweetmeats overmuch". It is hard to say that the stress in "Fie pleasure" and "No thing" at the initial position of each verse would not fall on the first syllable, thus the parts may phonetically form trochaic feet, violating the coherence of iambic pattern Gascoigne follows. Such a metrical pattern exposes Gascoigne's insufficient recognition of the decisive role of language in forming the rhythm of a line.

Sidney goes further on the experiment of language in poetry than Gascoigne. He proposes using elegant oral language in writing, exploring the musicality of the English, following the natural rhythm of language, and arranging the metrical patterns in accordance with the harmony of cadence. Sidney constantly experiments his ideas in his poems:

Nightingales seldom sing, the Pie still chattereth:
The wood cries most, before it thoroughly kindled be,
Deadly wounds inward bleed, ech sleight sore mattereth
Hardly they heard, which by good hunters singled be.
Shallow brookes murmure most, deep silent slide away;
Nor true love loves those loves with others mingled be (OA 7).

Sidney chooses for his verses the common words of his contemporary English spoken by those literate people at court, church and universities, webbing them into simple syntax, spotted alliterations, and easy parallelism with astute contrasts. That might remind the reader of Gascoigne's language style. But Sidney's verses are more flowing, more graceful and more harmonious. He separates a line into two parts, but makes the positions of pauses (in Gascoigne, caesuras) in the above lines shift when necessary, which partly results in flexibility of the metrical pattern, thus different from Gascoigne's immobility. The end rhyme Sidney practices here, rare in most western vernacular poetries, organizes, by imitating that of Dante Alighieri's *terza rima*, in an sophisticatedly skilled way, covering two or three syllables, exhibiting the musical effects that English can produce. When scanning the metre, the reader finds that the feet vary among trochee, spondee and iambus, the positions of pauses do not follow the rules of Alexandrine or the Italian caesura, though each of the lines is constituted by twelve or eleven syllables, but in a licensed way concordant with the natural speech rhythm which, of course, is one of the aesthetic aims Sidney's prosody concerns.

Duncan-Jones asserts that "Many poetic genres and motifs which occur in the Kenilworth entertainments were adopted and refashioned by Sidney in the next few years, some publicly, others more privately" (Duncan-Jones 98). In fact Sidney may have tried more poetry forms in his poetical construction, and invented some new genres that his predecessors never imagined①. Whether Sidney has read Gascoigne's "Certayne Notes of Instruction" or not, it is obvious that he is quite aware of Gascoigne's dilemma when the latter is trapped by the conflict between language and metre in making poetry. Sidney is far more powerful in manipulating language and metre when arranging his rhythm. Where Gascoigne is lost, Sidney finds his direction. Not letting metre rules a verse in precedence, Sidney makes language the dominant ruler in a line. When other poets are flustered in distorting language in catering to the rigid metre, Sidney changes metre in a leisured way. In Sidney's mind, rhythm, not metre determines a verse. Rhythm of a line comes from its imitation of the natural rhythm of language the line written. Metre is but helpful to enhance the rhythmical effect of language. When language conflicts with metre, he changes metre with no hesitation. This just explains why Sidney commingles metrical patterns in one verse, which becomes the common prosodic practice in English poetry writing after Sidney.

1.2.2 Foreign Prosodies and Native Tradition

Sidney experiments extensively on foreign prosodies. He tries to invent the English quantitative lines by observing the Latin metre, resulting in a series of imperfect species in English poetry. He works hard on the sonnet newly introduced into English poetry, devising his own pattern by amalgamating the Italian mode with what Surrey has just established. He also weaves the English Alexandrine line, intending to transplant this alien verse

---

① For example, the singing match between Therion and Espilus is, according to Walliam A. Ringler, Jr., "the earliest example in English" (362). Sidney's important innovations include those new poems in the *Old Arcadia*, and *Astrophil and Stella*, in which the elegant language, the effective rhythm, and the new poetical forms are new and fresh when compared with the works of Sidney predecessors and even many of his contemporaries.

from the French poetry. Not all these efforts have been made firstly by Sidney, however, his experiments, being at the beginning of the history of these genres in English poetry, have exerted profound influence on the English poetical construction. Therefore, people have formed a general idea that Sidney enthuses over the foreign prosodies while neglecting the native prosodic tradition. William A. Ringler, Jr. , the authoritative editor of the collected poems of Sidney and an expert of Elizabethan literature studies in the twentieth century, says, "When he commenced poet he followed classical and continental styles and forms more than he did those of his own country" (52).

Ringler's judgment may not be right. Sidney's purpose of transplanting the foreign prosodies is to anglicize them, and to integrate the alien rules into the English poetical system so as to enrich the native prosodic conventions. The English poetical tradition determines his practice. Sidney's exploration of Latin quantitative rhythm facilitates him to make an insightful evaluation of the quantity of English syllables to the aesthetic expression in poetry. He often intentionally makes use of the quantitative elements when composing his accentual-syllabic lines, yet he does not observe the Latin prosodic rules, but follows the English phonetic principles. The musical effects of his poems may largely due to such exploration. His transplantation of Latin hexameters, Anacreontics, Aristophanics, Asclepianics, elegiacs, Phaleuciacs and Sapphics, etc. into English results in a group of accentual-syllabic variants. His amalgamation of the Italian sonnet and the English counterpart is more like a native genre rather than a foreign one. His inventive writing of English madrigal appears far away from its Italian model in kinship. His English Alexandrine lines are endowed with only the tightness of syllable-count and the aesthetic taste of symmetrical balance of the French prosody, remaining mostly the native conventions deciding the characteristics of the lines. Two notable features in Sidney's Alexandrine, the position of pause (not the French caesura) and the stressed timed rhythm,① belong to the English poetical tradition.

The reason for the scholars of Sidney studies, like Ringler, allege that Sidney has "turned his back almost completely upon the English past" (Ringler lii), may lie in their understanding of what tradition is and what should be included in tradition. No one will deny that, in Sidney's time, Chaucer's poetry and even the poetry of Wyatt and Surrey have already become part of the English poetical tradition. The treasure of their poetry includes at least two parts, the prosodic conventions they have established and ways of their anglicization of foreign metres.

Chaucer is among the first poets who compose the first English iambic pentameter line, a kind of accentual-syllabic lines and which is also a kind of the most common English metrical lines in the history of English poetry:

> But for al this, whan that he say his tyme,
> He held his pees, non other bote him gayned;
> For love bigan his fetheres so to lyme,
> That wel unnethe un-to his folk he fayned
> That othere besye nedes him destrayned;
> For wo was him, that what to doon he niste,
> But bad his folk to goon wher that hem liste (Chaucer 478).

It is said that the device of his iambic pentameter lines is inspired by the Italian *endecasillabo* (Preminger and Brogan 515). The line "But for al this,

---

① In the description of the English rhythm, Koenraad Kuiper and W. Scott Allan define "stressed timed" as "A kind of rhythm, which English has, where the length of time between stressed syllables is roughly equal no matter how many unstressed syllables come between the stressed syllables" (Kuiper and Allan 207, 222).

whan that he say his tyme" has ten syllables, arranged in the iambic metre. The rhythmical contour of the first three feet is not so clear as that of the last two, reminding the reader of the rhythmical pattern of Latin hexameter. And the position where the pause occurs in the line reveals the learning of the Latin rules, or more directly, of the rules of French Alexandrine. There are also some other lines which share the similar structure with the first in this stanza. However, from a line like "He held his pees, non other bote him gayned" the reader still sees the traces of Italian *endecasillabo*—it contains eleven syllables and ends with the feminine rhyme. Of course, it is hard to say that Chaucer's lines do not contain the native elements. The narrative style, the orality of the language, and even the feminine rhyme are popular in the Middle English poetry. Another invention of Chaucer in his poetry, besides the rudimentary iambic pentameter, is the rhyme royal, a stanza coined by Chaucer in his "Troilus and Criseyde", which has been imitated by later poets, including Sidney (OA 22, OA 66). This invention has both native and foreign sources (Preminger and Brogan 1065). And, all Chaucer's endeavours on English poetry become part of the tradition in the eyes of the later generations. Therefore, when Sidney resumes the experiments on the accentual-syllabic lines, it is not proper to say that his designing of the substitution, the end rhyme and the position of pause is always inspired by the foreign prosodies.

Surrey's sonnets, though not appearing very much earlier than Sidney's poems of the same genre, have already imitated by Sidney and other poets of that time. Surrey's sonnets are new and with alien taints in the eyes of these poets, but they are English poems:

> The soote season, that bud and bloom forth brings,
> With green hath clad the hill, and eke the vale:
> The nightingale with feathers new she sings;

The turtle to her make hath told her tale.
Summer is come, for every spray now springs:
The hart hath hung his old head on the pale;
The buck in brake his winter coat he flings;
The fishes float with new repairëd scale;
The adder all her slough away she slings;
The swift swallow pursueth the flies smale;
The busy bee her honey now she mings;
Winter is worn that was the flowers' bale.
    And thus I see among these pleasant things
    Each care decays, and yet my sorrow springs (Ault 18-19).

The poem was published in 1557, but is already in the form of English sonnet, for the structure of the poem shows the traditional influence of English poetry. The fourteen lines are divided into four groups, forming three quatrains and a rhymed couplet. Quatrain stanza and rhymed couplet are prosodic conventions of English poetry from the Middle Ages. Many ballads are composed in such conventions. Surrey's design makes the English sonnet very different from its Italian model in the expression of feelings. There is a turning point in the construction of an Italian sonnet, locating between the octave and the sestet. The feelings expressed in the poem accumulate in the octave and reach a climax in the end of this part. Then in the sestet, there is a meditation of the feelings. The organization in this way is very similar to the structure of tragedy Aristotle explicates in his *Poetics*, being different only in that in a sonnet it expresses the turn of feelings, not an action. In an English sonnet, the accumulation of the feelings reaches a climax near the end of whole poem, that is, the end of the third quatrain, leaving almost no room for the speaker making a philosophical meditation in the remnant part. The ending couplet of an English sonnet is just enough for an aphoristic exclamation. Besides, the iambic pentameter of the lines and the stressed-timed rhythm belong to the English poetry, not the Italian one. The scenes described and the feelings expressed in the poem belong to the English as well.

Chaucer and Surrey certainly have set up an example for the English poets of the later generation in learning and absorbing the useful things from the foreign poetry. If this is regarded as part of the tradition of English poetry in the history, then Sidney's exploration of transplanting the foreign prosodies and foreign poetical forms is a practice of tradition too in this respect.

Even if the tradition is understood as the scholars like Ringler suggest, their comment on Sidney's neglect of native poetical tradition still does not hold water. For they cannot explain why Sidney traces the history of English poetry in his "Defence of Poesie", why he adopts the oral English as his poetic language, why he rebuilds the poulter's measure in his poems and why he applies the alliterations in his lines. In "Defence of Poesie", Sidney evaluates the works in the history of English poetry from Chaucer's "Troilus and Criseyde" to the lyrics of Surrey, *Mirror for Magistrates*, and Spenser's *The Shepherdes Calender*, affirming that they "have poeticall sinnewes in them" (Feuillerat 37). The writers of these works have established the most fundamentals for the English prosody at the beginning of the history of English poetry. The account of the history explains that Sidney does not "completely" neglect the native tradition. If the evidence of such tracing is not sound enough, the fact that Sidney using "the language of everyday polite conversation" may prove his following the native tradition in the choice of oral English in poetry. It might be from the facts that Sidney criticizes Spenser on "framing of his style to an old rusticke language" (37) and that Sidney "never wrote a ballad". (Ringler lii) Ringler draws his conclusion that Sidney is interested only in the foreign poetry. It seems that Ringler does not draw his conclusion convincingly, although he continuously relates some facts of Sidney's concentration on foreign models. Compare Sidney's stanza:

> Who has his fancie pleased,
> With fruits of happie sight,
> Let here his eyes be raised
> On nature's sweetest light. (CS 23)

with a ballad of the Middle Ages:

> There lived a wife at Usher's Well,
> And a wealthy wife was she;
> She had three stout and stalwart sons,
> And sent them o'er the sea (Abrams 391).①

Sidney's poem is lyrical; the ballad is narrative. However, the orality of language in both poems is almost the same—polite, conversational—belonging to the literate people. It is obvious that the revival of the obsolete words in order to achieve some archaic style is not the mainstream of the poetic language in Elizabethan era. The oral language of the educated people in the Elizabethan court is often regarded as a kind of standard speech of English, carefully cultivated, bearing enough dignity and lucidity when they express the sublime theme. And the familiarity and popularity of the conversational quality of this courtly orality is also suitable to a jovially ironical topic. It is part of the native practice of oral language in literature. Sidney strengthens the vigorous tradition with his delightful poems of daily English.

---

① Although the ballad has been modernized in spelling, it preserves the original linguistic style.

The poulter's measure "is almost the staple metre of the 1560s and 1570s" in England (Preminger and Brogan 972), being a native genre, having been used by Wyatt, Surrey and other poets before Sidney. Sidney himself has tries the metre in two ways, one direct practice on it (OA 3) and some quatrain stanzas adapted on the metre. In the *Old Arcadia*, Sidney uses the "awkward and old fashioned" couplet telling the praise of the honest Alethes to Mopsa, the ugly and ill-natured daughter of the boorish shepherd, Dametas (Ringler 384):

> Her haire pure Crapal-stone; her mouth O heavenly wyde;
> Her skin like burnisht gold, her hands like silver ure untryde (OA 3).

From the literal praise, the reader can sense the sarcasm. The "crapal-stone" (crapaud-stone) refers to the toadstone which is dark brownish-grey, with an etymologic meaning "dead rock". The "silver ure untryde" is the silver ore not smelted, which is black. How can the reader imagine that a girl is described as having the terrible dark brownish-grey hair, the big and wide mouth, the yellow skin and the black hands? The technique is of a frolicsome folksong. People can easily find some similar examples in the English ballads. If the long lines are divided from the pauses amid them, forming a quatrain rhymed with even lines, it will remind the reader the similarity it shares with the metre of English ballad, or the long and short measures, or other quatrains common in English poetry before Sidney:

> So shall my spryte be still upright
> In thought and conversation,
> So shall I bide well purify'd,
> From much abomination (PS xix)!

There are four stressed syllables in each of the first and the third lines, three in each of the second and fourth lines. The stanza is a hymnal stanza. The lines in the stanza are arranged in the common measure, the same metrical pattern of ballad metre. It is significant that Sidney has composed not a few such stanzas when his poetical art is rather fully developed. Sidney never has neglected the native tradition in the whole span of his career as a poet.

There is still one piece of strong evidence in testifying Sidney's attitude towards the native tradition of English prosody, that is, his use of alliteration in his verse. Indeed he only occasionally composes a few lines in the alliterative metre, for example, "Lady the life of all love (CS 25)". But he adopts very frequently the alliterations as most English poets do from the sixteenth century on:

Like late mowne meades, late cut from joy I live (CS 18).

To marre my minde, and with my hurt to please (CS 21),

Into your rimes, running in ratling rowes (AS 15):

For since mad March great promise made of me,
If now the May of my yeares much decline (AS 21)

The alliteration used in this way is generally categorized into rhetorical prosody today, as a kind of phonological decoration for the musical effect of a verse. Sidney inherits the native tradition in his poetry, and at the same time, he sets new tradition for English poetry. He exploits the rich resources of English phonology, handling artfully of poetical effects produced with consonants and vowels. His concentration on the assonantal patterns, terminal consonants, correlative consonants, and the repetition of vowels or the combination of vowels and consonants brings marvel musicality to his poems:

(a) Till wounded, blind, and wearied Spirites, lose
    Both force to flie and knowledge where to fall (CS 15).
(b) Brake bowe, brake shafts, while Cupid weeping sate (AS 17):

In the example (a), the ending "-ll", together with the scattered "l" which often belongs to different phonemic combinations, effects the cadence of the lines with their sonorous features, especially when they are in the stressed syllables. The sequential consonant /d/ which ends the words in the first line and the relating consonant /f/ which starts the words from the second enrich the lines with subtle acoustic qualities. It is also interesting to note that "force" and "fall", which are at the stressed positions of the initial and final foot respectively, form the repetition of the vowel /ɔ:/, corresponding to the atmosphere of the line with their pronunciation. One conspicuous thing in example (b) is the arrangement of two rolling consonant clusters /br/ assonated with the consonant /b/ between them and the repeatedly appearing consonant /p/ after them, linking the tensive first hemistich with the slacking second hemistich. The calculation of the sounds, being "touched into consciousness", "seems always perfectly natural" (Rudenstine 192). Sidney, together with Spenser, establishes a tradition of the poetical musicality for the coming poets.

Sidney has the native tradition as the foundation of his anglicization of the foreign prosodies. He absorbs the alien poetical forms and their rules into the English prosodic system so as to enrich the English poetry, to change the status quo of the poems written by his contemporaries, for he thinks that their poems do not have "sinnewes" in them and are in want of the "energia" (Feuillerat 37). He carries out a series of experiments on transplanting the foreign metres and poetical forms into English, intending to integrate them into the native poetry and amalgamate with the native conventions. His purpose is to cultivate the national culture through the improvement of the English poetry.

1.3 The Principles of Sidney's Prosody

Sidney does not specifically illustrate the prosody he establishes or helps to establish. There are several accounts in his "Defence of Poesie" and a "Nota" in his *Old Arcadia* relating to the subject. But those are only a small part. However, the general principles can be summarized from all Sidney's works as the following eight items, which are revealed through his composition.

I. The English for poetry should be "the language of everyday polite conversation" (Ringler lii).

As for the language used in the lines, the following example is common in Sidney's writings:

I sought fit words to paint the blackest face of woe,
Studying inventions fine, her wits to entertaine:
Oft turning other's leaves, to see if thence would flow
Some fresh and fruitful showers upon my sunne-burn'd braine. (AS 1)

The English in these lines is accordant with Puttenham's opinion that the language a poet uses in his poetry should be "the vsuall speach of the Court, and that of London and the shires lying about London within lx. myles, and not much aboue" (145). The English Puttenham describes is generally accepted as Standard English by the literate people of Elizabethan era (145). The words Sidney chooses here are common words frequently heard in daily conversations among those literate people. Most of them are active even at present. The compounds like "sunne-bunn'd" are abundant in the Early Modern English because of the popularity of the compound word-formation. There are no inkhorn words of archaism or foreignism. The grammatical structure of Sidney's English is rather simple. The subject-verb order is followed and the participle phrases and verb phrases are organized in an easy way, showing a style of daily speech by the educated people. There is only one inversion that appears unnatural in conversation, "her wits to entertaine". But it's a common practice in poetry. There is no twisted pronunciation in the lines, although the alternation of word pronunciation to meet the metre is permitted. The lines are natural and smooth, with no lack of elegance. Contrary to Sidney's tenet on language of poetry, the following lines by one of his contemporary poets exhibit a different style:

> To welter up and surge in wrathful wise,
> As did the flood where Helle drenchëd was,
> Would but procure defame of thee to rise;
> Wherefore let all such ruthless rigour pass, (Ault 53)

The vocabulary seems flaunty. Words as "welter", "surge" and "procure" are rather new and the meanings of them are in the change when the poem is composed. The complex grammatical structure is Latinate rather than that of natural sentence of the Early Modern English. The pronunciation of the suffix "-ed" (in the word "drenchëd") has been becoming outdated with the disappearance of most inflections in English. The poem is written earlier than Sidney's. Its style does not lead the trend in and after Sidney's time. Most of English poets have inherited Sidney's tradition from the late sixteenth century till today.

Ⅱ. The rhythmical system of English poetry is the accentual-syllabic one, which includes mainly two types, the accentual iambic and the accentual trochaic.

Sidney tries the dactyl in his experiments on English quantitative verse. In his mature poems he concentrates mainly on contriving disyllabic feet. The metre he observes is the accentual-syllabic, of which he contributes to English poetry the finalized design. He makes the accentual trochaic verse an important rhythm besides the accentual iambic one:

> But ô foole, thinke of the danger,
> Of her just and high distaine:
> Now will I alas refraine,
> Love feares nothing else but anger. (AS ii)

The contour of falling rhythm in the first and fourth lines is clear. Only in the second hemistich of the first line, one of the two weak syllables between the two stressed syllables cannot be counted when the line is scanned. This is a licence practiced by English poets in the past. The contour in the second and third lines is blurred by the end stress; however, the reader can distinguish the accentual trochaic from most part of the lines. The deliberate rhythmical design that Sidney invents can be seen frequently in metrical poems today.

Ⅲ. The musical effect, which is one important aspect of the

delightful form of poetry, must be fully considered and achieved in composition; and the melody of a poem should be fit for the theme and the meaning and the feelings the poem loads.

Sidney shows the musical effect of poetry in two ways, the sweetness of the lines themselves and the suitableness of the verse form to what the poet intends to express. He attracts the readers with the first layer of beauty but challenges the reader's intelligence with the second. From digging out the implications concealed in the lines, the reader may find more pleasures:

> Come shepheard's weedes, become your master's minde:
> Yeld outward shew, what inward change he tryes:
> Nor be abasht, since such a guest you find,
> Whose strongest hope in your weake comfort lyes. (OA 4)

The stanza is formed by four iambic pentameters, end-rhyming abab, with pauses falling between the boundaries of the second and third feet. The metrical structure shows the balanced symmetry. There are dotted alliteration and assonance enriching the musical colour. The melody is delightful—the leisure pace and clear cadence are satisfactory. The language is natural and easy, without slight cumbrance from the metre. The poetical form itself is delightful. And the reader's aesthetic experience will not end here if he carries on his further analysis of the lines. The poems from Sidney's *Old Arcadia* are better interpreted by putting them in the context of the stories accounted in the whole romance. Being part of the narrative, they are knitted into the plots, helping to present the theme of the stories and the feelings of the characters in the stories. This stanza is with no exception. The story related to the poem is like this: in order to approach Pamela, the beautiful princess he admires,

Musidorus, Duke of Thessaly, decides to disguise as a simple shepherd; he changes clothes with the shepherd Menalcas, and then sings these lines to himself. The strong desire and the agitated mood that the speaker reveals are partly suggested by the poet's control of the musical effects of the lines. The initial inversion of metre is matched with hyperbaton of syntax, augmented the acoustic emphasis of exclamation. The parallel structure both in metrical design and in linguistic organization suggests the conflicting thought and the contrast identity of the speaker. The alliteration and assonance are fit well for a wailful soliloquy.

Ⅳ. The balance between the English language structures and the metre of the poem should be kept. A poet should make his metrical design compatible with the natural state of English.

It is true that Sidney seldom alters the normal pattern of a word in pronunciation or the natural structure of a sentence in the line so as to follow the rules of metre. He always exerts himself to keep a balance between language and metre, making his metrical design accordant to his natural tongue:

> If I could thinke how these my thoughts to leave,
> Or thinking still my thoughts might have good end:
> If rebell sence would reason's law receave;
> Or reason foyld would not in vaine contend:
> Then might I thinke what thoughts were best to thinke;
> Then might I wisely swimme or gladly sinke. (CS19)

When reading these lines, the reader may not be quite aware of the metre, although they are arranged tidily in the iambic pentameter. The ictus fall naturally on the stressed syllables. The language structures fully stretch in the metrical pattern without being affected by the rigid prosodic rules.

V. If language and metre conflict, the pause, the orthography, and the foot substitution are allowed to maintain the harmony of the metrical rhythm and the language melody.

Of course the conflict between language and metre occurs no less frequently in writing, however, when the conflict appears, Not like many of his contemporaries who are eager to tame the language obeying the metre, Sidney solves the problem with the pause and the foot substitution:

> Till now, wrapt in a most infernall night,
> I find how heav'nly day wretch I did misse. (AS 33)

Basically, these two lines are in iambic pentameter. But the first two feet in the first line may be scanned as trochees ("Till now", "wrapt in"), or the first foot scanned as a spondee ("Till now"). Of course the first foot in the first line can be read as an iambus. Then the stressed syllable from the first foot abuts on the stressed syllable from the second foot. The constant stresses may violate the rhythmical profile of the line. Therefore, Sidney inserts a pause to separate the juxtaposed stresses. The pause here, serving as a weak syllable, maintains the rhythmical identity without violating the metrical pattern. Such a practice is very common today. The foot substitution in Sidney's prosody comprises two types, the initial foot inversion and the substitutes within the line. "Till now" as a metrical unit, when treated as a trochee, is the initial foot inversion. The trochaic "wrapt in" in the first line is a substitute which replaces an iambus in its position of the line. Substitution is not Sidney's invention, but strengthened as a poetical convention via his hand. The omission of one weak vowel in the word "heav'nly" belongs to the orthography that the Elizabethan poets often adopt in their composition.

VI. When a metrical line or stanza cannot match the syntactic structure of English, the enjambment is necessary to extend the metrical structure so as to make sure the flows of meaning and feelings smooth; the enjambment may cover two or more lines within or between the stanzas.

A reader may feel familiar with the enjambment when he reads Shakespeare's plays, Milton's epics, or Browning's dramatic monologues. He is not surprised when encountering the enjambment in a free verse written by a poet in the twentieth century. But reading poetry of Sidney's contemporaries, he finds most lines are end stopped. It is still a common practice for an Elizabethan poet of Sidney's time to end a line both metrically and syntactically. Even Edmund Spenser seldom employs the device of enjambment. Enjambment begins appearing in the English blank verse which is newly born just before Sidney's time. It is interesting that Sidney does not write a poem in blank verse, but replants the enjambment into his rhymed poems. It is conjectural to say that Sidney decides to break the limitation of an iambic pentameter so as to pursue a more "energia" expression in a larger metrical pattern:

> Come let me write, "And to what end?" To ease
> A burthned hart. "How can words ease, which are
> The glasses of thy dyly vexing care?"
> Oft cruell fights well pictured forth do please. (AS 34)

These lines are exceptional. Syntactical structures within the lines are arranged in a flexible way that when reading them, a reader is likely to neglect the existence of the metre, the iambic pentameter. The stanza behaves as a piece of free verse. Two enjambments here mediate well the disagreement between language and metre, ensuring the conversation between the two speakers in the stanza going on spontaneously and uninterruptedly, and enforcing a tension into syntactical structures so as to make it suitable to the strong feelings expressed.

Ⅶ. The quantity of the English syllables, being a part of the rhetorical prosody *de facto*, can be considered in the enrichment of the verse melodic contour.

Sidney experiments the English quantitative verse by following the Latin examples. Through those experiments he cultivates a sharp sense to the aesthetic effects of the English syllables in quantity. In his mature poems, for example, the poems from *Astrophil and Stella*, Sidney carefully controls the length of every syllable in pronunciation, achieving the unique musicality in his lines:

> G**o** my flocke, g**o** get you h*ence*,
> S**ee**ke a better pl**a**ce of f**ee**d*ing*,
> Wh**ere** you m**ay** have some def*ence*
> From the st**or**mes in m**y** breast br**ee**d*ing*,
> And sh**owers** from mine **eyes** proc**ee**d*ing*. (AS ix)

Sidney's practice on the quantity of English syllables coincides with the phonetic discoveries of today. There do exist short and long vowels in English. Allan Cruttenden has discussed the vowel length with the cited statistics (96), saying that the length of both short and long vowels varies in different phonetic contexts, and the variation expresses more obvious with the long vowels (monophthongs and diphthongs) (95-96). The distribution of the stressed syllables, most of which contain the long vowels (represented by the bold letters), slows down the tempo of the verse rhythm. And the end rhymes, which include the combinations of vowels and sonorants (alveolar nasal /n/ and velar nasal /ŋ/) (represented by italicized letters), prolong the acoustic effect of each line. The tempo matches the mood pervaded among the lines.

Ⅷ. Rhymes are important to the organization of a line and/or a stanza within a poem; to the former, the devices of rhetorical prosody, the alliterations and the internal rhymes, are suitable; to the later, besides the alliterations and the internal rhymes, the end rhymes, both the masculine ones and the feminine ones, are necessary.

Sidney thinks that "the chiefe life" of modern versifying "standeth in that like sounding of the words, which we call Rime" (Feuillerat 44), and does apply this emphasized idea into his practice. There are two kinds of rhymes he uses in his composition, one is the rhymes within a line, the other is the rhymes covering lines. People may have different terms to describe different repetitions of sounds within a line, alliteration for the repetition of consonants, assonance for vowels, etc., but a general name, rhyme within the line, might be convenient to illustrate the repetitions. As for the rhymes covering lines, the term end rhyme is exact, which mainly consists of masculine rhymes and feminine rhymes. Among the varied rhymes Sidney exercises, "His great innovation was to bring feminine rhyme back into English verse and to make it a formal structural element in the shaping of his stanzas" (Ringler lvi):

No m**or**e in thy sweetnesse gl**o**rie,
For thy knitting haire be sorie:
Use *th*y words *b*ut to *b*ewaile *th*ee,
*Th*at no *m*ore *th*y b**ea***m*es availe *th***ee**. (CS 27)

English does not provide a rich source for feminine rhymes, but Sidney manages to avail of it by realizing the feminine rhymes in the repetition of part of one word from different lines (as in "glorie" and "sorie") or in the repetition of part of two or more words (as in "bewaile thee" and "availe thee"). He is able to use the feminine rhymes from the beginning to the end of a whole poem, making them the principal device in knitting the lines. The stanza also shows some other methods Sidney chooses for the melody of the poem, for examples, the rhymes within the lines,① and the alliterations cover the lines.

Sidney's ideas on poetical form are concretized in the prosodical principles he follows. His exercises on these principles establish new conventions for English poetry and catalyze the maturity of the accentual-syllabic verse, the dominant metre in English metrical poems. Many of Sidney's ideas are still worthy of learning, not only because the ideas themselves are original, but also because the formation of these ideas is inspiring. His awareness of the poeticality of the English language is a good example on both sides.

---

① Bold letters represents the repetitions of vowels and italicized letters represents the repetitions of consonants.

Chapter 2 Sidney's Discussion on the English Poeticality

English Renaissance reaches its climax at the turn of the sixteenth and seventeenth centuries. The lyric, being called new poetry at that time, blooms in those enthusiastic literary activities. Accompanying the lyric prosperity is the rapidly developed English itself, which exerts the profound influence on the whole British society. The fact that the composition of new poetry is based on the English of great linguistic change, which provides opportunities to the ambitious writers, does draw people's attention to and thinking of the language they use when they carry on their poetical experiments. Sidney is one of their representatives. He explores the English poeticality so as to seek the theoretical support to his poem writing when dealing with the problems caused by the language in poetry. Being one important part of his poetic theory, Sidney's expoundation of the English poeticality helps to explain the rise of English lyric poetry during Elizabethan era.

2.1 Poeticality of Language and the Growth of English Poeticality

The poeticality of language refers to the definite language structures which evoke the concentrated imaginative experiences or some intense and specific emotional responses. ① The language structures comprise different linguistic layers of phonology, morphology, lexicology, and syntax. The structures are united, forming the poetical space, corresponding to the prosodic patterns of a poem, presenting the theme and the feelings the poet intends to infuse. The rhythm of language coincides with the rhythm of prosody, aurally or, less often, visually. The aesthetic experience, i. e. , the imaginative awareness or the emotional response, is acquired just through the poet's use of the poeticality of language, through his specific choice and arrangement of the language.

The reason why language of poetry is often different from that of daily conversation might be the stronger colour of its poeticality. The word chosen may be of no difference from ordinary talk; the syntax arranged may be similar to common speech; but the regularity of the language structures, either in syntactic or in phonetics, exalts these average things to the rank of poetry:

> The apple cap sinks down to your faint hopes,
> sprawled in the sun on the grassy hillside,
> shirt over the soft
> haemal arch. ... (Prynne 219)

Division of lines, forming phonological order, restrains the language from rampancy. The first two lines are counted to ten syllables each. The third has five, a half of the previous line in the length when considering the number of

---

① This definition is corresponding to the explanation of poetry in the Britannica Encyclopaedia, or rather, is derived from the explanation. *Britannica Encyclopaedia* defines the poetry as "literature that evokes a concentrated imaginative awareness of experience or a specific emotional response through language chosen and arranged for its meaning, sound, and rhythm" (*Britannica Encyclopaedia*, "poetry").

syllables. The repetitions of the consonant /s/ produce a constant effect, linking the sounds of words into a sliding cadence. There are also contrasts between words, for instance, "sink" versus "faint" and "sprawled" versus "grassy", etc., for their stressed positions in the lines, which inspire the reader's imaginations. Of course the metaphor and the image the language presents here belong often to poetry, not daily conversation.

In fact, the poeticality that a language possesses is not limited in poetry. It is extensively applied to other literary genres as well, for example, the prosaic writings:

> It was the *best* of times, it was the *worst* of times, it was the age of *wisdom*, it was the age of *foolishness*, it was the epoch of *belief*, it was the epoch of *incredulity*, it was the season of *Light*, it was the season of *Darkness*, it was the *spring of hope*, it was the *winter of despair*, we had *everything* before us, we had *nothing* before us, we were all going direct to Heaven, we were all going direct the other way—in short, the period was so far like the present period, that some of its noisiest authorities insisted on its being received, for good or for evil, in the superlative degree of comparison only (Dickens 1).

The poeticality displays mainly through the audio effect achieved in the arrangement of the language rhythm, especially in the parallel construction of the phonological structure, in which the sharp semantic contrast was given prominence to. The aesthetic symmetry is shown through the measured rhythm. There is an almost identical cadence contour between each pair of the paralleled clauses. Each of the italicized words, because of the contrast meaning and positions in the linguistic structure, is emphasized and given the primary stress on its word stress in the rhythmical patterns. These isochronous stresses, which are joined with the almost equal numbered weak syllables, establish a musical melody of poetry. In some pairs of the paralleled clauses, the focused words of the second clause have more syllables than that of the first part. And because of the ending position of these words, they give the prominence of the words on one hand, avoiding the monotonous of the repetition and keeping the stability of the contrastive sentence structure with a more substantially phonological design on the other. The clear rhythmical pattern of the passage illustrates that the poeticality of the language does not only express in poetry though it is generally seen in poetry.

The rapidly growth of English in its early modern time leaves poets a new space to display their arts. Those intelligent people are aware of the poeticality of their native language. Sidney's discussion on the poeticality of the English language is among people's first inspection of their mother tongue, being important to the boom of Elizabethan lyrical poetry.

There are generally two tendencies existing in the growth of a language. One is that the language becomes elegant, lucid and productive in expression. The other is that it turns standard, precise and effective in organization (History of English 12). The two tendencies are reflected in English of Sidney's time in different linguistic structures of the lexical, the syntactic, and the phonological.

One noted thing of the growth of English is the speedily expanding of English vocabulary. "During the sixteenth century and the first decades of the seventeenth century, there were thousands of new words added to the English *verborum copiae*. (291)" Compared with the Middle English, the abundant words directly borrowed from Latin and modern European vernaculars greatly changed the formation of the English vocabulary. Some obsolete native words were revived with new meanings and the new usage. Words derived from different sources but share the same or similar meanings enriched not only the synonyms and synonymical structures, but also the styles of expression. People thus have more choices in their writing and have their writing more deliberate, accurate and energetic. And at the same time, because of the spread of the printed books, together with the literate people's awareness of regulating the spelling, large numbers of variants of words decreased in a short time. The following two passages may explain this tendency:

(a) And *sithence* it hathe pleased God, (as I gave you humblie to understande my last *lettres*) to call unto his mercie one Thomas Daie by meane whereof it restethe in your honorable favor to *præsente* (accordinge to your former pretence) him, aswell for whose cause as divers others I do accounte my selfe no lesse bound then I oughte (Feuillerat 77).

(b) When we heare Musicke, we must be in our eare in the vtter-roome of sense, but when we intertain iudgement, we retire into the cabinet and innermost withdrawing chamber of the soule: ... (Smith 381)

Passage (a) is written by Sidney in about 1569. Passage (b) is written by Samuel Daniel at the end of the sixteenth century. Although there are only less than three decades between the two writings, the variation of words in the Daniel's occurs less than that of Sidney's. The italicized words in passage (a) have variants at that time, for example, "since" for "sithence", "letters" for "lettres", "presente" for "præsente". Sidney only chooses one type from among the variants in his writing. The fact shows that the use of words has not been unified in orthography. But the situation changes quickly. In passage (b), almost all the words are fixed to one standard, ① demonstrating that writers have accepted the regulation of spelling.

The lexical and syntactic structures of the Early Modern English become simplified and standardized in its evolution. Most lexical inflections are disappearing. The grammatical rules become universal in both word-formation and sentence construction. The regulations of the lexical structure and the syntactic structure unite into the identical set. The Modern English grammatical system has established preliminarily, very close to the Standard English grammar of today (Lass 187-189). Two principal methods of word formation, the compoundation and the derivation for example, act on the rules same as syntactic structuring:

(a) In the waine of my little wit, I am forst to desire your protection, else every *Ballad-singer* will proclaime me *bankrupt* of honesty (Gebert 143).

(b) Yet in despight of my indevors, I *understand*, some have bin most *unadvisedly over-cunning* in *mis-interpreting* me ... (152)

The formation of the italicized words is based on a free combination mode, just like the organization of a sentence in essence. Two independent elements join together, either equal in importance, or one being subject to the other. The phenomenon exists ubiquitously in Modern English.

The phonetic changes of English during the Elizabethan era have not

---

① The use of letters "u" and "v", or "i" and "j", follows the standard of spelling in the second half of the sixteenth century. Charles Barber explicates that "for the first letter of a word, the printer invariably selects *v*, and in other positions he invariably selects *u*" (15). Letter "i" is used commonly in Early Modern English, while "j" is merely treated as a variant form of "i" and "used only in the combination *ij*; ... for example, ... *diversifijing*, 'diversifying'" (16).

occurred as intensely as the vocabulary does. Yet, "the subject of sound-changes is just as important in the history of languages as the changes in grammar and vocabulary" (Baugh and Cable 235). Compared with the past, the Early Modern English is richer in musicality, for the changes of vowels are noteworthy. The numbers and types of vowels have increased and the pronunciations have been regulated. After the Great Vowel Shift, some vowels have merged and more diphthongs have come into being, which can be illustrated in the following table (ModE represents Modern English):

1400	1500	1600	ModE
i:	ei	ɛi	ai
e:	i:	i:	i:
ɛ:	ɛ:	e:	
a:	a:	ɛ:	ei
u:	ou	ɔu	au
o:	u:	u:	u:
ɔ:	ɔ:	o:	əu

(Lass 72, figure 12)

The preliminary form of the Modern English diphthongs /ai/, /au/, /ei/, and /əu/ has been emerged around the turn of the 16th and 17th centuries, which enriches the sound of English and expands the spectrum of the audio colours of the language. Specific explanation should be given to the English diphthong: though sharing the same name with those of the Romance languages, it represents a different phonetic phenomenon:

(a) Des*ire*, des*ire* I have too d*ear*ely bought,
With price of mangled mind thy worthlesse w*are*, (CS 31)

(b) Credis me potuisse m*eae* maledicrere uit*ae*,

ambobus mihi qu*ae* car*io*r est oculis? (Catullus 140)①

The English diphthong is a fixed and independent phoneme (as is presented in the bold letter in example (a)), existing abundantly in English syllables which form the phonological words, making the English vowels impressive in achieving the musical effect. On the contrary, languages like Latin or its modern vernaculars, French and Italian for example, do not have the same diphthongs of the English language. Generally, their diphthongs depend on definite phonetic conditions, in which two vowels are combined into one diphthong through liaison (as is presented in italicized letters in example (b)). The difference of the diphthongs between English and the Romance languages shows that an English poet may have much freedom and more advantages than an Italian or a French poet when applying the diphthongs in their verse. ②

When a language becomes abundant in vocabulary, precise in grammar, and colourful in phonetics, it is expressive, possessing qualities needed in literature, i. e., the poeticality. The rapid growth of English from the Middle English to the Modern English paves the way for the prosperity of the Elizabethan poetry; the increasing poeticality of the language might be one reason in explaining the prosperity.

The growth of English in the 16th century is accompanied with the growth of the English nation and the English culture. It is not difficult to understand that after defeating the Spanish Armada and as the Great Britain becoming a world-influential power, how eagerly her elites want to improve their mother

---

① Guy Lee translates the two lines as: "Do you believe I could have cursed my life / Who's dearer to me than both eyes?" (141)

② In (a), there also exist diphthongs or triphthongs similar in the formation to the Latin examples.

tongue so as to develop their national culture to compete with the European continental cultures which they admire as the advanced while which look down on their island culture as barbaric. The cultural significance is clearly reflected in people's concentration on the cultivation of English. The complaints of the ill-treatments to the language in its development, the fervent endeavours in the pillage-like borrowing the *copia verborum* from Latin and the vernaculars they admired, and the diligent digging and reviving their native linguistic resources—all directly poimt to one aim—the perfection of English.

The English people's cultivation of their language can be regarded as one part of the trend of the rise of modern vernaculars in Europe of the time. Just as the modern nations have come into being, so their native languages have replaced Latin and acquired the official status in their social life. However, most of those vernaculars appear rustic and vulgar, rough in style and poor in vocabulary. These languages need developing. This is a task not only of improving a language, but also of constructing a national culture. And people had their reason to do so—the Latin had been as barbarous as their native languages when the Roman firstly met the brilliant Greek. The dignity of Latin comes from thousand-year cultivation by generations of its learned people. Therefore, the opinions of improving the vernaculars are raised:

> i. The language needs cultivation in order to become a fit medium of literary and scholarly expression. ii. Great writers such as Cicero and Quintillian play a vitally important part in ennobling the language. iii. *Copia verborum*, "copiousness of vocabulary, wealth of lexical resources", had to be created. iv. The language needs to be "fixed" or "regulated" with rules (Law 232).

The English elites are invigorated by these opinions too. The shamefulness was cast away when they feel that even the mighty Latin needs cultivation. It is natural and glorious for them to complete the same task. They are also encouraged by those successful vernacular writers. Dante, Boccaccio and Petrarch have proved with their writings that they could reach the same achievements with their native language as those great writers like Cicero and Quintillian do with Latin. The creativity of the English people during the Renaissance spurs the growth of English, which in turn promotes the development of the English nation and the English culture.

Sidney's exploration of the poeticality of English is influenced by the rapid maturity of English. The progress of the great change of the language from Middle English to Modern English is in the completion in his time, which provides a vast new space for English poets displaying their talents in the competition with their foreign rivals. Yet, how to make full use of the new features of English in their poems urges them to study the language. Sidney's discussion on the English poeticality is also inspired by the growth of the English nation and the English culture. Being proud of the rise of the Great Britain, Sidney was anxious to promote the development of his society. He treats the study of language and poetical construction as a task of their cultural construction.

2. 2 The Accounts of Sidney's Ideas on English Poeticality

Sidney discusses his reflection of the English poeticality intensively in his "Defence of Poesie" and dispersively in his *Old Arcadia* and *Astrophel and Stella*. These accounts contain his insightful understanding of the growing language, significantly contributing to cultural construction. The concentrated observation of Sidney's ideas in his treatise "Defence of Poesie" might be convenient to describe a precise but complete view of his consideration of the poeticality of the English language.

2.2.1 English "Is Capable of Excellent Exercising"

Sidney praises English, saying that, "our language giveth us great occasion, being indeed capable of any excellent exercising of it" (Feuillerat 43). He explains his idea with the discussion of English from the characteristic of its grammatical, lexical and phonological elements.

The English grammar is praiseworthy. Sidney thinks that the aim of using the language is "uttering sweetly and properly the conceit of the minde", the grammatical rules of language must not be the fetter of thought expression (44). English, as Sidney sees it, just meets the demand of such an aim:

> for Grammer it might have, but it needs not, being so easie in it selfe, and so voyd of those combersome differences of *Cases*, *Genders*, *Moods & Tense*, which I thinke was a peece of the Tower of *Babilons* curse, that a man should be put to schoole to learn his mother tongue (43-44).

Sidney points out the advantages of English grammar and the reason why many of his contemporaries have not seen these advantages. ① The English language of that time behaves more strongly as the analytical rather than the synthetic. However, the grammatical system of English is based on the Latin mode, which makes some linguistic phenomena difficult to explain. Latin is a synthetic language (Baugh and Cable 56). The relations of words in a Latin sentence depend largely on the inflections of words, i. e. the connection and meaning are shown by means of the forms of words (word endings, for

① The meaning of grammar Sidney discusses is the same with the definition of today, "using 'grammar' to include both SYNTAX and that aspect of MORPHOLOGY (the internal structure of words)" (Quirk et al. 12).

example). The word order in a sentence plays almost no importance in indicating the relations. Therefore a Latin sentence "Puellae aquam portant" (which means "The girls carry water") may be arranged as "Aquam puellae portant" or in other orders without changing the meaning the sentence expresses. The word "puellae" is the plural nominative form of "puella"—the nominative case determines its subjective status; but not relate to its position in the sentence. The similar rule explains the use of the word "aquam"—the ending "-am" indicates its status of a noun in accusative case. The word will be used as the object in the sentence no matter where it is placed. The inflections make a Latin sentence precise and concise in expression without causing ambiguity. However, the inflections of the synthetic language also cause problems. The rules of the inflection are too complex, like "the Tower of *Babilons* curse". And these rules are only applicable within the formation of words. Latin grammar, thereafter, is mainly the grammar of word inflection. The rules of word-formation are different from the rules of the sentence construction. Two sets of grammatical system in one language force a man "be put to schoole to learn his mother tongue". The Modern English is different. It is simple in grammar, for there are universal rules being applicable both in the word-formation and the sentence construction. Such a characteristic appears even in the Early Modern English. An analytic language adopts extensively the prepositions and the auxiliary verbs. It depends on the word order to show the relationships of words and to indicate the meaning of a sentence. "Water carry girls" is not acceptable in English, but people have the solution to it. A preposition "by" and the auxiliary verb "is" are used in the construction, "Water is carried by the girls". That is the reason why Sidney utters that English is equally "capable of any excellent exercising" in expressing what other languages can express. This is only one merit of Sidney's mother tongue. The greater merits of English in grammar, if they are explained with the grammatical theory of today, are the unity of the principal rules of word-formation and the rules of sentence construction. There exist a set of universal grammar applicable to both aspects. Randolph Quirk et al. have summarized four main types of English word-formations, prefixation, suffixation, conversion and compounding, among which the first two, according to the authors of *A Comprehensive Grammar of the English Language*, "can be referred to as 'affixation'" (Quirk et al 1520). "The main EModE① word-formation processes can be described in terms of free lexemes or bases and bound affixes" as these four categories (Lass 377). The essence of affixation is that a prefix or a suffix being added to the base, i. e., a determinant being added to the determinatum; the essence of conversion is "assigning the base to a different word class without changing its form"; the essence of compounding is adding one base to another, i. e., combining two determinata (Lass 377; Quirk et al 1520).

> This classification reflects the important typological change in English from stem-formation in Old English to word-formation as we know it today. In the course of the Middle English period invariant free lexeme came to be established as bases for word-formation, and the rich stem allomorphy of OE was largely lost in derivational morphology. In this respect Early Modern English is already Modern (Lass 377).

The structure of the compound word is similar to the typology of syntax. Although grammarians have different terms to describe each structure, the word-formation and the sentence construction share actually the same principles. New English words may be formed under the simple rules of

---

① Early Modern English.

coordinate, principal-subordinate, etc., the same principals from the syntactic. English is rich in compound words, phrases, and fixed expressions. The consistency of the rules from the lexical layer to the syntactic layer makes the English grammar simplified, which liberates the productivity of the language with its very limited grammatical limitations. The expressiveness of the language is thus further strengthened.

The merit of English word-formation in the production of new words is obvious. Compared with the enumerable stems, the free lexemes are innumerable. That means far more new words may be produced through word-formation than through stem-formation. It also means that the rapid growth of English becomes possible with the support of the abundantly increasing vocabulary. Sidney praises the word-formation "is particularly happy in compositions of two or three wordes togither, neare the Greeke, farre beyonde the Latine, which is one of the greatest bewties can be in a language" (Feuillerat 44). The capability of word-formation is theoretically infinite. The other aspect of the advantage of the word-formation is that the new word is easy to be remembered. A word formed through the stem-formation in the Old English or Latin usually cannot be learned with the meaningful memorization. Because of the internal inflection of the stem, there is a big difference between the word and its stem in spelling in most cases. For example, the stem of the word "collide" is "laedere" (meaning "hurt by striking") (Trumble and Stevenson 449), from which it is hard to guess the meaning of the word by its stem. A mechanical memorization of every new word often means much hard labour. On the contrary, it is convenient in many occasions to learn a new word of word-formation with the help of the meanings of its base(s) and the affix(es). For instance, the meaning of "heartbreak" can be roughly inferred through the combined meanings of its lexemic components "heart" and "break". The merit of word-formation in Early Modern English has proved what Sidney acclaims the "beauty" "in a language".

Sidney analyzes the features of English pronunciation, believing that the phonological structure of his mother tongue is fit for either the quantitative metre or the accentual metre; and English surpasses both the ancient languages like Latin and the modern vernaculars like French and Italian in versification:

> Now of versefying, there are two sorts, the one auncient, the other moderne. The auncient marked the quantitie of each sillable, and according to that, framed his verse: The moderne, observing onely number, with some regard of the accent; the chiefe life of it, standeth in that like sounding of the words, which we call Rime. Whether of these be the more excellent, wold bear many speeches, the ancient no doubt more fit for Musicke, both words and time observing quantitie, and more fit, lively to expresse divers passions by the low or loftie sound of the well-wayed sillable. The latter likewise with his rime striketh a certaine Musicke to the ear: and in fine, since it dooth delight, though by an other way, it obtaineth the same purpose, there being in either sweetnesse, and wanting in neither, majestie. Truly the English before any Vulgare language, I know is fit for both sorts: for, for the auncient, the *Italian* is so full of Vowels, that it must ever be combred with *Elisions*. The *Duch* so of the other side with Consonants, that they cannot yeeld the sweete slyding, fit for a Verse. The *French* in his whole language, hath not one word that hath his accent in the last sillable, saving two, called *Antepenultima*; and little more hath the *Spanish*, and therefore verie gracelessly may they use *Dactiles*. The English is subject to none of these defects. Now for Rime, though we doo not observe quantitie, yet we observe the Accent verie precisely, which other languages either cannot do, or will not do so absolutely. That *Caesura*, or breathing place in the midst of the Verse, neither *Italian* nor *Spanish* have: the *French* and we, never almost faile off.

> Lastly, even the verie Rime it selfe, the *Italian* cannot put it in the last sillable, by the *French* named the *Masculine* Rime; but still in the next to the last, which the French call the *Female*; or the next before that, which the Italian *Sdrucciola*: the example of the former, is *Buono*, *Suono*, of the *Sdrucciola*, is *Femina*, *Semina*. The *French* of the other side, hath both the Male as *Bon*, *Son*; and the Female, as *Plaise*, *Taise*; but the *Sdrucciola* he hath not: where the English hath all three ... (Feuillerat 44-45)

What Sidney talks in this passage are some facts he has observed within his limited knowledge of languages and prosodies from the ancient Greco-Roman era to the Elizabethan time. His impressive comment on the advantages and disadvantages of the European languages when they are judged with the prosodic rules comes largely from his experience, affected by his patriotism as well. It is not possible for him to give a convincing explanation to his conclusion that English is better than all other languages, especially those vernaculars. Sidney insists that English fits for both the quantitative metre and the accentual metre. But his poetical practice has proved that English is not suitable to the former metre. The reason for this contrast might be due to the education Sidney received and the strange linguistic phenomenon in the Early Modern English. Latin grammar is taught "as the basis for school education" in Elizabethan England and "ortographia", "etymologia", "syntaxis" and "prosodia" are the four main parts of the grammar (Attridge 41; 47).① Latin "prosodia" is instilled into the pupils by the school training, which makes it possible for these educated people observing the English language with the Latin grammatical concepts when they grow up and when there are only the borrowed Latin terms in their description of English phonetics. On the other

① One general textbook of Latin grammar that Sidney used at Shrewsbury School is Gaultherus' *De Syllabarum et Caminum Ratione* (Attridge 41).

hand, there coexist two types of stress systems in the Early Modern English, the Germanic Stress Rule (GSR) and the Romance Stress Rule (RSR), which means that the syllable in an English word of different origin may be given prominence through the stressed accent or through the length of pronunciation (Lass 125-128). But both GSR and RSR describe the stress patterns of the phonological words with a tendency of focusing on the word accents. Even if in the RSR the rule that the length of a long syllable equals two short ones is neglected. But the influence of Latin pronunciation, the existence of long and short syllables in English and the fact that a syllable emphasized is shown in loudness, length and pitch at the same time are enough to cause Sidney's confusion. Anyway, the coexistence of GSR and RSR in English provides the possibility for poets to adopt the phonological elements from both sides. In this respect, Sidney is right to say that English fits for both versifications of the ancient and modern, surpassing Latin and its modern offsprings. Sidney's discussion on the concept of caesura may not be absolutely correct when it is linked with Italian and Spanish, but is insightful in English. The practice of the English poets, including that of Sidney, has proved that the use of caesura in an English line can be free in any position between the first syllable and the last. The poets from Italy, France or Span cannot compete with them in this practice, because the stress systems of these languages are different. The word-stress of English is preserved when it is organized into a sentence, so that the sentence generally contains more than one stress. To adjust the rhythmic contour, the writer usually appeals to the stop(s). In an English line, such a stop is better named as "pause" than "caesura", for caesura has its fixed positions in the middle of the line. Most Romance languages assign stress of a sentence by following penultimate prominence (like Italian), or the end prominence (like French), meanwhile neglecting the original word-stresses, automatically generating a fixed cadence-profile of the sentence. When Sidney talks about the rhyme, he, like most of his contemporaries, often mixes it with rhythm; therefore, his "rime" may refer to either the rhythm or the rhyme. His comparison between English rhymes and the Italian and the French rhymes is convincing. The syllable, the constitution of a foot, comprises three parts in general, the onset (On), the nucleus (Nu) and the coda (Co). The onset is made up of the beginning consonant or consonants of the syllable. The nucleus, which is the core of the syllable, usually is held by a vowel. The coda is made up of the consonant or consonants after the nucleus (Aronoff and Fudeman 71). It is the nucleus, or nucleus and coda together, that forms the rhyme of a poetical line. The English rhyme, according to the combinations of nucleus and coda, falls into three categories: Nu+Co, bare Nu and sonorant Co. When the rhyming rule of poetry is taken into account, the situation might be more complicated. In a poetical line, the last stressed Nu and all the sounds following it make up the rhyming part. Therefore, the rhyming part of an English line may consist of one Nu-Co combination if the line ends with a right-head foot (iamb or anapaest), or two such combinations if the line ends with a binary left-head foot (trochee), or theoretically three Nu-Co combinations if the line ends with a ternary left-head foot (dactyl). (The first kind of rhyme is masculine rhyme, while the second is the feminine rhyme. No specific name given to the third but it is actually one kind of feminine rhyme.) The rhyming structures are richly varied, offering poets more choices in their compositions; while the dominantly penultimate stress pattern of Italian determines not only the syllable count of a line but also characteristic of the rhyme. Though the Italian poetry surpasses the English in types of rhymes, it lacks the sonorant Co rhyme, for its words end with On + Nu or bare Nu, which makes the ending Co impossible, and explains why Petrarch practices most commonly the feminine rhymes in his *Il Canzoniere*.

The rhythm of English gives stronger prominence to stress (accent) than Latin and its modern descendants, like Italian and French. The accentual, especially the accentual-syllabic, metre, is one of the most conspicuous features of the English metrical poetry. The other three languages focus on, more or less, the aesthetic effects of the phonological quantity in a poem. Different emphases are linked with different linguistic characteristics of different languages, resulting in different poetry. Sidney's poetical practice has proved this. The comparison of his poems with those of Latin poet Gaius Valerius Catullus, Italian poet Torquato Tasso and French poet Joachim Du Bellay might manifest Sidney's ideas on the unique merits of the English pronunciation:

Sidney: With how sad steps, O Moon, thou climb'st the skies (AS 31)
Catullus: Vale puella, iam Catullus obdurat (8)
(Goodbye lass, now Catullus sticks it out)
Tasso: il gran Sepolcro adora e scioglie il voto (*Gerusalemme Liberata*)
(Prostrates himself at grand Sepulchral and delivers his vow)
Du Bellay: Si les larmes servaient de remède au malheur (*Les regrets*)
(If tears can be used to cure misfortune)

One common feature of these four lines is the slow-paced tempo of the rhythm. However, they have their own way to reach it. Sidney combines the element of syllable quantity into the stress-timed (the stresses are isochronized in scansion), delaying the appearance of the coming stresses. The fragmented grammatical structure enhances the effect. The line is in iambic pentameter, consisting of ten monosyllabic words, "but the words are not low, nor is the line dull" (Ringler liii). The melody of the verse is not monotonous, for the diphthongs play an important role in adjusting its cadence contour. The words "how", "thou", "climb'st" and "skies" all contain the diphthongs which enrich the sound quality of these words. Interestingly, "how", "climb'st" and "skies" are put in the stressed position in the metrical pattern and distributed significantly if considering the sound arrangement of the whole line. The word "how" is in the stressed position of the initial foot of the line. Its stressed nucleus /au/ is distantly echoed in the stressed nucleus /ai/ in the words "climb'st" and "skies" which are in the stressed positions of the fourth and fifth feet. The seriate diphthongs imitate, with their gliding sounds, the mood that the line conveys. The voice of the speaker in the verse is spread by the repetition of the stressed diphthongal vowel /ai/. Sidney also makes the line imitate the rising of the moon—a personified celestial body climbing up the sky with heavy steps and sad feelings. Almost all the long vowels and the diphthongs are distributed in the stressed positions of the metrical pattern, lengthening the time of reading. Two pauses fall in front of and behind the third foot, each between two stressed syllables, enhancing the time delay with two distinct stops. The dispersed short vowels, most of them being weakened, and the irregularly arranged consonants illustrate vividly the tottering steps of the moon. The simple words Sidney uses have achieved surprising effect in which the function of the gliding diphthongs is noteworthy. They enhance the beauty and charm to the line, saving it from the common.

Sidney realizes the merit of an English diphthong for the aesthetic purpose of the poetical form. He exploits extensively such a feature in his poetical design, resulting in many beautiful lines which "yeeld the sweete sliding, fit for a Verse" (Feuillerat 44). The English diphthongs, which form the majority of the English long vowels and, of which Sidney has touched the charm, are indeed unique. Unlike the diphthong in Latin, Italian and French, the English diphthong is one self-complete and independent phoneme. Its status does not rely on the combination of two monophthongs, which means that the sound quality can be changed within a smallest phonological unit (Kuiper and Allan 127). Such a wonderful linguistic phenomenon cannot be found in the other three languages. The diphthongs in these languages are combined ones, many of them being temporarily combined through liaison of the two juxtaposed monophthongs. This kind of combined diphthongs exists in English as well. English is more affluent in the species of vowels than in those of Latin, Italian, and French, which provides more choices for a poet to compose his poems.

Catullus decelerates the tempo of the line rhythm by caesura and several polysyllabic words. Although the words "puella" and "iam" in the line contain diphthongs, the factual effect they make is not the same as those in Sidney's line because the pronunciations of these two diphthongs are influenced by the quantitative metre. Tasso relies on the teeming vowels to get to his aim. Du Bellay appeals to the French Alexandrine conventions—the quantitative measure, the function of caesura and the quite enough number of syllables—in accomplishing his poetical design. It is not possible to conclude all the features of these four languages with these four short lines. However, they provide enough support to Sidney's idea that English is capable of excellent exercising.

2.2.2 English "Is Fit to Honour Poesie, and to Be Honoured by Poesie"

In "Defence of Poesie", Sidney explores the expression of English poeticality in the lyrical poems. After comparing the performances of English and the major Romance languages in poetry, he concludes that English, "is most fit to honour *Poesie*, and to bee honoured by *Poesie*" (Feuillerat 45). He raises four examples as the evidences, which are regarded as the representatives of new lyrical poetry, to prove that English does have the strong poeticality. These examples include Geoffrey Chaucer's "Troilus and Criseyde", the poems of Henry Howard, Earl of Surrey, some poems in the lyric selection entitled *Mirror for Magistrates*, and Edmund Spenser's *The Shepherdes Calender.* Among these examples, Chaucer's work belongs to the fifteenth century, written in the Middle English, not proper to be cited here to serve the discussion of the poeticality of Modern English. The other three examples are suitable. The poems of Earl of Surrey had been produced in the first half of the sixteenth century, composed in the Early Modern English. The works of Sackville and Spenser, Sidney's contemporaries, are written in the same English Sidney uses in his poems. Sidney praises their creative practice of English in the newly emerging poetical forms.

Although Chaucer writes in Middle English, he leads the way of improving the English language. Sidney exclaims that "hee in that mistie time could see so clearly, or that wee in this cleare age, goe so stumblingly after him" (37). Chaucer walks far ahead of his time in writing "Troilus and Criseyde": he is conscious in cultivating a standard English. The effort to regulate and enrich the language is obviously reflected in his writings. On the one hand, he uses the generally accepted English as his language for his poems. On the other hand, after introducing extensively the writing skills from the Italian vernacular poetry which has just reached the aesthetic height that even the classical poetry could not compete, Chaucer establishes foundamentally the prosodic rules for the English poetry, among which is the iambic pentameter, a metrical pattern coinciding harmoniously with the natural rhythm of the English language. Chaucer's contribution to English language is people's acceptance of the foreign poetical forms with a standard language they are familiar with. The accentual-syllabic verse, the tidy and regular end-rhymes, the ordered stanzaic forms, the apt arrangement of monosyllabic words and polysyllabic words, etc. —all the new things in the English poetry first come into being in the hands of Chaucer. His efforts to cultivate English through his poetic experiments are in fact meant to develop the poeticality of his mother tongue.

Surrey has partly inherited Chaucer's creative style. Though his poetic diction is archaistic, the clarity and mellowness of his verse are not impaired. Sidney comments that "in the Earle of *Surreis Lirickes*, manie thinges tasting of a Noble birth, and worthie of a Noble minde" (37). Together with Thomas Wyatt, Surrey learns and transplants the sonnets and blank verse into English poetry, opening the new ways for Tudor literature. A. C. Partridge thinks that Surrey does not match Wyatt in the poetic talent, but exceeds Wyatt in the poetical language. Surrey has a more exquisite taste:

> Surrey's service was the good taste with which he combated the diffuse and prolix in poetic language, to give his style meaningful lucidity. For the existing state of the language, this was more valuable than gifts of imagination (Partridge 46).

Surrey has re-written a sonnet from Petrarch's *Il Canzoniere* (sonnet 164), following the poetical form which he establishes and which is called by the later generations the English sonnet. The form is brand-new when it appears, and the skills Surrey uses in such a form are unusual. He abandons the principal rules of prosody handed down from the Middle English poetry—the alliteration and the mechanical caesura, which often distort the natural Englishand and cause the stiffness of a line if it is not well designed. Instead, he gives prominence to the natural rhythm of his contemporary English:

> Calm is the sea; the waves work less and less:
> So am not I, whom love, alas, doth wring,

Bringing before my face the great increase
Of my desires whereat I weep and sing (Ault 19),

The language is lucid and fluid, used in the daily conversation of those well-educated people. The rhythm-profile of the lines is smooth, coinciding with the natural language rhythm, projecting the accentual feature of English into an exact but flexible way. The feeling reflected in the lines sounds a bit artificial though; it is unhindered in expression. Because of the free distribution of pauses in accordance with the expression and the language structures, the metrical pattern of the poem appears not rigid as the following one:

No force for that, I price your beauty light,
  If so I find you steadfast in good will.
Though few there are that do in age delight,
  I was your friend, and so do purpose still (Chambers 141);

One defect of the poetical design is that the language is twisted to meet the metre, which is revealed in the poet's exertion in end rhyming and observation to the rule of mid-line caesura. The end rhymes are arranged with the sacrifice of the natural language structures. The rigid uniform of the position of caesura reduces the lines into "mechanical regularity" (Ringler liv). If the language of a poem cannot be well organized, is it possible for its writer to express his idea clearly in the poem? It's obvious that Surrey has overcome these disadvantages. He tames the foreign poetical forms, making them compatible to the English language. In Surrey's hand, the Italian sonnet becomes the English sonnet, the Italian blank verse becomes the English blank verse, and the Italian endecasyllabic line becomes the English iambic pentameter. Perhaps unconsciously but actually, Surrey has exploited the poeticality of his contemporary English in his poetry.

Sidney accounts *Mirror for Magistrates*, "meetly furnished of beautiful partes" (Feuillerat 37). These "beautiful partes", as Sidney sees, comprise the application of the English poeticality. Among the selected poems, Thomas Sackville's works are praised frequently by the later generations. They are gloomy and labourous, but effectively convey the majestic mood. The poet's endeavour to the rise of Elizabethan lyrical poetry has gained him praise:

> When all temptation to flattery had long passed away, Pope chose him out for special commendation among the writers of his age as distinguished by "a propriety in sentiments, a dignity in the sentences, an unaffected perspicuity of style, and an easy flow of numbers..." (Ward and Waller 200)

Sackville's own poems may be good evidence to people's recognitions:

> The wrathful winter, 'proaching on apace,
> With blustering blasts had all ybar'd the treen,
> And old Saturnus, with his frosty face,
> With chilling cold had pierc'd the tender green (Chambers 110);

There remain some traces in diction of Middle English poetry; however, the metre of the poem becomes regular and easy. The syntactic structures are kept complete in the metrical patterns. A complex sentence stretches from line one to line two, containing two complicated phrases, each in one line. This organization is repeated in line three and line four. So the first two lines and the second two constitute a pair of counter-balanced parts. The reader may assume that such a parallel construction is intentionally designed, for an aesthetic symmetry is achieved and further more, the progress of winter's coming in the fierce wind is imitated. Different layers of parallel constructions of language are frequently used in poems to contrapose the repetition of the metrical patterns. The phonological characteristics of English are also explored in conveying the mood. The plosive consonants /p/, /b/ and /f/ scatter in the lines, responding to each other or forming the alliterations, imitating acoustically the fierce winter wind. Long vowels (diphthong in especial) and the delaying end rhymes make the reader feel the moving of the winter in the chilly wind. The arrangement of pauses is flexible, breaking away from the rigid Middle English poetical conventions. Sackville inherits Chaucer's innovations in stanza design and the end rhymes. His poem benefits from the development of the Early Modern English in syntactic structures, morphological choices and phonological expressions.

Spenser's *The Shepherdes Calender* is considered by Sidney as having "much Poetrie in his Ecloges, indeed woorthie the reading" (Feuillerat 37). The word "poetrie" refers just to the poeticality. Spenser is eager for language experiments in his poetry, very original in displaying the musical beauty of the English language. This is acclaimed by many people:

> ... a metrical writer had arisen who excelled all his predecessors in his sense of the capacity of the English language for harmonious combinations of sound: whether he takes an irregular lyrical flight, or employs the iambic rhythm in uniform stanzas, he shows that he can use the courtly style of diction to the utmost advantage (Ward and Waller 228).

Such harmony may be explained through Spenser's own poems. The following stanza is one of the two stanzas W. J. Courthope had cited in *The Cambridge*

History of English Literature and is sung highly of by Courthope himself. The language of Spenser is influential for it meets the rise of a national Standard language (Lass 539):

> Colin, to heare thy rymes and roundelayes,
> Which thou were wont on wastfull hylls to singe,
> I more delight, then larke in Sommer dayes:
> Whose Echo made the neyghbour groues to ring,
> And taught the byrds, which in the lower spring
> Did shroude in shady leaues from sonny rayes,
> Frame to thy songe their chereful cheriping,
> Or hold theyr peace, for shame of thy swete layes (52).

Spenser chooses the simple words spoken in people's daily life and selects the simple sentences used in people's usual conversations. But he invigorates them with his control of melody of the lines. The end rhymes arranged in the stanza is *ababbaba*, a combination of *rime alternate* and *rime chiuse* based on the Italian prosody, making the ending sounds of the lines rolling on. The scattered consonants of post-alveolar approximant /r/ and labial-velar approximant /w/, either forming the alliterations within a line or echoing with each other within the whole stanza, manifest the rolling effect of the natural sounds described in the poem. Matching with the diphthongs, long monophthongs and the light consonants without much obstruction, the whole stanza well imitates the scene that the song of Colin echoes in the woods rousing the responding singing of birds. The weaving of the songs of a human being and the sounds of nature is expressed as well through the deliberately distribution of the polysyllabic words among the lines, which make the stresses of words coincide with the stresses of the lines, forming a natural and elegant style. The whole stanza sounds melodiously delightful, rich in musical moving. Spenser is extraordinary in exploring the poeticality of his mother tongue.

The above evidences might support Sidney's idea that English is fit to honour Poetry and to be honoured by Poetry and that English is capable of excellent exercising.

2. 3 The Cultural Significance of Sidney's Ideas on English Poeticality

The ideas on the poeticality of the English language expressed in Sidney's "Defence of Poesie" clearly reflect his attitude to his mother tongue. His approval to the standard national language, which just emerges, reflects the constant increase of sense of nativeness the English elites of Sidney's time possessed. The sense of nativeness is exposed through the proudness of English nation in the ambitious and active construction of their national culture. Language is one of the most important carriers of culture. It is also the important part of the culture. When a nation rises, many people of the nation will give their enthusiasm to the improvement of their national language, attentive to the application of the language in every field of their social life. The attentiveness itself is significant in the cultural construction, which is illustrated by the abundant evidences in the history. Plato regards the language as the route to reality (Law 17). Aristotle discusses the poetical practice of the ancient Greek with three chapters in his *Poetics* (Adams and Searle 62-65). Dante debates the poeticality of the Italian in "De vulgari eloquentia" (Bec 59). Joachim Du Bellay probes the ways "pour donner perfection ȧ la langue française" (for presenting perfection to the French language) with his treatise "Déffence et illustration de la langue française"

(Longeon 152). It is obvious that all these writers, especially Dante and Du Bellay, have shown their strong sense of nativeness when talking about their native languages. The reader can easily feel the national feelings flowing with the words, "Je n'estime pourtant notre vulgaire, tel qu'il est maintenant, être si vil et abject, comme le font ces ambitieux admirateurs des langues grecque et latine" (150).① Although the English nation grows in a different way from those of the European continent, and the English language evolves differently from other European modern languages which are called vernaculars then, the island country has been profoundly influenced by the cultural trend on languages. What Sidney expresses in his "Defence of Poesie" are very much like the ideas of Dante in "De vulgari eloquentia" or Du Bellay in "Déffence et illustration de la langue française". They convey the same thought of culture.

Sidney realizes the importance of the English poeticality to the commencement of the English new poetry of the Elizabethan era. His realization prepares a theoretical support for his conscious experiments on the language in his poetical construction. Being an influential literary patron of the late sixteenth century in England, Sidney plays a decisive role in shaping the Elizabethan lyrics. His idea about the poeticality of the English language has become one important source of English literary criticism of his time and of the later generations. Poets' attention to the practice of language has led to the extensive beautiful lyrics flourishing in a short time. Sidney's contemplation on English poeticality urges many poets to both theoretically compose and examine their poems. Thus, the custom of being a poet and critic has come into being Sidney's time. Such a custom has guaranteed the constant blooming of the English poetry from the Elizabethan era to the present.

---

① The French words may be translated as, "But I don't think that our vernacular, as it is at present, is so inferior and so wretched as those eager admirers of the language of Greek and Latin thought."

Chapter 3 Sidney's Experiments on English Quantitative Verse①

Sidney tries the English quantitative verse in his early works, the *Old Arcadia* and *Certain Sonnets*. These poems of quantitative verse are only a small fraction of Sidney's experimental works in his poetical construction; however, their poetic value has attracted many people to probe into them. The emergence of Sidney's English quantitative verse is linked with some historical events at the beginning of the Elizabethan lyrics blooming, especially the activities of the "Areopagus"②. People have observed Sidney's struggle with the foreign verse design, postulated that Sidney's experiment on quantitative verse is but an endeavour to enrich the English lyric forms. However, they neglect a more significant poetical value in Sidney's anglicization of the classical prosody during his exploration in the establishment of an ideal English verse rhythm.

---

① This chapter is derived from a published paper, entitled "The Areopagus and Their Experiments on English Verse Metre", of Chinese version that Professor Ou Hong collaborated with the author of this book. Professor Hu Jialuan had helped to revise the paper with some pertinent suggestions when it was publishing.

② Areopagus is the place where, in ancient Greek time, the highest judicial court of ancient Athens held its sittings. Areopagus also refers to the court itself. Here the Areopagus refers to a literary salon in Elizabethan era.

3.1 The Background of Sidney's Experiments

The reason for Sidney's experiments on the quantitative verse might be that he feels the prevailing English metre of his time does not well reflect the prosodical feature of the English phonology on the one hand, and does not well meet people's expectation of musical effects in lyrics on the other. The essence of poetry metre is the verse rhythm. The English prosodic history before Sidney has bequeathed three kinds of verse rhythms to the Elizabethan poets, namely, the accentual, the syllabic and the immature accentual-syllabic verse rhythm. The first one represents the English metrical tradition which can be traced back far into the Old English poetry, the second shows the influence of the French prosody on the English counterpart, and the third is the result of the exploration of verse rhythm by the English poets from Chaucer on (Larry D. Benson xxxix). Chaucer's innovation on the English verse rhythm has submerged in the history and became obscure in Sidney's time because of the rapid change of English herself. The syllabic verse has not been frequently used by Elizabethan poets, possibly because the verse rhythm of such a poem cannot be easily compatible with the English natural speech rhythm. The accentual verse turns to be the dominant type, for its rhythm is in accordance with the English rhythm. People feel natural when composing a line of poem with such a verse rhythm. However, the poets of Sidney's time, limited by their understanding of the expressiveness of the accentual verse, assumed that if people did not pay enough attention to the length the syllables in a verse, the stressed rhythm could not fully meet the demand of their finely lyrical verse composition in which they regard the musical effects produced as a very high aesthetic and poetic achievement. The accentual verse in their mind is crude and clumsy, and cannot be musical. Sidney is influenced by this idea too. He, like his contemporaries, turns his eye to the classical prosody, finding that the anglicization of the quantitative verse might be a solution to the development of English lyrics.

In this respect, Sidney's experiments on English quantitative verse can be understood as being guided by the need of the national cultural construction of his time. There is a trend of the rise of vernacular and the national cultures in the Renaissance Europe. Literate people from the newly born nations are fascinated with cultivating their own language and their own culture. Often they are not satisfied with the status quo of their own languages and cultures, feeling them humble when compared with the classical ones. These people decide to improve their own languages and cultures by learning from the classical ones. The quantitative verse is what they want to explore in their creation of the vernacular poetry. In fact, some Continental poets, and the English poets, have already introduced or have been ready to introduce the classical verse rhythm, especially the Latin verse rhythm, into their own vernacular poetry.

Among those Continental poets, Italian and French poets are worth mentioning. Poets in these countries even held academic societies and formed their own schools to promote their proposition of adapt the quantitative verse to meet the demand of composition of their vernacular poetry. In France, Jean-Antoine de Baïf, Joachim Thibault de Courville and his followers founded "Académie de Poésie et de Musique". Baïf's experiments of the quantitative verse in French are included in his *Les Étrennes de Poezie Fransoeze en vers mezurés*. Baïf's proposal about the quantitative verse was spread through "la Pléiade", and particular the "Académie de Poésie et de Musique", which foreshadowed the form of the Alexandrine, the principal metre of French verse, came into being (Sabatier 177). In Italy, Claudio Tolomei founded the "Accademia della Nuova Poesia" in Rome, advocating the idea of writing

Italian poems in quantitative verse. He published in 1539 his *Versi*, *et regole de la nuova poesia Toscana* which inspired his contemporary poets and those of the later generations (Hardson 89).

Compared with the active movements in France and Italy, the English poetical construction seems to lag behind. Yet, they determine to change the situation. The "Areopagus" urges poets to anglicize the foreign prosody, and "prescribed certaine Lawes and rules of Quantities of English sillables for English Verse" (Smith 89). Sidney, one of the leaders of "Areopagus", is familiar with the English prosody this literary salon proclaimed. Yet, before Sidney and his friends, some scholars have already noticed the possibility of grafting the classical metre into the English poems. As early as in 1570, Roger Ascham, in his *The Schoolmaster*, had acknowledged that,

> In deed, our English tong, hauing in vse chiefly wordes of one syllable which commonly be long, doth not well receiue the nature of *Carmen Heroicum*, bicause *dactylus*, the aptest foote for that verse, conteining one long and two short, is seldom therfore found in English; and doth also rather stumble than stand vpon *Monasyllabis*. (30)

Ascam was aware of the difficulty in introducing the quantitative verse into English poetry, because English and Greco-Roman languages emphasize different phonetic features in shaping their own verse rhythms. However, he was optimistic when looking toward the future of English,

> although *Carmen Exametrum* doth rather trotted and hoble than runne smothly in our English tong, yet I am sure our English tong will receiue *carmen Iambicum* as naturallie as either *Greke* or *Latin.*" (30-31)

Ascam was confident that the iambic metre can be accepted in English poetry, but he did not put forward the solution to the acceptance of dyctylic metre for English poets. At that time, it was Thomas Drant, an elder poet of Sidnian circle, who had preliminarily designed certain rules for English quantitative verse prosody after careful study. Drant's rules were not kept on the historical record, and it is said that he gave them to his close friend Sir Philip Sidney (89, 99) who, after talking over the "Areopagus", writes the rules down in his *Old Arcadia* as "Nota" (Sidney 71-72; Ringler 391).

Sidney's "Nota" mainly includes the following: (1) some Latin prosody rules are applicable to the English poems; for example, the position; (2) English has its own phonetic characteristics, rich in consonants and monosyllabic words; (3) English words should be pronounced in their natural way, even if they are borrowed from the foreign languages; (4) particles can be pronounced long or short, depending on the context.

"Nota" is a product of Sidney's observation to English poetry writing under the rules of the Latin prosody. It reflects to some degree Sidney's understanding of and expectation on English and her performance in poetry; that is, English can compete Latin in the quantitative verse. Furthermore, because of her unique phonological features, the English quantitative verse may display the musicality different from that of the Latin verse. He believes that in English, poets can adjust the length of a syllable as in Latin so that they can explore the musical effect in the verse in a Latinate way.

3. 2 Application of Latin Prosody into English Verse

Sidney admires the musicality expressed by the classical quantitative verse. The quantitative verse, being improved by those Latin poets, represents the major classical verse metre. Its rhythm is embodied through the feet of the measured syllables in a line, that is, the rhythm echoes through the quantity of syllables. Because the length of a syllable and the arrangement of such a syllable are important to the verse rhythm, the Latin poets have strived for digging out the possible elements of Latin phonetics which could realize their amibition. Then they summarize the rules of prosody and perfect these rules in their practice. Taking Latin verse as his model, Sidney composes eighteen English quantitative poems—thirteen from the *Old Arcadia* and five from the *Certain Sonnets*—in which the rhythm is arranged within a system of measured syllables long and short.

The position is one of Sidney's experiments; however, it is also a difficulty that often traps Sidney into awkwardness. In Latin prosody, when a short vowel is before two or more adjacent consonants, including the combination of the ending consonant of a word and the initial consonant(s) of another word next to it, or when a vowel before x or z, the vowel should be pronounced as a long one. This is called "positio", or "position" in English (Trumble and Stevenson 2293; Cruttenden 53). The rule of position in Latin prosody, being frequently used by Latin poets, forms a unique feature of Latin poetical rhythm. It privileged the poets to prolong the vowels whenever necessary, and thus making it easier for them to seek the musical effect they want. However, once the rule is applied into English, Sidney finds it hard to naturalize it. The rhythm of English is not due mainly to a systematic arrangement of long and short syllables, though the length of a syllable is often linked with the emphasized part in a metrical foot. It is the stress that decides the English verse rhythm. Sidney is not successful in his position experiment:

– ˘ ˘ – ˘ ˘ – ˘ ˘ – – – ˘ ˘ – –

Lady, rese*rvd* by the hea*v*' *ns* to do pa*s*tor*s*' company honor,

– – – – – ˘ ˘ – – – ˘ ˘ – –

Joyning your sweete voice to the rura*ll* muse of a dese*rt*e. (OA 13)

The italicized letters show the possible combination of the consonants in front of which the vowels are to be lengthened according to the rule of position. Sidney uses the methods of elision and double-writing the consonant letter, etc. to produce the position so that the syllable at the place where the ictus falls would be treated as an accepted long one. But, it seems that Sidney only achieved a visual effect to those who are familiar with the Latin prosody. It is none of the help to those who know nothing about the Latin prosody. In the words like "reserved", "heaven" ①, and "desert", the stressed syllables are longer than the unstressed syllables. Such an English phonetic phenomenon has nothing to do with the Latin rule of position. In the words like "pastor" and "rurall", the second syllables are shorter when read than the first one because it is unstressed in the word, though Sidney has made the positions here by adding a genitive case and double writing the letter "l". When "pastor" and "rural" are read in the line, people would naturally give compensation to the length of the second syllables in conforming to the "borrowing rule" (Cruttenden 251), but that's not the result of Sidney's position. In English, there is no equation that a long syllable equals to two short ones when they are pronounced, nor an equivalent ratio between a stressed syllable and two weak ones.

The same clumsiness of Sidney's application of the Latin position to his English quantitative verse can be found in other poems of his experiments:

– – – – – – – – – ˘ ˘ – –

① The combination of the letters "ea" in Early Modern English was pronounced as /eː/ (Barber 292).

> With strong foes on land, on seas with contrary tempests
>
> – – – – – – ˘ ˘ – ˘ ˘ –
>
> Still doo I crosse this wretch, what so he taketh in hand (OA 11).

These lines, according to Sidney, are set in the elegiacs①. The classical metre of the elegiac distich consists of a dactylic hexameter and a dactylic pentameter, which shows a balance of the long and short syllables in the line and creates a slow and smooth tempo. Sidney gives out the scansion: "– – – – – ˘ ˘ – ˘ ˘ – ˘ ˘ – – // – – – ˘ ˘ – – ˘ ˘ – ˘ ˘ –". It is possible for Sidney to draw the reader's attention to the mood he wants to show among the lines. But it is also possible to arouse the reader's uneasiness when he scans the lines by Sidney's formula. According to the rule of Latin prosody, the vowel /i/ in the words "with" and "still", and the vowel /e/ in the second syllable of the word "tempests" should be lengthened by position. Such pronunciations are against the natural ways when these words are read. In fact, the length of a syllable is fixed within a word, with exceptions only when the syllable is at the beginning or the ending of the word, and the word is arranged in a larger linguistic unit, e. g. a phrase or a sentence, the length of the syllable might be affected by its phonetic context which is different from the Latin position:

> ' * x ' * ' * ' ' * ' * *' *
>
> – ˘ ˘ – – – – – ˘ ˘ – ˘ ˘ – –
>
> Ere that I should consent to doo such excessive a dammage

---

① The possible metrical scansion for Latin elegiacs, or elegiac couplet, is:

˘˘ ˘˘ ˘˘ ˘˘ (¯)
– – – – – – – – – ˘˘ – +

– –
– ˘˘ – ˘˘ – – ˘˘ – ˘˘ + (Flewett and Pantin xxxiii-xxxiv; Howaston and Chilvers 346).

' * * ' * * ' * ' * ' * * ' *

– ˘ ˘ – – – – – ˘ ˘ – ˘ ˘ – –

Unto the earth by the hurt of this her heavenly jewell (OA 74).

The acoustic quality of the vowel /ai/ in the word "I" should be pronounced *de facto* with a certain length and prominence even if it is located in a weak position (Cruttenden 132-133), which conflicts with its position in the dactylic scanned in Latin prosodical rule. The first syllable /kən/ in "consent" does not likely acquire enough length that Sidney expected. It is a weak syllable, both in the word and in the phonological utterance.① However, some syllables, like /midʒ/ in "dammage" and /əl/ in "jewell" do have been prolonged a little, due to the ending positions of the utterances and the combinations of vowels plus the voiced consonants (53). But the length of the prolonged syllables is only phonetically noticeable but not long enough to meet the demand of Latin metre. The significance of Sidney's experiments here might be his perception of the musicality of English in the acoustic spectrum of speech.

In order to make full use of the phonetic resource effectual in arranging the long and short syllables in a line to form the quantitative verse, Sidney might have dug very carefully in the English language. Yet it seems that he exerts in vain in many cases. Sidney points out that "vowel before vowel or diphthong before vowel always short, except such an exclamation as 'ōh'; else the diphthongs always long and the single vowels short. (Sidney 72)"

---

① In the popular theory of prosodic phonology, a set of domains are hierarchically ranked, namely, the phonological utterance, intonational phrase, phonological phrase and phonological word, from the largest to the smallest. These domains of different layers have connections but not always identical coincidences with their equivalent counterparts from the grammatical system covering both the syntax and the morphology, like sentence, phrase and word (Gussenhoven and Jacobs 239-255; Roca and Johnson 444-494).

Unfortunately, phoneticians of the later generations have not reached the same conclusion (Cruttenden 92, 94-96; Kuiper and Allan 127).

In Sidney's "Nota", two features of English are noted: English is rich in consonants and consonant clusters, people frequently use the one-syllable words and two-syllable words in their communication: "... our tonge being full of consonantes and monasillables, the vowell slydes awaye quicklier then in Greeke or Latin, which be full of vowells and longe wordes. (Sidney 72)" This shows Sidney is awareness of the phonological difference between English and the ancient Greek or Latin, thus he would have to consider the unique characteristics of his native language when naturalizing the Latin prosody. Most of Sidney's English quantitative verses sound smooth; possibly because he does not neglect these characteristics:

> ¯ ˘¯ ¯ ¯ ˘ ˘ ¯ ˘ ¯ ¯
> Yet dying, and dead, doo we sing her honour;
> ¯ ˘ ¯ ¯ ¯ ˘ ˘ ¯ ˘ ¯ ¯
> So become our tombes monuments of her praise;
> ¯ ˘ ¯ ¯ ¯ ˘ ˘¯ ˘ ¯ ¯
> So becomes our losse the triumph of her gayne;
> ¯ ˘ ˘ ¯¯
> Hers be the glory (OA 12).

The lines are written in Sapphic metre. Although a few words, like word "dying" and "triumph", appear artificial if they are treated strictly in the given metre, the melody of the whole stanza is not affected too much by them. The musical beauty comes from the poet's control of the short and long of the syllables and from the poet's understanding of the phonological qualities in English. The monosyllabic words occupy the majority in these lines, but the verse itself is not monotonous at all. The verse rhythm is retouched by diphthongs in a way that English can acct but Latin cannot. The rich consonants allow the poet to create easily the special sound effects, e. g. alliteration through the alveolar plosive /d/ in the line "Yet ***d***ying, and ***d***ead, ***d*** oo we sing her honour", and the continuity through the bilabial nasal /m/ in the line "So beco**m**e our to**m**bes **m**onu**m**ents of her praise". Sidney's efforts show that the English poets can pursue their own poetical musicality through the advantages of English pronunciation.

3. 3 Quantity and Stress

Sidney comes across the problem of balancing the syllable quantity and the syllable stress when carrying out the English quantitative verse experiments. The Latin verse rhythm is delivered through the arrangement of the long and short syllables in a line, which means the quantity of the syllable is the decisive factor in forming verse rhythm. In an English line, the stress dominates the verse rhythm. It is an arduous work to make the artificial metre coincide with English natural rhythm so that the words in a line are pronounced in their natural way. Of course the stressed syllables, because they are emphasized, sounds longer than they are not emphasized. The question is that the English syllables, whether in a word or in a sentence or in a poetical line, seems never in concord with the Latin equation that a long syllable equals two short ones in length. This is the obstacle that Sidney hardly surpasses.

It seems not possible for Sidney to keep the length of the syllables by following the rules of Latin prosody in his experiments on English quantitative verse. He cannot walk out of the influence of the English stress. The poet's perplexity is reflected in the lines like this:

' ' ' * ' ' ' ' * *' * ' ' *

¯ ¯ / ¯ ˘ ˘/ ¯|| ¯ /¯ ˘ ˘/¯ ˘ ˘/¯ ˘

Faire seeke not to be feard, most lovely beloved by thy servants,

(CS 14)

With fifteen syllables and a caesura at the place where the comma falls, the line seems to follow strictly the metrical pattern of Latin hexameter. The marks above the verse indicate the possible Latin hexameter scansion. The upmost line of marks above the verse shows the natural rhythm stress pattern of English. When reading in a Latin way, the reader would feel that he is not reading an English verse. When reading in its natural rhythm, the reader would feel that he is not reading a metrical line.

In the front of poem thirty-one in the *Old Arcadia*, Sidney writes explicitly that his poem follows the Latin hexameter. He even lays out the metrical scansion. But the lines have betrayed Sidney when the conflicts occur between English stress and Latin metre of quantity. For example, the first line "Faire Rocks, goodly rivers, sweet woods, when shall I see peace?" is rather smooth though not like a precise metrical verse when it is read in the natural English rhythm. Once being treated as a Latin quantitative verse, the discord of the English language and the Latin metre would come forth. When "faire rocks" scanned as a spondee foot (in fact it should be scanned in that way), the words "goodly" and "rivers" would be affected by such scansion. To meet the demand of the metre, the reader either reads the first syllable of the word "rivers" as a short one and takes the second as the long, which makes the words sounded very artificial, or reads all the syllables in "goodly" and "rivers" as the long syllables, which is against the natural pronunciation of these words.

Being well taught and trained with Latin in his education, Sidney should know that Latin has stress. He should know that the stress in Latin does not decide the verse rhythm, though it impinges on the metrical lines. He should know that Latin poets, in order to keep the balance of the whole line and avoid the over-emphasis concentrating on some specific part, often shun the coincidence of stressed syllable and ictus:

> "When stress and ictus do not coincide, the accentuation of syllables is more regular, and the flow more stately; it is the avoidance of coincidence in the body of the hexameter that is largely responsible for its stately character." (Flewett and Pantin xxxii)
>
> "The effect of their falling on different syllables was that the weight of emphasis was more evenly distributed, and each syllable therefore more clearly and carefully pronounced, a valuable result when the quantities were so important. (Flewett and Pantin xxiv)"

Roman poets would deliberately cope with stress in their poems. Virgil's verse that describes the scene of Aeneas and Sibyl walking into the realms of Hades serves as a good example:

ˈ ˈ ˈ

-| - ˈ|- ˈ|- |- |-

ibant obscuri sola subnocte per umbram

They went lonely into darkness beneath the night shades (Book VI, line 268)

The ictuses coincide with the long syllables, but not with the stressed syllables in most places. This arrangement makes ictus and stress "balance and offset one another and the syllables flow evenly in consequence" (Flewett and Pantin xxxiii). The verse rhythm here therefore is controlled to a slow tempo so that the "quiet flow and perfect smoothness is exactly fitting to the picture of the dim figures walking quietly down that dreadful path in the darkness" (xxxiii).

Of course the coincidence of ictus with stress or with long syllable depends on the poet's choice. The poet's licence allows him to achieve the effects he wants in the verse without following the convention. A line from the poem of Catullus may explain this to some degree:

ˈ   ˈ   ˈ   ˈ   ˈ   ˈ
˘ – ˘   – / ˘   –   ˘ – / ˘   –   ˘ –

Phaselus ille quem udetis hospites
The sailing-boat you see there, visitors (4)

Catullus makes the ictus, stress and long syllable coincide completely, exaggerating the contrast between the emphasized syllables and those not emphasized, adding a haste tempo to the iambic trimeter. Here, "the rushing iambics of 'Phaselus ille' were chosen to suggest the swift motion of the boat" (Flewett and Pantin xxxviii). A verse like this is not common in Latin poems. Catullus has to replace iambuses by spondees in other lines of the same poem to avoid monotony.

The practice of Virgil and Catullus explains that different control of coincidence of ictus and stress may form different sound effects.

Sidney might be enlightened by the exertion of the ancient Roman poets. However, he can learn the skills of those precursors, but cannot overcome the difficulties caused by the nature of English as he tries to anglicize the quantitative metre. The Latin poets can successfully restrain the stress in a line. Sidney cannot. Readers may find that Sidney, for most occasions in his experiments, yields to English stress:

> – ˘ ˘ – ˘ – ˘
>
> With violence of heav'nly,
>
> – ˘ ˘ – ˘ – ˘
>
> Beautie tied to vertue,
>
> – ˘ ˘ – ˘ – ˘
>
> Reason abasht retyred,
>
> – ˘ ˘ – ˘ – ˘
>
> Gladly my senses yeelded (CS 25).

The above lines are in the metre of aristophaneus①. William A. Ringler says that "Since Sidney measures his lines by artificial rules that are divorced from phonetic actualities, a passage such as" the above "may have the appearance of, but cannot be read aloud to sound like verse" (392). The words "violence" and "tied" cannot be read in the natural English speech as they are scanned in the above lines. The phonological structure of "violence" is /ˈvaiə-ləns/, consisting of two syllables. Since the stress falls on the first syllable, the triphthong /aiə/ will acquire the prominence both in stress and in length. The syllable /vaiə/ may not be necessarily twice longer in pronunciation than syllable /ləns/; however, it is certainly not shorter than /ləns/ in the real phonetic conditions. Even if the triphthong is separated into two parts, a diphthong plus a monothong (/ai-ə/), the phonological structure of the word "violence" changed to /ˈvai-ə-ləns/, the number of syllables meets the Latin prosodic rule but the lengths of the three syllables are not possible to be scanned as /˘ ˘ –/. The possible scansion which near Sidney's

---

① Aristophaneus is one metrical form of the Aeolic, the scansion of aristophaneus is: "– ˘ ˘ – ˘ – +" (Preminger et al. 9).

result might be /¯ ˘ ¯/, for the combination of the vowel /ə/ plus the sonorous nasal /n/ has a longer effect in pronunciation than a pure weak vowel or a nasal. And because of the position that /ləns/ is amid three weak syllables, it will be promoted to prominent status. Sidney scans the word "tied" (/ˈtəiid/ or /ˈtəiəd/)① as /˘ ¯/ by the Latin rule of position, for there are two consonants, the italicized part in "tie*d t*o", after the vowel of the second syllable. Of course the scansion reflects only Sidney's wish, not the factual linguistic phenomenon. There are also other things resulted from Sidney's artificial rules. However, if the lines are really read aloud in natural English rhythm, they do sound like verse:

> * ˈ * x ˈ *
> With violence of heav' nly,
> ˈ * ˈ * ˈ *
> Beautie tied to vertue,
> ˈ * * ˈ * ˈ
> Reason abasht retyred,
> ˈ * * ˈ * ˈ *
> Gladly my senses yeelded.

The lines are roughly arranged in accentual trimeter. The second and the third feet in the first line have altered the norm of a standard iambic trimeter, shaping the line with a falling rhythm. The second line depicts the cadence of a trochaic trimeter. The third line follows the metre of iambic trimeter except for an initial inversion. The fourth line repeats the design of the third, but

① The diphthong /ai/ in Sidney's time might be pronounced as /əi/, and the suffix "-ed" was often treated as one non-reduced syllable of a nucleus plus a coda (Cruttenden 245-246; Schipper 158).

there is an extra weak syllable at the end. The substitutive feet (either initial inversion or substitutes within the line) and the extra syllable were acceptable as poetical licence in the second half of the sixteenth century, which would not affect the rhythm of the accentual-syllabic verse. These lines, in which the metrical pattern is compatible with the language rhythm, express a harmonious melody of poetry.

When analyzing Sidney's quantitative verse, Ringler says:

> Sidney himself was aware of the clash of his measures with normal English pronunciation, and though he never succeeded in writing truly quantitative verse in which the rhythmical pattern is determined by the natural quantity of English syllables rather than by arbitrary rules, in two of his poems (OA 32 and CS 5) he did succeed in so ordering his syllables that the artificial and natural quantitative patterns coincide, and in which in addition the quantitatively long syllables are also those that normally receive stress in English, so that the quantitative pattern produces a regular stress pattern. But he did not continue his experiments in this kind ... (393)

Ringler has pointed out Sidney's progress in the quantitative verse experiments, but not stated the reason why Sidney abandons the Latin metre eventually. In his "Defence of Poesie", Sidney proclaims that English is "fit for both sorts" of versification, that of the quantity and that of the "number (with some regard of the accent)" (Feuillerat 44). That might be the reason for Sidney carrying out his quantitative verse experiments. Yet, Sidney also acknowledges that "for the rhyme, though we do not observe quantity, yet we observe the accent very precisely" (44). It is obvious that Sidney realizes the difficulty in his experiments, because English is more suitable for poets to compose the lines with the rhythm of accentual-syllabic verse. Actually, in *Astrophil and Stella*, a sonnet sequence composed later in his life and as his main achievement in lyrics, Sidney follows almost strictly the accentual-syllabic, a dominant verse rhythm of English metrical poems adopted by poets from Sidney's times on. This might be the reason for Ringler not further accounting for it.

An accentual-syllabic verse presents appropriately the notable English phonological features in a disciplined way. The rhythm is displayed through the arrangement of the stressed syllables which appear at equal intervals in the line. And all syllables (including both the stressed and unstressed) are counted precisely and distributed iso-numerically to the metrical units (feet). Poets are offered limited freedom with some variations in verse designing, such as the inversion, the substitute and the feminine rhyme. There is another kind of significant freedom that the strict accentual-syllabic verse furnishes a poet: he can organize the definite syllables within the specific metrical units to achieve the musical effects he expects with observation of the stress timing and stress pattern of the line. The quantity of the syllables within a metrical unit is allocated according to its natural linguistic context. The syllables from different metrical units may not be admeasured like the ones in a Latin verse. That is to say, the distribution of the syllabic quantity is accomplished within a metrical unit, but not among metrical units. The stressed syllable may not be equal to two unstressed ones in length. In an accentual-syllabic verse, the poetical elements, the ictus, number, stress and quantity, are deliberately considered. The verse rhythm reflects the natural state of English rhythm. The establishment of the dominant position of the accentual-syllabic verse incarnates the maturity of English metrical poems. It is monumental.

3. 4 Conversion to the Accentual-Syllabic Verse

Sidney gives up his experiments on quantitative verse as he realizes the value of the accentual-syllabic verse; however, it does not necessarily mean that he gives up his pursuit in the English poetry of the musicality expressed by the quantitative elements that the English syllables have. The length of a syllable in the poem is "important aesthetically" (Cuddon 544). It is true that most of Sidney's poems are written in the accentual-syllabic verse, especially those in his *Astrophil and Stella*, which follow almost the pure rhythm that an accentual-syllabic verse possesses. However, with the stressed timed rhythm, the reader can feel the musical beauty of sounds Sidney expressed through the artful allocation of those short and long syllables:

> The fourth song alone, with its hurried and (as it were) whispered metre, its inimitable refrain, its perfect selection of images, is enough to raise Sidney above all his contemporaries. (Lewis 329)

The "hurried and (as it were) whispered metre" and the "inimitable refrain" Lewis mentioned are certainly related to the musicality the song conveys. How does Sidney create this sound effect? The following lines may prove his intention:

' * ' * ' * '

ONELY joy, now here you are,

' * ' * ' * '

Fit to heare and ease my care:

' * ' * * ' * '

Let my whispering voyce obtaine,
' * ' * ' * '
Sweete reward for sharpest paine:
' * * ' * ' * '
Take me to thee and thee to me.
' x ' x * ' * '
"No, no, no, no, my deare, let be." (AS iv)

This is the first stanza of the fourth song from Sidney's *Astrophil and Stella*. The first four lines, rhyming *aabb*, form the main part of the stanza, and the last two rhymed lines are the refrain repeated in the following strophes. At least four features the passage expresses may show the charm Lewis admires. First, the verse rhythm of the poem. Sidney adopts the trochaic tetrameter, making the stressed syllable determining the rhythmical contours of the lines. A careful reader can feel the falling rhythmical characteristic of a trochaic verse, although it may not be differentiated much from an iambic line. The falling rhythm suppresses the ending part of the metrical units, thus weakening the sonority of the line. This weakening is even exaggerated by the insertion of a dactyl in the line "Let my whispering voyce obtaine" and by the contrast of the metrical structures which form the contrast phonological styles between the imploration and the refusal in the refrain. The metre itself may possibly quicken the tempo of the verse rhythm. Secondly, the arrangement of the monosyllable words and the polysyllable words. The continuous monosyllable words may not make very distinctive the stressed words and the unstressed words in a line, for a monosyllable word, if it is notional, can be pronounced in a stressed way, even in the weak position of a metrical poem, when read with a natural language rhythm. The indistinctiveness of the pronunciation to some degree just imitates the "whispered" manner. The disyllable words are interspersed intentionally in the lines, adding variety to the monotonous sound effects, or intensifying such effects. For example, the word "onely", at the initial position of the verse and of the stanza, creates a clear falling tone of the voice, thus, suggesting the mood of the whole passage. Following "voyce", the word "obtaine" not only meets the demand of the metre, but also, because of its unstressed first syllable, prolongs the weak voice produced by the ending part of the diphthong /ɔi/ and the following voiceless consonant /s/. As a result, it causes a clear weak part between two accents. The word "reward" is used to reply the verse metre. It is also used to serve another phonological aim: the word boundary of "reward" here does not coincide with the metrical template, so it is likely for the reader to stop for a while after reading "Sweete", then, the tempo and sound effects here will be slightly changed. Thirdly, the short lines. A short line may not necessarily result in the "hurried" metre. But when it is combined with the above-mentioned two features, the short line is effective in enhancing the "hurried" metre. Fourthly, the quantity of the syllables. Almost all the long vowels in lines are distributed in the stressed positions, and the short ones in the unstressed positions. This arrangement reminds the reader of the metrical design of Catullus's "Phaselus". The sharp contrast between the double emphasized syllables and double weakened syllables in a short line hastens the tempo of the melody. Besides, the lines are teemed with soft sounds. For example, the repetition of the falling diphthong /iə/ in the words "here", "heare" and "deare" from different lines echoes the mild voice throughout the stanza. ① Such examples can be found in Sidney's *Astrophil and Stella*.

① When one pronounces the diphthong /iə/, "The lips are neutral throughout, with a slight movement from spread to open (Cruttenden 142)." There is not much tension in the process of pronunciation, which makes the sound not very forceful.

' ' * ' * ' * ' * '

Come sleepe, O sleepe, the certain knot of peace (AS 39)

This is a typical accentual-syllabic verse in Sidney's sonnet sequence—the iambic pentameter line with the initial inversion of a substituted spondee. The comma after the first foot acts as a pause, separating the melody flow and highlights the initial foot. Verse rhythm concords with the phonological characteristics of natural English speech. The sound delivers the verse meaning in a delicate imitation, and the musicality of the verse is expressed through the poet's control of the short and long syllables. "Come" and "sleepe" form a spondaic foot in which the vowel /ʌ/ of "come" is prolonged since the syllable is stressed, and connected with the long vowel /iː/. The sound of the foot creates the effect of imitation and symbolization, leaving the reader space for imagination. The initial position, together with the pause immediately following the spondee (allowing the long vowel /iː/ last more longer), intensifies the imitation. The pronunciation of the word "O" in the second foot is also exaggerated, which works with the following pause after the second foot, forming another emphasis. In this way, the first two feet present vividly the feeling when a man is in his weariness through the sound imitation. The last three feet echo the first two feet. The vowel /əː/ in the first syllable of the word "certain" diminishes the length because of the voiceless consonant /t/ after it, causing the pressing and instability of the third foot. The stress falls on the word "knot" in the fourth foot, advancing the climax of reading in the vowel /ɔ/. Then in the ending foot, the stressed long vowel /iː/ reappears, echoing the sound in the first two feet, makes the musical imitation continuous. Suppose that Sidney does not experiment on the English quantitative verse, he may not design such delicate musicality in this way. Sidney combines the accentual-syllabic verse with the elements of a quantitative verse, producing an effective musicality in his poem. The effects of his experiments are obvious.

3. 5 The Influence of Sidney's Experiments

The exertion of Sidney's experiments on the English quantitative verse has influenced his contemporaries. The quantitative movement in Elizabethan England "did not really get under way until Sidney started writing quantitative poems for the *Arcadia*, probably between 1577 and 1580, and discussing the subject with Drant, Dyer and Spenser" (Attridge 130). Sidney and these people, together with Greville and a few young poets (e. g. James Reshoulde, Robert Mills and Abraham Fraunce) are the probable members of "Areopagus" (130). Of course Sidney's influence has not been limited within the salon. Gabriel Harvey was not the member of the "Areopagus", but he was influenced by Sidney. These people did not compose many English quantitative verses, and the preserved ones are much less. However, the poems written by Spenser and Fraunce are enough evidences to demonstrate Sidney's influence.

Spenser accepted partly the "Lawes and rules of Quantities of English sillables for English Verse" prescribed by "Master SIDNEY and Master DYER" (Smith 89). When Spenser delivered his "Iambicum Trimetrum" to Harvey in the October 1579, he remarked that Sidney and Dyer "had thereof already greate practise, and drawen mee to their faction" (Smith 89-92). Spenser's apprentice-training on English quantitative verse seems no better than Sidney's earlier experiments:

- - ˘ - / - ˘ - - / ˘ - ˘ ˘ -

Tell hi*r th*at hi*r p*leasures were wonte to lull me asleepe (qtd. in

Smith 91);

The line is written under the rules of Latin iambic trimeter. ① The noted licence in the line is the pronoun "hir". ② The positions where the word "hir" located are the places where the ictus falls. Therefore "hir" in these places should be read as a long syllable. Spenser prolongs the syllable by following the Latin prosodic rule of position. The italicized letters show the combined consonants after the vowel /i/. However, Spenser's efforts seem as nonsense as what Sidney has tried. The length of the syllable is not determined by the juxtaposition of two consonants after it in English pronunciation. And the clumsiness also lies in the metrical design of this line: in "to lull me asleepe", there is an extra weak syllable, which violates the metre. To solve the violation, one should neglect one of the weak syllables in scansion. Besides, the position of the word "lull" is also arguable. If the sound of "lull" is not prolonged, the continuity of four short syllables is against the "promotion rules" of English pronunciation (Attridge 165). Spenser's practice also proves that the direct transplantation of foreign prosody is impossible.

What Spenser differentiates from Sidney is that Spenser is "concerned above all with the Latin rules of quantity", and "attempt[s] neither an imitation of the Latin stress-patterns nor an approximation to the stress-rhythms of the native English tradition" (196). It seems that Spenser cares only the pure quantitative verse.

The influence of Sidney on Fraunce in the experiment appears stronger than on Spenser. Being "the most prolific and the most popular of the

---

① The Latin iambic trimeter consists of three iambic metron, that is, three couple of iambus. A Latin trimeter line is equal to an English hexameter in the number of syllables.

② The pronoun "hir" was the objective and genitive form of "her" in the history of English from the thirteenth century to the sixteenth century (Blake 118).

Elizabethan quantitative poets", Fraunce's method in metrical designs "is close to that of his master, Sidney" (192). Both Sidney and Fraunce "seem to be more conscious of the accentual structure of the line, as well as giving vowel-tenseness an important role in decisions about quantity" (198). The following three lines are quoted and scanned by Derek Attridge from Fraunce's *Amyntas*:

¯ ¯/ ¯ ¯/ ¯||¯/ ¯ ¯ /˘ ˘ ˘/¯ ¯

But Pan, and Fauni, but garden greene of Amintas,

¯ ¯ /¯ ¯ /¯ ||¯ / ¯ ¯ /¯ ˘ ˘/¯¯

But you springs, and dales, and woods aye wont to be silent,

¯ ¯/¯ ¯ /¯|| ¯/¯ ¯/ ¯ ˘ ˘/¯¯

Leave of your mourning, Ile give you leave to be silent (qtd. in Attridge 193),

The lines sound unnatural when the syllables read in long and short way. But they will be natural when read in the natural stress of the English speech rhythm. Accentually, Fraunce's hexameters are more regular than Sidney's (Attridge 193).

But neither Fraunce, nor Spenser, nor any other people who are influenced by Sidney and are enthusiastic in the experiments of the English quantitative verse can adhere to it. Almost all of them had turned to the construction of the English accentual-syllabic verse. The mature poetical works of Dyer and Spenser indicate the conversion: their giving up of the experiments on the quantitative verse does not mean that they have stopped the exploration of the quantitative elements the English language possesses. The length of an English syllable is significant aesthetically (Cuddon 544). The poem "My Mind to Me a Kingdom Is" may serve as a note to this exploration:

> My mind to me a kingdom is,
>   Such present joys therein I find,
> That is excels all other bliss
>   That earth affords or grows by kind.
> Though much I want which most would have,
> Yet still my mind forbids to crave (Ault 123).

The form of this poem is madrigal. For the need of singing, Dyer has to consider the lines being harmoniously matched with the musical melody. The stanza comprises a long measure (or long metre) and a rhymed couplet, and the lines are arranged in accentual iambic metre with ictus falling on stresses. With four isochronously appeared stresses arising in an octosyllabic line, the structure is possible to decelerate the reader's reading speed. Some unstressed syllables are long when pronounced, reinforced the slow tempo, adding the beauty of smoothness to the melody. The musical effect shown by the quantitative elements enriches the English prosody.

Spenser's "Epithalamion" is also a good example of assimilating foreign prosodies. The stanzaic form of "Epithalamion" is similar to the Petrarchan *canzone*. ① The verse rhythm is the accentual-syllabic, but the quantitative tint is tangible. Such a design makes the melody suitable to the theme expressed in the poem:

---

① Canzone is an Italian word, meaning "song". As a literary term it refers to "various kinds of medieval Provencal and Italian lyric poems" (Baldick 30). Petrarch composed lyrics in the form of canzone. This influential form consists five or six stanzas and a half-stanza envoi. The length of the stanza may vary from seven to twenty lines in different poems but identical within one (30).

Wake, now my love, awake; for it is time,
The rosy Morne long since left Tithones bed,
All ready to her silver coche to clyme,
And Phoebus gins to shew his glorious hed.
Hark how the cheerefull birds do chaunt theyr laies
And carroll of love praise (*Edmund Spenser's Poetry* 494).

The ending of the lines is emphasized with trochees or spondees put in the end of the accentual iambic line and with the coincidence of the stressed syllables and the syllables with long vowels. The beginning of most lines adopts the initial inversion, a device of foot substitution similar to the Latin technique, to enhance the musicality of the line. The initial foot "Wake, now" in the first line forms a spondee, or a trochee sounds like a spondee, attractive with its sonority. The comma amid the foot causes a temporary pause when the line is read, producing a trough of sound. The design outlines a falling-and-rising shape of the cadence. The diphthongs in the two words make the shape clearer. The acoustic effect is appropriate to a calling. The semicolon in the first line, functioning as a Latin caesura, divides the line into two hemistiches and maintains the balance of the two parts at the same time. There is a contrast in structure between the first hemistich and the second. The first hemistich is cut into pieces by two commas, loosing its continuity and steadiness. The second hemistich, though short, appears smooth and sonorous. Spenser integrates the first hemistich with the silence caused by semicolon and amalgamates it with the second half-line so that the calling effect of the first part of the line could be projected and the harmonious completeness retained. The design of the initial foot in the fifth line is similar to that in the first line except the pause. The vowel in the word "hark" is shortened before the voiceless consonant, leaving a feeling of haste for the reader. Such a feeling just matches the image the line illustrates. In the line, many syllables containing long vowels arranged regularly, do not completely coincide with the stresses, but ensure the progression of the vocal tone. It is reasonable to conjecture that Spenser's deliberate design of the metrical patterns has benefited from his experiments on the English quantitative verse.

Sidney's experiments on the English quantitative verse touches the reform of the English verse rhythm, which might influence the direction of the English poetical evolution. Verse rhythm is the soul of poetical form and the precondition (or basis) in forming the metre (or metrical pattern). Verse rhythm displays a poet's poetical style. Verse rhythm reveals the general poetical feature of the poems written in one language. Verse rhythm, which is the result of generations of people exploring the essential phonological characteristics of a language, reflects the cadence of a language. The forms of poems may vary from time to time according to the needs of poets, but the verse rhythm keeps stable. The settlement of a verse rhythm often decides the visage of poetical form. And the endeavour to change the verse rhythm often becomes an exertion of breaking the poetry tradition and creating a new one. Sidney's experiments on the English quantitative verse have helped the English poets fully realize the significance of the accentual-syllabic verse to the English poetry. And the latter represents the maturity of English metre.

Chapter 4 The Accentual-Syllabic Verse

Sidney forges his accentual-syllabic verse from the practice of melting English and foreign prosody. In the experiments on the English quantitative verse, he realizes the poetical value of the accentual-syllabic verse to the construction of English poetical forms. Both the foreign influences and the native traditions are reflected in his metrical design of the new verse.

4.1 Influences on the Rhythm Contours

Two phonological elements are counted in composing an English line, the syllable and the prominence of the syllable (the stressed syllable, or in short, the stress). Either of them may be determinate or variable in number, decisive to the types of metrical design—the accentual verse, the syllabic verse, the accentual-syllabic verse, and the nonmetrical verse (free verse).

The accentual verse (also named tonic verse or strong-stress verse) has the number of stresses fixed but the number of syllables variable. It is frequently used by English poets of almost all generations from the Old English time to the present, showing a constant vitality. The reason for the continuous blooming of this traditional convention lies in the principle that guides the metre formation. In an accentual verse, the rhythm of the metre imitates the natural rhythm of English speech, as R. Bridges puts it, "the stress must all be true speech stresses" (92), thus making the line sound less artificial in cadence. The ictuses fall isochronously on the counted stresses, which guarantee the metrical pattern being observed, and leave the freedom for poets to make the metre coincides with the language structure in the line. G. M. Hopkins's sprung rhythm verse is a modern development of this tradition.

English syllabic verses exist mainly as theoretical beings, lacking in enough supports of practice except those rare experiments of Marianne More, W. H. Auden and Thom Gunn (Baldick 217). However, it is significant to the emergence of accentual-syllabic verse. In the lines of a syllabic verse, the number of syllables is counted while the number of stresses is not taken into account. In the languages whose syllabic criterion is identified, like Chinese and French, the stress pattern is fixed once a sentence is completed, and in the same way, the stress pattern fixed when a line completed. Because of the regular stress pattern in words, phrases and sentences, poets of these languages do not need to care for the rhythm of a line when they set a definite number of syllables in it. Different from most of those languages in the Indo-European Family and seeming of no importance to the development of English metre though, Chinese is helpful in the explaining the syllabic verse: every syllable is counted so that the total number of syllables in a line is fixed; every syllable is given prominence in a line, especially in the metrical verse, because every syllable is a phonetic correspondent of a character (*zi*). What frustrates an English reader most is that the stress seems useless in determining the cadent contour of a Chinese metrical verse, for the cadence of such a line is dominated by the tone (*ping* and *ze*) (Roca and Johnson 394), even if the number of syllables (or rather, characters) is determinate. The French syllabic verse demands the number of syllables fixed in a line, regardless of the prominence of a stress, because the ascensive positions of a French line is rather fixed and the stress might not be a prominent factor of the language both in phonetic and in metrical system. The French prosody has influenced the English counterpart profoundly, and accordingly the syllabic pattern of a French line effects on the English poets.

The English accentual-syllabic verse, involving such a French effect, will be discussed thoroughly after the analysis of the nonmetrical verse.

Some people assert that the nonmetrical verse equals to free verse. This may not be true. In fact, an absolute free verse does not exist; therefore, such a term will easily lead people to the wrong understanding. It might be better to term a free verse nonmetrical verse. Although both syllables and stresses are variable in a nonmetrical line, they are carefully arranged so as to project the contour of rhythm. The techniques of forming parallel structures, grammatically and phonologically, constitute at least part of the nonmetrical versification that share similarities with the accentual verse. They both allow some liberty of the language structures in organizing a line and they both emphasize on the agreement between the rhythm of language and the rhythm of verse:

(a) Love me little, love me long,
Is the burden of my song (Warren and Erskine 73)

(b) Landscape plotted and pieced—fold, fallow, and plough;
And áll trádes, their gear and tackle and trim. (Ramzani et al. 78)

(c) Give me the splendid silent sun with all his beams full-dazzling,
Give me juicy autumnal fruit ripe and red from the orchard,
(Whitman 446)

The (a) lines are accentual verses, for there are four isochronous stresses in the first line and three in the second, following the metrical pattern of a ballad. The (b) lines are a kind of accentual verse, "sprung rhythm", a metrical pattern designed by Gerard Manley Hopkins, which may be regarded as an intergrade state from metrical verse to the nonmetrical one. ① The (c) lines are nonmetrical verses which break away from the metrical convention but reserve the general principles of verse design, like cadence. These three examples show at least two important similarities between the accentual verse and the nonmetrical verse, the language structure is naturally accepted as the verse structure and the language rhythm is also naturally adopted as the verse rhythm.

Nonmetrical verse may be regarded as a counteraction to the accentual-syllabic verse in structure. The former displays the extremity of freedom in a poem, and the latter exhibits the extremity of discipline.

When both the number of counted stresses and counted syllables are invariable in a line, and when the number-fixed stresses in it are equally distributed on the isochronous positions where the rhythmical ictus fall and which are intervened by the similarly equal distribution of weak syllables, a standard accentual-syllabic verse is formed. It is worth noticing that the accentual-syllabic verse does not arise automatically from the accentual verse even if the syllables are regulated in the latter verse, because "the placing of the stresses in the line" is different: "syllabotonic metres have specific patterns of stress, while accentual metres do not" (Preminger and Brogan 770).② Yet, when comparing an accentual-syllabic line with an accentual verse, the reader finds that the stress pattern and the traditional metrical

① Gerard Manley Hopkins's sprung rhythm is a kind of accentual verse based on nursery rhymes and on medieval alliterative metres. It counts the number of stresses in a line, regardless of the number of those weak syllables, and permits the frequent juxtaposition of stresses and the "outrides", or additional weak syllbles. He devises four feet for his metre, "a monosyllable and the so-called accentual Trochee, Dactyl, and the First Paeon [/ × × ×]". (Preminger and Brogan1208-1209; Baldick 210)

② The accentual-syllabic verse is also called syllabotonic verse.

convention linked with the latter in origin have passed into the former with a new design. It reveals the inheritance of accentual-syllabic verse from the ancient accentual verse. Some exotic elements are combined into the metrical design, thus distinguishing the accentual-syllabic verse from the pure native species. The count of syllables and the variation of metrical units within a line are poets' creation when they are inspired by the foreign versifications.

The idea of counting syllables in a line, which is mainly from the French metre, can be traced back to Chaucer's time (or even earlier), when he tries to forge the English accentual-syllabic verse. Two evidences show that French prosody acts as a foreign tint in it. On the one hand, that after 1066, the French language has dominated the lives of those English literate people for more than three hundred years and still been a language of culture and fashion thereafter. ① English writers in the Middle English period write in French or translated literary works from French. ② On the other, that counting syllables to a fixed number in a line, which is a French prosodic tradition, ③ "was known in English poetry as far back as the second half of the thirteenth century, and has been a favourite metre from Chaucer's first poetic attempts onward to the present" (Schipper 209). Chaucer's lines may reflect this

---

① The Middle English literature once was the literature in French after the Norman Conquest for quite a long time when French literature flushed on the island. It is hard to say that the English literature, even if it is popular lower class literature, had not been affected by the noble French sentiment. In 1362, English was restored legally to its dominant place, but French was used as an accomplishment of gentlemen (Baugh and Cable 149-156).

② For example, Chaucer translated the French "Livre de Mellibee et de Prudence" and put it into his "Tale of Melibee" (Blake 504).

③ Determining the number of syllables is also the prosodic tradition in the verse of Greek, or Latin, or a vernacular descending from Latin like French and Italian, so it is possible that the influence the English metre accepted is a blended one. However, since the French was the most influential language in England at that time, and such a tradition is perhaps both the oldest and commonest of French metre, it is reasonable to say that the idea counting syllable in an English line comes mainly from a French origin (Saintsbury 161).

foreign colour:

> To you, | my purse, || and to non other wight
>
> Compleyne I, || for ye be my lady dere ("The Complaint of Chaucer to His Empty Purse")!

The number of syllables in each line is limited to ten, similar to the French decasyllabic verse:

> Oliver est || desur un pui muntet;
>
> Or veit il ben || d'Espaigne le regnet
>
> E Sarrazins, || ki tant sunt asemblez (*La Chanson de Roland*).①
>
> (Upon a peak is Oliver mounted,
>
> Kingdom of Spain he sees before him spread,
>
> And Sarrazins, so many gathered.)

Chaucer's lines are more flexible than the lines from the ancient French epic. The use of caesura is noted. In a French decasyllabic verse, the caesura generally comes after the fourth syllable, almost equally dividing the line into two hemistiches, as shown in the above lines, and this position is fixed in most cases. The lines appear rigid when they are unchangeably identical in structure; both the caesuras and the stresses are strictly restricted to a fixed pattern. Chaucer's caesura, or to be more exact, pause, "does not always occupy a fixed place" in a line, but "is liable to shift its position" (Schipper 213). The different arrangements link with different metrical structure and

---

① The English translation is cited from *The Song of Roland* (http://omacl.org/Roland/r1-87.html).

different phonetic characteristics, expressing different aesthetic tastes indeed.

The variation appearing in Chaucer's lines is caused by his recognition of the stress-timing rhythm of the English language and his admiration of the diversity of the classical metres which are panegyrized by the vernacular poets as prosodic canons. The above lines sound natural and harmonious with English rhythm contour on the one hand, and accord with the iambic pentameter on the other, although there is a slight deviation from the norm in the second half of "To you, my purse, and to non other wight". The shift position of caesuras and the substitution of feet, (which also frequently occurs in modern French metrical poetry but rarely in the ancient decasyllabic verse,) are restrained techniques in classical versification. Chaucer may be the first English poet who consciously introduces these techniques into the English composition. He designates the direction of the development of the English accentual-syllabic verse.

More fervent enthusiasm that poets pour into the construction of the accentual-syllabic verse is witnessed by the second half of the sixteenth century, when Sir Thomas Wyatt and his friend Sir Henry Howard, Earl of Surrey opened the torrent of new English lyric poetry as they contacted with the Renaissance on the continent of Europe. They met foreign poets and accepted foreign influences. Under these influences, the English accentual-syllabic verse grows to its maturity in *Tottel's Miscellany* (1557), *Phœnix Nest* (1593) and *England's Helicon* (1600), which prepares an effective poetical form for William Shakespeare and English high Renaissance.

Wyatt brings the Italianate element into the Tudor poetry through his translation of Petrarch. Maybe influenced by the Italian vernacular mood, or maybe inspired by the vague model of Chaucer, he is willing to make the poetical lines decided by the living speech rhythm. Being "apparent [ly] disregard of the iambic metrical pattern", Wyatt prefers "a certain effect" in his lines "as of the speaking voice" (Thompson 15). His poetry is an effort of breaking away from the rigid and clumsy lines of his contemporaries:

× ' * ' × × * '
Now cease, my lute! this is the last
' * * ' * ' * '
Labour that thou and I shall wast (Ault 7),

It is acceptable if the lines are scanned as the iambic tetrameter, but disputes may arise. At least the initial foot inversion in the second line is not common until Sidney popularizes the technique. The caesuras and the enjambment have already shattered the fetters of the metrical convention during the first half of the sixteenth century. Although Wyatt's lines are crude compared with those of masters as Shakespeare, Milton, etc., they are helpful in Elizabethan poets' exploration of the expressiveness of the accentual-syllabic verse.

Surrey contributes to the English accentual-syllabic verse with his various iambic metres. He employs the accentual iambic meter with enjambment in blank verse and poulter's measure, taming lines into the metrical pattern,

' ' ' ' (') '
Ye winds, | I you conjure, || in chiefest of your rage,
' ' ' ' ' (') '
That ye my Lord me safely send, || my sorrows to assuage ("Good Ladies").

There is a controlled smoothness. Surrey decides that metre comes first but not language rhythm though, he carefully corresponds the syntactic structure with the metrical pattern so that the natural melody in a sentence could echo effortlessly in a regulated verse. The couplet here follows the metre called poulter's measure, a heavy and clumsy metrical pattern in the eye of many a poet, popular in 1560s and 1570s under the definite influence of classical and the possible influence of French (Alexandrine in especial) iambic hexameter and heptameter, and equally definite influence of the native ballad metre. ① The first line is divided into two equal groups with a primary caesura. And the second line is divided into an eight-syllable group plus a six-syllable group with the same method. Both lines are almost pressed into the regular iambic metres with only a few words appearing stubborn. That is the reason John Thompson regrets that "Surrey sometimes employed the iambic pattern in ways that would not be fully developed until Sidney took them up (Thompson 31)." "Metrically, he [Surrey] is one of the great road-makers (Lewis 235)."

4. 2 Sidney's Prosodic View on the Accentual-Syllabic Verse

Since the aim of poetry, in Sidney's opinion, is to teach through delightful moving, is through the spread of the pageant of beautiful vineyard, the poetical form must be delightful too. But how could one organize this

① (1) English poets invent the iambic hexameter and heptameter (fourteener) in their translation of Latin epics. The native influence of ballad metre on the fourteener is also clear (Preminger and Brogan 424). (2) There are similarities between the French Alexandrine and the iambic hexameter in English poulter's measure, the application of caesuras, the principle of stress distribution, etc., and the origin of French Alexandrine, which was germinated from the Latin prosody, is much earlier than the English hexameter. In addition, the French poetry has influenced the English poetry strongly in history, especially during the Renaissance period. It is reasonable to speculate the relationship between the French Alexandrine and the English hexameter.

delightful form? In this aspect, Aristotle's idea must have guided Sidney,① "The chief forms of beauty are order and symmetry and definiteness, which the mathematical sciences demonstrate in a special degree (*Metaphysics*: book 13: 3)." The aesthetic form is often shaped and perceived by conventions (Townsend 58). The art does not consent to any casual form in the appearance of a work (Hegel 9). Sidney believes that English is fit "to honour the poesy, and to be honoured by poesy". He equips his lines with beauties he finds in language, in rhetoric and in the prosodies both from the native and from the foreign.

Sidney's idea on forming an accentual-syllabic line consists of three parts, the use of language, the arrangement of metrical pattern and the exploitation of rhetorical devices. In his opinion, an ideal English used in a poem should be easy and clear. Words are common among the literate people of "everyday polite conversation" (Ringler lii); grammatical structures are simple; phonetic features that reveal the musical effects of English are fully exploited. The language a poet uses in his poems should be "fittest to nature" (Feuillerat 43), not for displaying his art. The poet's skills are hidden in the natural language so that the language could be in accord with his skills. Once he "flieth from nature", indeed he "abuseth art" (43). Therefore, the poet should make "words set in delightful proportion" (20), that is, "everie word having his natural seat, which seat must needs make the word remembered"

① In his letter to Hubert Languet (February 4th, 1574), Sidney mentions that "De Græcis literis tantum haurire vellem quantum ad benè intelligendum Aristotelem sufficeret, esti enim quotidiè traductiones nonnullæ fiunt, tamen ego suspicor eas non satis dilucidè et aptè sensa authorris exprimere..." ("Of Greek I wish to take in only enough for a proper understanding of Aristotle, for though translations are made almost everyday I suspect that they do not express the author's meaning clearly and aptly enough."), explaining that Sidney and his literate contemporaries read Aristotle to a certain degree. The Aristotelian ideas on aesthetics mentioned here is very popular in Sidney's time (Feuillerat 84; Duncn-Jones 280).

(27). Sidney displeases with the archaic and inkhorn dictions. His criticizing Spenser in "framing of his style to an old rusticke language" (37) may not be correct. However, it does show his attitude to the issue. It is true that he seldom revives an outdated word in his verse. Almost all of his vocabulary is limited to the standard usage of his time. Sidney also likes the common and short words in English because they are frequently used in English. He intentionally values the virtue of the common English monosyllabic words, which is carried on by the later poets as an English poetical convention. ① On the other hand, Sidney disagrees with some poets' neologism, decrying that

> Now, for the outside of it, which is words, or (as I may tearme it) Diction, it is even well worse: so is it that honyflowing Matrone Eloquence, apparrelled, or rather disguised, in a Courtisanlike painted affection. One time with so farre fet words, that many seeme monsters, but must seeme straungers to anie poore Englishman: an other time with coursing of a letter, as if they were bound to follow the method of a Dictionary: an other with figures and flowers, extremelie winter-starved (Feuillerat 42).

He points out three affected styles among his contemporaries: strange and clumsy foreign words, heavy dependence on alliteration, and over-euphuistic figures of speech. Sidney condemns them as artificial. The same idea is reflected in Sidney's poems:

> You that do search for every purling spring,

---

① Edward Bysshe, when talking about the rules of English versification, accepts Sidney's preferrence as the fifith rule of "conduing to the beauty of our Versification" (Chapter One, Section III).

> Which from the ribs of old Parnassus flowes,
> And everie floure, not sweet perhaps, which growes
> Near thereabouts into your Poesie wring;
> You that do Dictionarie's methode bring
> Into your rimes, running in ratling rowes:
> You that poore Petrarch's long-deceased woes,
> With new-borne sighs and denisened wit do sing (AS 15);

He criticizes a poet who always dreams of writing a splendid poem by seeking fancies from the distant and alien places, piling the rhymes as if compiling a dictionary and imitating other poets' expression which only appears sham and morbid in his composition. "You take wrong waies." "And sure at length stolne goods do come to light (AS 15)." Yet, Sidney does not turn his back totally to the foreign dictions. For example, his inventive use of the epithets which is recognized by later writers as one of his distinctive achievements:

> But for the uttering sweetly and properly the conceits of the mind (which is the end of speech), that hath it equally with any other tongue in the world; and is particularly happy in compositions of two or three words together, near the Greek, far beyond the Latin, which is one of the greatest beauties can be in a language (Feuillerat 44).

The epithets, the "compositions of two or three words together", which had been frequently used by Homer (thus, Homeric epithets) and which is admired by Sidney as one aspect of beauty of a language for it appeals to the mind, is significant to a line not merely of the ornamental beauty but more chiefly of the distinctive purposes to do with allusion, connotation, repetition and metre (Preminger and Brogan 378). English poets before Sidney seldom allow the epithets in their poetry. ①

Sidney accomplishes a normal order of concise words in his lines, which reflects his idea of the English grammar, "for the uttering sweetly and properly the conceit of the mind, which is the end of speech" (Feuillerat 44). English grammar is far simpler than most of European languages, which is obvious a merit of this international language. Sidney praises that the grammar limits the least people's practice on English.

Sidney advocates that the rhythm of a line should be an imitation of the natural language and that the metrical rhythm should be in concord with the rhythm of the natural language. And that to achieve the concordance, the feet within an accentual-syllabic line are allowed to vary under the precondition of keeping both the stressed syllables and the unstressed syllables determinate in number and the stresses at the equally-timed prominent positions. He promotes at least two important techniques with his practice, making them ideas of English prosody in shaping a metrical line: substitutes and pauses. The tempo of the line and rhythm contour are adjusted through varying substitutes of feet and shifting positions of pauses. Thus he naturalizes an entirely new rhythm (the accentual trochaic, a kind of accentual-syllabic verse) (Ringler lv).

Sidney's innovation on the metrical pattern is inspired by his ideas on reducing the mechanical regularity strictly followed by the poets of his time. ② He turns to the classical prosody to find the solution to shatter the rigescent

---

① The idea from George Puttenham's *The Art of English Poesie* may represent the common attitude on this question, "Some of our vulgar writers take great pleasure in giuing Epithets and do it almost to euery word which may receiue them, and should not be so, yea though they were neuer so propre and apt, for sometimes wordes suffered to go single, dogiue greater sence and grace than words quallified by attributions do (Puttenham 182)."

② George Gascoigne recognized that there was only one metrical pattern existing in the works of the poets just before Sidney (Smith 50). Unfortunately, the lines of most of their poems are rigidly produced in unchanging pattern, the unvaried iambic feet, and the immovable caesura position, which, in Sidney's eye, is lack of energy, not able to express the poetic matter well.

mode. He believes that the English language offers poets great opportunity, "being indeed capable of any excellent exercising of it" (Feuillerat 43). Sidney relates two sorts of prosodies in his "Defence of Poesie": the classical, marked by the quantity of the syllables in a line; and the modern vernacular, noted by "observing onely number, with some regard of the accent" (44), standing on another kind of rhythm. He further explains the different musical effects applied by these prosodies. For the classical prosody, "both words and time observing quantitie, and more fit, lively to expresse divers passions by the low or loftie sound of the well-wayed sillable" (44). And for the modern one, "with his rime striketh a certaine Musicke to the eare: and in fine, since it dooth delight, though by another way, it obtaineth the same purpose" (44). Lines composed either in the classical prosody or in the modern vernacular one are appropriate, for "there being in either sweetnesse, and wanting in neither, majestie" (44). Sidney alleges that an English line can be written in either the classical way or the vernacular way, because both kinds of prosodies are applicable to the English poetry. He believes that English exhibits more poeticality than any modern European languages, like the Italian, the French, the Spanish, the Dutch, etc., for English has no defects that other languages possess when a poet displays his skills in "Elisions", "sweete slyding", "Antepenultima", "Dactiles", and "Cæsura", etc (44). So English "is more to honour Poesie, and to be honoured by Poesie" than other languages (44). The patriotism Sidney expresses deserves people's respect though, his understanding of the application of the classical prosody to the English poetry proves that he is far from the truth. Just because of his misunderstanding of the foreign prosody, Sidney launched an experiment on the English quantitative verse among his friends in a literary salon that Edmund Spenser banteringly called "Areopagus". However, Sidney cannot neglect the actual practice of English poets, acknowledging that for the English verse rhythm, "though we doo not observe quantitie, yet wee observe the Accent verie precisely, which other languages either cannot do, or will not do so absolutely" (44). His recognition comes from his perception of the poeticality in his contemporary English. However, Sidney does adopt some techniques from the classical prosody. He varies the feet in an accentual-syllabic verse and sets free the caesuras from the fixed position in a line in order to add the flexibility and "energeia" to it. ①

The reason of Sidney's variation of the lines may be initiated by the classical prosodies, for Romanized metrical patterns seldom exist in a traditional English accentual verse. The strong trend of a metrical line composed in Sidney's time and the time just before, as Gascoigne noted, follows strictly one pattern from the very beginning to the very end. Metrical foot substitution is regarded not appropriate. The result of such a trend is certainly the mass production of rigid poems in England when Queen Elizabeth ascended to the throne. Even so, the rigid metrical lines mark a great progress in the history of English poetical evolution. Compared the lines

ˊ ˊ ˘ˊ ˘ ˊ ˘ ˘ ˊ ˘ ˊ ˘ ˊ

What sweet relief || the showers to thirsty plants we see,

ˊ ˊ ˘ ˊ ˘ ˊ ˘ ˊ ˘ ˊ ˊ ˘ ˘ ˊ

What dear delight the blooms to bees, || my true Love is to me ("A Truelove")!

with

˘ ˊ ˘ ˊ ˘ ˊ ˘ ˊ ˘ ˊ

But still to look; || and thought I look too much,

---

① energy (Feuillerat 41). Katherine Duncn-Jones explains it as "the clarity with which the poetic theme has been realized in words" (note 246-1; *The Major Works* 388).

ˈ ˈ ˘ ˈ ˘ ˈ ˘ ˈ ˈ ˈ
Needs much I look || because I see none such.
("The Looks of a Lover Enamoured")

the reader marks easily the differences between the two groups of lines. The metrical pattern of the first group seems rougher than the second. The two lines of the first group do not have identical stress patterns, nor do they keep equivalent number either in stresses or in the whole spectrum of syllables. The only close link between the two lines is the ending rhyme. The second group consists of two iambic pentameters which form a rhymed couplet. Although the lines sound rather clumsy and mechanical, the repetition of words seems unnatural and unwitty and the position of caesuras in the lines lacks variation, they are closely integrated with the established metrical patterns.

Sidney has greatly developed the poetical ideas of Gascoigne and other people of the early Elizabethan age. He endows the strictly regulated metrical pattern with gracefulness and intelligence which once had been sparkled in Chaucer's brilliant lines and flashed now and then among those of Wyatt and Surrey. His lines, as is pointed out above, are flexible and expressive, due to the feet varied and caesuras set free from the fixed position,

ˈ ˘ ˘ ˈ ˘ ˈ × ˈ ˘ ˈ
Doubt you to whom my Muse || these notes entendeth,
ˈ × ˘ ˈ ˘ ˈ ˘ ˈ ˘ ˈ
Which now my breast || orecharg'd to Musicke lendeth (AS i)?

In fact, different readers may have different scansions from these lines of Sidney, but all the scansions could display a harmonious beauty, as in the following:

' × ˘ ' ˘ ' × ' ˘ '

Doubt you | to whom || my Muse | these notes entendeth,

' × ˘ ' ˘ ' ˘ ' ˘ '

Which now | my breast || orecharg'd | to Musicke lendeth?

The scansion might be derived partly from Sidney's learning from the classical prosody and partly from his own innovational thought. Poets of Sidney's time knew that there exists the "Archilochean" in Latin poetry and that Latin prosody accepts the weld of different feet within the same line. However, not many a poet dared try it in English metrical verse. It's hard to say that "inversion", especially the "initial inversion", set as a norm or convention to the English prosody by Sir Philip Sidney, is not tinged with a certain color of the Greco-Roman poetry. The controlled elegance revealed from the delightful form declares the maturity of English lyric in poetical construction.

Sidney, like his predecessors and many of his contemporaries, cultivates the rhetoric assiduously in his writing; unlike them, he primarily subdues the style to serve for the theme of a poem, not just to exhibit the splendid panoply of schemes and tropes (Ringler 460). He expresses his idea in Sonnet 3 of *Astrophil and Stella*:

Let daintie wits crie on the Sisters nine,
That bravely maskt, their fancies may be told:
Or Pindare's Apes, flaunt they in phrases fine,
Enam' ling with pied flowers their thoughts of Gold:
　Or else let them in statelier glorie shine,
Ennobling new found Tropes with problemes old:
Or with strange similies enrich each line,
Of herbes or beastes, which *Inde* or *Afrike* hold.

For me in sooth, no Muse but one I Know:
Phrases and Problemes from my reach do grow,
And strange things cost too deare for my poor sprites.
How then? even thus: in *Stella*'s face I reed,
What Love and Beautie be, then all my deed
But Copying is, what in her Nature writes. ①

The affected ornaments to the poetical lines displease Sidney, the cadged "fancies" "bravely maskt" (gorgeously arrayed), the borrowed rhetorical devices "flaunt they in phrase fine", the dazzling thoughts "enameled with pied flowers" (splendid styles) or garnished with "statelier glorie". "Ennobling new found Tropes" with "problems old" (the proposition and discussion of the moral precepts) and decorating the line with absurdly "strange similies" (a Euphuist style) are merely behaviours of those mediocre poets, which are unnatural and far away from the true art. With the rhetorical devices dangle in the line like the garish gems without any help to the flow of feelings, they are not persuasive, as Sidney describes

Doubt there hath bene, when with his golden chaine
The Oratour so farre men's harts doth bind,
That no pace else their guided steps can find,
But as he them more short or slacke doth raine,
Whether with words this soveraignty he gaine,
Cloth'd with fine trope, with strongest reasons lin'd,
Or else pronouncing grace, wherewith his mind

---

① Ringler takes this sonnet as a brief review Sidney made of the literary movement of Elizabethan era (Ringler 460). And Duncan-Jones thinks that "Sidney catalogues four current ways of ornamenting or elaborating verse" ("Notes"; *The Major Works* 358).

> Prints his owne lively forme in rudest braine (AS 58).

Such rhetoric is not what Sidney wants. His ideal art must be "copying" "what in her Nature writes". Those "strange things cost too deare for my poor sprites (soul)", yet they are useless to express the theme Sidney founds. Sidney believes that in poetry the graceful use of language is to express the subject effectively. ① A good style must be "clear" and "appropriate" (Adams and Searle 71). The figures of speech not only "give 'charm' and 'distinction' to our expression", but also, they "give 'clearness' and 'liveliness' to the expression of our thoughts" (Corbett 424). Like a "faire vineyard" (Feuillerat 19), it is thus

> able in many ways to infuse vehemence and passion into spoken words, while more particularly when it is combined with the argumentative passage it not only persuades the hearer but actually make him its slave (Adams and Searle 105).

It is notable that Sidney has treated almost all the schemes and tropes the Elizabethans know. This practice incurs criticism from the later generation as indulgence in mannerism. When Sidney tries his hand in literature, there is a fashion of mannerism. John Lyly and his *Euphues* are noticeable examples, in which the ornate language style is conspicuous. If Sidney is judged with such a standard, he is in mannerism. But Sidney's rhetoric serves his theme much better than Lyly, and it seems that Sidney is more conscious of the purpose of rhetoric than Lyly. And, if the Elizabethan mannerism is considered in the

---

① Sidney explains that a poet has to carry on two tasks, to deliver much "matter" "expressed by words" and to find "words to expresse the matter". The latter includes the question of style in which rhetorical devices play an important role (Feuillerat 37).

historical background, some people's feeling of strong dislike might be weakened. Seeing that in a time when English begin to get the full plume that English writers can display with proud patriotism, who will blame their naive but ambitious indulgence in new techniques they have just been trained with? Anyway, no matter how absurd their similes appear, no matter how shallow their poetry themes look like, and no matter how puerile their thoughts are, the early Elizabethans are creating history, as the pioneers of the coming great era, attempting all the new things. They may have done improperly a little in craving for polite letters though, their optimistic confidence echoes in that upward epoch. The Elizabethan mannerism is very different from the styles effused from the dispirited pornographic poetry and *pianwen* of Liang and Qi dynasties in ancient China.

Formal classical rhetoric, and especially its division dealing with style (*elocutio*) was assiduously cultivated in the later sixteenth century—one of the main characteristics distinguishing Sidney's own poetry from the earlier work of his countrymen is its complex rhetorical elaboration (Ringler 460). He combines naturally many rhetorical devices into his lines.

When comparing Spenser with Sidney, Ringler says that Spenser, "sought to vitalized English poetry by amalgamating the native and the continental traditions", whereas Sidney "turned his back almost completely upon the English past" (lii). Although Ringler plays a little trick here in his statement, he makes clear that Sidney has neglected the English native prosody. This, of course, is not completely true. Sidney turns his eyes to the foreign poetical conventions, "almost completely", though, he never forgets to find treasures from the "English past", like the expressiveness of the common monosyllabic words and the figures of speech in traditional English prosody (the alliteration, for example).

4. 3 From Latin Caesura to English Pause

Sidney has employed different kinds of metrical patterns in his poems and gradually concentrated on the practice on the accentual-syllabic verse, of which the *Astrophil and Stella* is a quintessential result. A careful observation on the lines in the *Astrophil and Stella*, compared with the other lines of accentual-syllabic verse in his other works when necessary, may reveal the value in Sidney's assiduous exertion to his poetical construction. Seven aspects that Sidney effects on the accentual-syllabic verse are worth discussing: the count of syllables, the arrangement of basic metrical pattern (feet), the pauses, the substitutes, the application of schemes and tropes, the choice of diction, and the consideration of the language structures. It is noticed that his designs of pauses and substitutes are more influential than others in the history of English poetry.

The principle that an English poet follows in designing the pause within a line is different from that of a Latin caesura. A caesura often refers to a metrical division amid a line where a word boundary falls within a metrical foot, dividing the line into two length-equal hemistiches. A pause refers oftener to the respiratory rest of speech within a line, linked with the language structures (phonological and syntactical) of the line. While the position of a caesura is rather fixed, that is, in the middle of the line. The purpose of using caesura is to keep a symmetrical balance of the line with the two hemistiches paralleled metrically. The position of pause can be varied according to the language structures of the line. And these two layers of language structures, the phonological and the syntactical, coincide in most cases. With the design of pauses in a metrical line, an English poet is able to reach further aesthetic purpose than a Latin poet admired. This is shown firstly in Elizabethan poetical practice, especially in Sidney's practice.

George Puttenham analyses the reasons for the use of caesura, which lie in two: to make the reading of poetry comfortable and not difficult to be understood, and to construct an aesthetic symmetry within the metrical design. He summarizes the basic usage of caesuras in different lines:

> If there be no *Cesure* at all, and the verse long, the lesse is the makers skill and hearers delight. Therefore in a verse of twelue sillables the Cesure ought to fall right vpon the sixt sillable: in a verse of eleuen vpon the sixt also leauing fiue to follow. In a verse of ten vpon the fourth, leauing sixe to follow. In a verse of none vpon the fourth, leauing fiue to follow. In a verse of eight iust in the middest, that is, vpon the fourth. In a verse of seauen, either vpon the fourht or none at all, the meeter very ill brooking any pause. In a verse of sixe sillables and vnder is needefull no Cesure at all, because the breath asketh no reliefe: yet if ye giue any Comma, it is to make distinction of sense more then for any thing else: and such Cesure must neuer be made in the middest of any word, if it be well appointed (75).

To construct an aesthetic symmetry of the line seems very important in Latin poetry and the early Tudor poetry, which becomes almost a fetter to Sidney and his contemporaries. But Sidney tames the caesuras. He makes the caesura playing some functional roles to help to convey the feelings of the speaker and to express the theme in his poem in addition to the two common purposes. So caesuras in Sidney's lines are used for adjusting the rhythmical tempo so as to change the patterns metrical units to meet the demand of the themes and feelings he expresses on one hand; and to balance the language structures and the metrical contours on the other hand. In this respect, a caesura in Sidney's verse is better named as a pause.

When one distinguishes Sidney's innovation on using pauses in an English accentual-syllabic verse, it is convenient for him to match partly the positions of pauses with the punctuations in a line, for, in modern English poetry, pause, as a metrical phenomenon corresponding to the break in the syntactic structure in a line, is not only suggested by the boundary of language structures, but more often emphasized by the punctuation. Sometimes an Elizabethan poet may equal the concept of pause with the idea of punctuation. ①

There are two kinds of referential practice on caesuras before Sidney: the native tradition from the Old English poetry and the foreign prosodic influence. Sidney arranges the positions of caesuras in a line of iambic hexameter basically on the principles of the Latin prosody rigidly borrowed by the Old English alliterative verse, and also on the practice of the French Alexandrine greatly developed during the French renaissance. He makes the caesura falls just after the sixth syllable in a line, and thus separating equally the long line into two pieces, like "He burnt un*w*ares his *w*ings, || and cannot fly a*w*ay (AS 8)." The line shows the imprint of the Old English verse tradition. The repetition of the consonant "w" forms one prominent feature kept in the native poetical convention before Sidney's time, the alliteration. ② Compare

*M*eotodes *m*eahte || and his *m*odge Þ anc,

---

① George Puttenham had matched the syntactical comma with the metrical caesura when he talked about the English caesura (Puttenham 74).

② Here the consonant "w" is placed on the positions other than the beginning of a word or stressed syllable, following the Old English verse practice.

(the Measurer's might and his mind-plans,)①

and

Sithen the *s*ege || and the a*s*saut was *s*esed at troye,
(After the siege and the assault was ceased at troy,)
(*Sir Gawain and the Green Knight*; Abrams 201)

The similarities are clear between the three lines on the surface—they all have caesuras separating the lines and the alliterations integrating the lines. But the structural differences exist, revealing the progress of the English prosodic tradition. Bede's line explains well the two features of the Old English verse. On one hand, the caesura falling on the middle of the line is so strong that it splits *de facto* the line into two halves and divides the four principal stresses of the line into two symmetrical groups; on the other hand, the consonants of the two principally stressed syllables in the first half-line alliterate with the consonant of the first principally stressed syllable in the second half-line, thus linking the separated line with alliterative metre. However, caesura and stress distribution in Bede's verse is regular though, it performs somewhat mechanical. The line from *Sir Gawain and the Green Knight* inherits the merits of Bede's line and the defects of Bede's as well. The position of such a strong caesura makes the number of the stressed syllables in two half-lines unequal. This may add a little flexibility to the line. The virtual symmetry caused by caesura is limited to the noun phrase "Sithen the sege and the assaut" without violating the completeness of the whole line. But such a

① The line is quoted from Venerable Bede. "An Ecclesiastical History of the English People" (Abrams 17). "Þ" is a runic symbol which equals to modern "th" (Abrams 14).

strong position of caesura breaks the balance of the verse rhythm. Sidney organizes his line in a way different from that of Bede's and of *Sir Gawain and the Green Knight*, though he dyes his line with the Old English prosodical convention. Grammatically, he pauses between two juxtaposed predicates, leaving the subject "he" in advance to rein the parallel parts. Metrically, he exactly controls both the stressed syllables and the unstressed syllables, weaving them into iambic hexameter, thus creating naturally the beauty of symmetry within the meter by caesura with no stamp of the mechanical separation. Sidney's line is not stiff. The regular iambic feet coincide harmoniously with the language rhythm, like "His paper, | pale dispair, || and paine his pen doth move (AS 6)." And frequently, Sidney's line marks much foreign colours when the caesura falls just after the sixth syllable, as in "That in no more but these || I might be fully blest (AS 77)", which reminds the reader either of the Latin hexameter, or of the French Alexandrine.

Firstly, the trail of caesura practice of Latin prosody in Sidney's line is perceptible. In a Latin hexameter, the basic pattern of the position where a caesura falls is within the third foot, either after the first syllable or the second of a dactylic foot, making a pause of reading amid the long line, like "arma vir/umque can/no || Tro/iae qui / primus ab / oris (*Aeneid*, I, i)", and "exsili/um tac/tusque || lo/ci na/talis a/more (*Metamorphoses*, VIII)". The "strong" or "masculine" caesura is more common and more influential in the history of prosody. The "weak" or "feminine" caesura is not very popular among the Roman poets. In fact, "the Roman poets show an increasing tendency towards word-division within (rather than between) the central feet of line—not only the third foot" (Raven 94). This tendency reflects also clearly in Latin iambic trimeter. The caesura often falls after the first syllable of the third foot, as in example "crinem / solu/tis || squa/lidae / serpent/

ibus (qtd. in Raven 52)". However, it is also acceptable when it falls after the first syllable of the fourth foot, as in example "exul / pavens / invi/sus ‖ in/certi / laris (qtd. in Raven 52)". All these examples reveal one idea: the position of a caesura in a Latin line can be varied to meet the demand of the cadence. Sidney has learned the essence of the Latin prosody on caesura.

Secondly, the influence of the French Alexandrine is conspicuous. This might be an old and tough question when Sidney's iambic hexameter is studied in the history of English poetry. Many poets before Sidney or in his time were acquainted with the prosody of French Alexandrine; some of them are even quite familiar with the reform on French Alexandrine by the Pléiade. With regard to the design of caesura in an iambic hexameter, the difference between Sidney's and others is his more flexible design. In the line "That in no more but these I might be fully blest", the reader may find a common Alexandrine caesura, with its position in the middle, dividing the line into two syllable-equal halves, but may not find Sidney's line rigid with such a caesura. More common features of Sidney and the French Renaissance poets who improved the techniques of their Alexandrine may display in a line like "The onely light of joy, ‖ the onley warmth of *Love* (AS 76)." The pause not only emphasizes the symmetry of the metrical structure between the two halves of the line, but also projects the parallel structure in three layers of language (syntax, phonology, semantics) and the pattern of metre, emphasizing the roles of caesura in conveying the theme, the feelings and other poetic expressions. Compared with the French Alexandrines, "Dessus le mur troyen, ‖ voyant passer Hélène" (Under the wall of Troy, seeing Helen passes) ("Les Amours d'Hélène", lxvii), the position of Sidney's pause in a line is not fixed in the middle but extended to any suitable place in accordance with the demand of expression and the natural respiratory stop within a sentence. His pauses appear natural and harmonious in language structures, thus enhancing the musicality of the metrical pattern. For example:

(a) That face, | whose lecture shewes || what perfect beautie is: (AS 77)

(b) Those looks, | whose beames be joy, || whose motion is delight, (AS 77)

(c) "Foole," | said my Muse to me, || "looke in thy heart and write." (AS 1)

(d) His paper, | pale dispair, || and paine his pen doth move. (AS 6)

(e) Loving in truth, | and faine in verse | my love to show, (AS 1)

There are two pauses in (a): the principal pause dividing the whole line into two metrically equal halves, and the subordinate pause isolating the initial foot from the others. The first foot is emphasized by the subordinate pause; the symmetrical balance is kept through the principal pause. (b) shares the similarity with (c), the subordinate pause protruding "Those looks" to a prominent place, the principal pause organizing a parallel structure with an obvious punctuation mark, the comma. Both (c) and (d) have a principal pause cutting the line into two hemistiches. However, the subordinate pause in (c) falls after the first syllable, which is also a monosyllabic word, of the line, dividing the initial foot; the subordinate pause in (d) falls after the first syllable of the third foot, counterpointing the two parts of the first half-line, so the line is kept integrated with the combination of both the English native prosodical convention, the alliteration, and the foreign metrical design, the caesura. The practice of pauses in (e) looks like that of the French trimètre (the tripartite form of the Alexandrine) that matures quite late in France. ①

Sidney is able to deviate freely from the general practice of caesura in his iambic hexameter, as in "That hue, whose force my heart still unto thraldome ties (AS 102)?" He makes a pause after the first foot, or "That presence, | which doth give darke hearts a living light: (AS 77)" amid the second foot, etc. Such bold innovation is not common among poets before Sidney, nor frequent in his French counterparts. Only when the French Alexandrine evolved to the end of the nineteenth century, the free design of the position of caesuras appeared. In the line "Au ciel, | dont elle seule ouvre | et ferme la porte ('Sagesse I')" the two caesuras fall after the second syllable and the eighth syllable. In the line "Et qui n'est, chaque fois, ni tout à fait la même ('Mon Rêve familier')" the caesuras come after the third syllable and the seventh. These lines reveal the spirit of Sidney's idea on caesura, i. e., naturalness and helpfulness to the expression of the theme and feelings. To some extent, one may say that the greatness of Sidney lies in his innovative maneuver of the poetical form, not in the themes of his poems, for he is always able to find a suitable verse to convey his not-so-profound thought. A single line may not fully show the expressiveness and flexibility of the pauses that Sidney arranges, however, a stanza may do:

She comes, | and streight therewith her shining twins do move
  Their rayes to me, | who in her tedious absence lay
  Benighted in cold wo, | but now appeares my day,
The onely light of joy, | the only warmth of *Love.* (AS 76)

---

① For instance, in "Tison de gloire, | sang par écume, | or, tempête ('Plusieurs Sonnets')!" or "Andromaque, | je pense à vous! | Ce petit fleuve ('Les Fleurs du mal', LXXXIX, Le Cygne)," two caesuras of the same prominent divide the line into three metrically equations.

Obviously, the comma from each of these four lines labels a pause falling. It is also obvious that the falling of the pauses in the stanza is not on the same position, which disobeys the Latin prosody. But such an arrangement breaks the usual mechanism and monotonousness of the lines that his precursors composed. If examining carefully, the reader may find that the language structures suggest more hidden pauses within the stanza, such as the possible pauses after the third foot and before the last foot in the first line and the possible pause amid the last foot in the second line, etc.

If Sidney often depends on the rules of the Latin Hexameter and the French Alexandrine when he distributes a caesura to his English iambic hexameter, which makes his poems more or less look like apprentice training, he behaves very artful as a master when practicing a pause in his later iambic pentameter line, the "energia" English verse. ① In such a verse, a pause may appear in any necessary position between the first and the last syllable, sometimes breaking a foot, more often between two feet without violating the integrity of anyone. And sometimes, two or more pauses are used in the same line to intensify the onomatopoeic effect.

The most common position of a pause in Sidney's iambic pentameter is the one after the fourth syllable, between the second foot and the third. This convention reminds the reader of the Latin and French prosodic practice; therefore some people call such an English iambic pentameter the English Alexandrine. Actually it is not a copy of those two foreign modes, and the name of English Alexandrine seems more exact when considering the dominance of the Latin Hexameter, the French Alexandrine and the English iambic pentameter in each of its own poetry. The pause in Sidney's iambic pentameter, being a natural demand of the language rhythm, is rather a

---

① The *Astrophil and Stella* contains 102 sonnets of iambic pentameter, totally 1428 lines, displaying Sidney's exquisite innovation of the metrical construction on English iambic pentameter.

spontaneous result of the language structures than a metrical discipline, or a careful coincidence of both. The lines like "I saw and liked, I liked but loved not (AS 2)," "What may words say, or what may words not say (AS 35)," "With rage of love, I cald my Love unkind (AS 62);" and "When Sun is hid, can starres such beames display (AS 88)?" display the dominance of language or the coincidence of language structures with metrical pattern.

The next position that Sidney's pause frequently falls is the one after the sixth syllable, between the third foot and the fourth, which also is a position common in Latin hexameter or iambic trimeter, and in French Alexandrine or decasyllabic verse. But, as is mentioned above, Sidney's pauses are rather natural stops in the lines "Upon thy cheerfull face, joye's livery weare (AS 103)" and "But ere I could flie thence, it pierc'd my heart (AS 20)." And this spontaneity that a pause displays can be seen clearer in the positions other than the one after the fourth syllable or the sixth.

In the cases that a pause falls after the first syllable, breaking the first foot, as in "True, that true Beautie Vertue is indeed (AS 5)," after the second syllable, between the first foot and the second foot, as in "Stella, whence doth this new assault arise (AS 36)," after the third syllable, breaking the second foot, as in "Of reason, from whose light those night-birds flie (AS 71)", after fifth syllable, break the third foot, as in "Out traytour absence, darest thou counsell me (AS 88)," after the seventh syllable, breaking the fourth foot, as in "When Nature made her chief worke, *Stella's* eyes (AS 7)," after the eight syllable, between the fourth foot and the fifth foot, as in "Let *Vertue* have that *Stella's* selfe; yet thus (AS 52)," and after the ninth syllable, breaking the last foot, as in "Flie, fly, my friends, I have my death wound; fly (AS 20)," the metrical convention, either from the native tradition or from the foreign influence, is almost completely reformed.

Sidney further demonstrates his talent in designing an iambic pentameter line with two or more pauses, of which the line "Nature's praise, Vertue's stall, Cupid's cold fire (AS 80)," might be a good example for explaining his liberation of a caesura from its inflexible position. The parallel construction of different layers in the language structures, syntactical, phonological and semantical, forms naturally with the division of the first line by two pauses. In the repetitions of the juxtaposed structures, the last part of the line has one more monosyllable word than the previous two parts, which enriches the line with variety of both language structures and the metrical patterns. The musical effect is enhanced with the whole design. The metre of the line is almost imperceptible, but its scansion helps the reader appreciate its subtlety: " ' * / ' | ' / * ' / | ' * / ' ' ". Among the first six syllables of the line, the rhythm contour appears falling generally. Such an effect comes from the existence of the two pauses, which is a natural result of the boundaries of the phonological phrases. The falling rhythm is conversed in the last four syllables which form one linguistic unit as well as two metrical feet, because the ending spondee, especially the ending diphthong of the spondee of the line raises the tune with its acoustical feature. A line of five feet has four substitutes, which makes the label of iambic pentameter almost impossible. However, the melody of the line is not consequently affected. And whether the line is in rising rhythm or in falling rhythm, Sidney seems always able to show his art in devising the pauses:

(a) With arms crost, yet testifying
Restlesse rest, and living dying (AS viii).
(b) Absence sure will helpe, if I
Can learne, how my selfe to sunder (AS x)

These lines are trochaic tetrameters. The rhythm contours of them are all falling ones. The design of pause in each line conforms naturally with the boundaries of language structures from different layers, so that the position of the pausecould not be fixed metrically. A pause may falls in the middle of a line, as in (a), or in the end or in the beginning part of a line, as in (b), depending on the need of expression.

Sidney balances the symmetry of a line with more than one pause, as in "Fy, schoole of Patience, Fy, you lesson is (AS 56)". The pause between the words "Patience" and "Fy" divides the line into two equal hemistiches. The pause after the "Fy" in the first hemistich and the pause after the "Fy" in the second form jointly the phonological parallelism. The design is fresh with ringing musicality. He even tries to reverse the positions of principal caesura and subordinate caesura that a Latin poet maintained, as in "Of reason, || from whose light | those night-birds flie (AS71)". Thus he shifts the focus of sound effect onto the word "reason" at the beginning of the line, emphasizing the significance of its meaning. Sidney's success in the design of pause in the lines still relies on his combined use of the device:

> "What he?" say they of me, "now I dare sweare,
> He cannot love: no, no, let him alone (AS 54)."

The metre exists, but becomes yielding by the side of language. The pauses in the two lines illustrate mainly the boundaries of linguistic structures. The sentences presented like a short daily conversation. The pauses consolidate the style.

4.4 Substitutes in the Accentual-Syllabic Lines, Excluding the Iambic Pentameter

From the indulgence of "go-as-you-please" to the strict discipline,

English verses were over-regulated by prosodists like Gascoigne. Yet, the works of some poets show that they had not answered Gascoigne's calls. Wyatt's decasyllable iambic lines are mostly irregular in metrical pattern. Surrey's verses are not perfectly regular too, although in his lines "the principle of the iambic metrical pattern is perfectly clear (Thompson 29)". And the poets from the "Areopagus" often neglect Gascoigne's rule. All these poets keep in their mind that the rhythm of natural language cannot be twisted too much. They break the sameness of metrical units of a line to balance the rhythm of language and the rhythm of metre. However, every poet has his particular method to achieve it, and so does Sidney.

Sidney follows the basic design of a metrical line but varies the metrical pattern with pauses and substituted feet to avoid the mechanism. He can weave a regular accentual-syllabic line by following strictly the metre and at the same time maintaining the natural state of English. What he surpasses most of his contemporaries is that he also can knit an accentual-syllabic line containing substitutes and settle such designs as prosodical conventions for poets from his time to the present. The initial inversion, a kind of the foot substitution, and the substitution of a foot inside the line are Sidney's skillful practice in composing a metrical verse. The variation serves for three purposes: to conform the metrical rhythm to the rhythm of language, to make the metre contribute to the meaning of the verse, and to echo the feelings the line conveys.

Sidney's accentual-syllabic verses include the lines of which the length varies from the trisyllabic to the fourteeners, with the basic metrical pattern either the iambic or the trochaic. Among these lines consisting of different numbers of syllables, the decasyllabic line, or iambic pentameters, which will be discussed in the next section, may represent Sidney's achievement in establishing the prosodical conventions of substitutes. However, a survey of

Sidney's other lines might be a proper preparation for further discussion.

The shortest accentual-syllabic line in which Sidney tries the substitutes is the trisyllabic one:

    '/ '*
What? ever (PS 13)?

The pause after the word "what" produces in the initial position of the line a monosyllabic foot *de facto*, which may also possibly be regarded as a semi-foot or half-foot by many a prosodist. Anyway, the law that a "foot of one syllable is always long, stressed, accented (Saintsbury 83)" is observed by Sidney and his contemporaries. The second foot of this line appears to be a trochee, but, since the foot belongs to the feminine rhyme scheme of the poem from which this line is cited, the last weak syllable is often not counted in the metrical scansion. So, the metrical analysis reveals clearly that such a line deviates more or less from the norm through the varied metrical pattern. The design itself testifies Sidney's breaking away from Gascoigne's mechanism. Sidney uses quite rarely a trisyllabic line in his poem and often treats it as an extension of the line it follows:

Behold me, lord, let Thy hearing creep
My Crying
Nay give me eyes, and light, least that sleep
In dying (PS XIII).

The four lines here would rather be treated as a hexameter couplet ending with feminine rhymes—each of the enjambements links a trisyllabic line and a decasyllabic line.

The tetrasyllabic line is, just like most trisyllabic lines Sidney designs, mostly a continuation of the line just before it, as a line *de jure* attached to the other:

x * / ' * / ' * / ' *
For so faire a flame embraces
' * / ' *
All the places (CS 13),

or a beginning part of the unity it forms with the following line:

* ' / * '
And who abroad
* ' / * ' /* '
Of world a dweller is (PS 33).

or both,

* ' / * '
(a) And look into
* ' / * '
His Temple too (PS 27).
' * / ' *
(b) *But to* mortall
' * / ' || x / ' */ ' *
Fetters *tyed*, *do* waite the hower
* ' / ' *
Of deathe's power (CS 26),

with the syntactic structure covering the run-on lines, and the metrical patterns keeping approximately the identity. The substitution exists, as is labeled in the italics. There are also some tetrasyllabic lines independent in syntactic structure and in metrical design:

> x /' */* ' / * '/ * '/* x
>
> Yea even my songs thy name shall magnify,
>
> x '/ x '
>
> O Lord most high (PS 9).

The second line is a tetrasyllabic one. Its relation with the line before it is not as close as "And look into / His Temple too", neither grammatically nor metrically. The independence of the line is strengthened by the foot substitutions as well. And in the following example:

> * '/*' /' */ * '/* '
>
> Alas, I lie: rage hath this errour bred,
>
> ' */x '
>
> Love is not dead (CS 30).

The tetrasyllabic line here deviates strongly from the basic iambic design. There is an initial inversion, and the second foot of the line can be read, either as an iamb, thus forming a prosodic contrast to emphasize the meaning and the feelings conveyed by the words, or as a spondee, in order to create a climax with the help of the intensified sounds. Sidney makes substitutions behave naturally, even if it is a very short line.

Sidney uses rarely pentasyllabic lines; he uses it as the sub-line segments to his verse experiments, the tag lines of the accentual (iambic) Sapphic stanzas, for example:

' ' /* '/ *'/* '/* '

(a) Fore-felt Desire, begin to savour parte

* ' / * ' *

Of comming gladnes (OA 59).

' */* ' / * ' / * '/* '

(b) Can of thy prayse the tongues entombed make

* ' /* '*

A heavnly story (PS 6)?

The scanned lines in these examples remind readers easily of the breaking up of a long fourteener—the enjambment has linked up the decasyllabic line and the pentasyllabic line following it. The extra weak syllable in the end of the pentasyllabic line is the result of the ending feminine rhyme. Not much variation of metre appears in the ending line of Sidney's accentual Sapphic stanza. But when he put the pentasyllabic line into the construction of his own six-line (trochaic) stanzas which he coins in his translation *The Psalms of David*, Sidney greatly increases the substitutes:

* ' / '* / '

To God's Altars tho①

* '/' */'

Will I boldly go

' */ ' */' *

① "tho" here means "then" (Trumble and Stevenson 3246).

shaking off all sadnes,

* ' / ' * / '

To that God that is

' */ ' * / '

God of all my blisse,

' * / ' * / ' *

God of all my gladness (PS 43).

Considering the feminine rhymes of the third and the sixth lines, the whole stanza can be treated as a complete pentasyllabic-line one. It might be arguable, but the basic metrical pattern of these lines is trochaic. The substitutive feet have crammed into every line—the initial inversion and the monosyllabic foot in the end—making the trochaic design almost undistinguishable. But the musical contour is clear and beautiful.

If it seems that Sidney treats the trisyllabic line, the tetrasyllabic line and the pentasyllabic line as sub-segmental stiches, it is obvious that he regards the hexasyllabic line and the over-six-syllable lines as the fully stretched ones that he is able to show his arts. Among the total two hundreds and ninety-one poems composed by Sidney, twenty-three are constructed partly with the hexasyllabic lines, occupying 7.9% of Sidney's poetical products. One poem in these twenty-three, the sixth song from his *Astrophil and Stella*, is formed with sheer hexasyllabic lines that Sidney weaves into nine six-line stanzas he invents. His hexasyllabic lines sound pure, easy and beautiful:

* ' /* ' /* '

But both to both so bent,

* '/* ' /* '

As both in both are spend (AS vi).

The natural language structure conforms naturally to the English iambic trimeter, a strict accentual-syllabic verse; and the rhythm, together with the alliteration, a traditional prosodic feature, describes the cadence of the melody. Yet, such lines are not short of variation:

x ' /' x / * '
Go snake hide thee in dust,
x ' / x ' / * '
Ne dare once shew thy face (OA 63),

Putting the choice words in choice positions, Sidney leaves quite enough room for the reader to choose his scansion. If the words "go", "thee", "ne" and "once" are all read in stressed way, the two lines are identical in metrical structures—each containing one spondee at the beginning of the line as an initial inversion and, each including a spondee in the middle of the line as a substitution—in which the poetical licence is skillfully practiced. If these anceps are scanned as the weak, then the lines deviate less from the norm of the iambic pattern, except a trochaic foot "hide thee" in the first line which replaces an iambus. A reader may have other choices when coming to these delicate words, and the variations continue. Sometimes the metre is definite, like

' * / ' ' / * '
Happy man, happy wife (OA 63).

And the variations are salient. An expert as David Keppel-Jones① may borrow a Greek prosodic term "second epitrite" or "crētic" to scan this simple line, with the result "' * ' ' / * '" or "' * ' / ' * '". Then it is hard to decide the English iambic trimeter of the line to an ordinary reader. Sidney writes a few of the accentual hexasyllabic lines in his *Old Arcadia* (in OA 63 and partly in OA 7, 52, 55), *Certain Sonnets* (CS 23, 26, 28, 30) and three other poems not included in these works. Then after having forged a pure hexasyllabic-line poem in his *Astrophil and Stella* (AS fifth song), he plays with the device abundantly in his translation of *The Psalms of David* (eleven poems among the total thirty two, occupying 34.4% of the collection). The short line in Sidney's hand becomes brilliant and expressive. Comparing the lines

* '/* '/* '/* '
(a) I cannot eat but little meat,
* '/* '/* '
My stomach is not good (Ault 41);

and

x ' /* ' /* '
(b) Though thou, my ring, be small,
* '/* '/ * '
And slender be thy price (Ault 54),

---

① David Keppel-Jones is the author of *The Strict Metrical Tradition*, an extraordinary work on the variations in English iambic pentameter from Sidney to Matthew Arnold. Some uncommon terms from the Greek prosody appear in Keppel-Jones' criticism, very accurate for the description but very difficult for a beginner. The book was published by McGill-Queen's University Press in 2001.

with Sidney's verse

        * ' /* ' /* '
(c) I layd me down and slept,
    * '/* '/* '
For he me safely kept (PS 3)

the reader will find the differences between them. The syntactical structures of the lines in (a) are regular and smooth, harmoniously agreeing with the standard accentual iambic metre, but the euphonious melody loads a vulgar subject and a low theme, degenerating the style of the poem. The phonological arrangements in (b) do not accord with the prosodic metre in some place, which cause some clumsiness when the lines read. The initial foot "Though thou" in the first line sounds embarrassing because of the repetition of the paired dental fricatives. The word "be", which seems not emphasized in the syntactical structure, is put to a stressed position, becoming ascensive. Such arrangement exposes that the poet is not able to recognize fully the relationship between language and prosody or that he just cannot control the poetical form. Besides, what the lines express makes the verse style too affected. Sidney's lines (i. e., (c)), though with slight flaws in concordance of phonetic rhythm and metrical ictus, as in the initial foot of the second line, certainly have reached the sublimity both in style and theme.

The hexasyllabic lines are also practiced in Sidney's early sonnet experiments in his *Old Arcadia*. In this experimental sonnet form, the hexasyllabic lines are combined or paired with those decasyllabic lines. This makes the reader to conjecture the relationship of Sidney's experiments with the classical long lines of sixteen syllables. The lines of Sidney, "Why doost thou haste away // O Titan faire the give of the daie (OA 52)?" seem reflecting some trace of the classical dactylic hexameter:

> ¯ ˘ ˘ / ¯ ˘ ˘ / ¯ || ¯ / ¯ ˘ ˘ / ¯ ˘ ˘ / ¯ ¯
>
> Omnia possideat, non possidet aëra Minos (*Metamorphoses*, VIII).①
>
> (Minos may own all else, but not the air)

The dactylic hexameter is used extensively as a ubiquitous line in the classical poetry. It becomes "the vehicle for heroic epic, for didactic, satirical, pastoral and much other poetry, and plays its part in such combinations as the elegiac couplet and certain lyric structures (Raven 90)". Poets during the Renaissance period were fascinated with the grace, eloquence and stateliness exhibited through the dactylic hexameter in the classical poetry. In that sense, the same characteristics shown in Sidney's combination of the hexasyllabic line and the decasyllabic one is probably the crystalization of his learning from the classical poetical structure.

Sidney's heptasyllabic lines seem always irregular to the duple metres. An extra syllable always floats in a disyllabic-foot line. Yet, the extra syllable is integrated into the metrical pattern, not isolated. Prosodists have summarized the techniques of arranging the extra syllables in a metrical verse—monosyllabic foot, feminine ending, orthography, or just being uncounted in scansion—which are practiced skillfully by the modern poets and are accepted naturally by the readers of today. But these were challenges to a poet at the court of Queen Elizabeth. When Sidney applies them in his composition, it is more or less innovative. Sidney does not use the heptasyllabic line in his early works. Only when he is able to maneuver

---

① The scansion is cited from the work done by H. W. Flewett and W. E. P. Pantin (xxx). The English translation adopts partly from the work by A. D. Melville (177).

artfully the lines of different kinds and different length, does he weave them flexibly into the stanzas of his mature works. Sidney controls it successfully. He designs two kinds of accentual-heptasyllabic lines, the iambic and the trochaic, in which he employes different techniques. In the iambic line, Sidney devises an initial inversion and a feminine ending:

' '/* '/* ' *

(a) Time runs away for sorrow: (CS 3)

' */ * '/* ' *

(b) Who hath his fancie pleased, (CS 23)

With a foot like "Time runs" (/ ' ' /) or "Who hath" (/ ' * /) to begin a line, which may make some people like Gascoigne feel uncomfortable, is one of Sidney's favorite and frequent tricks. The feminine ending combines the falling rhythm with the rising rhythm of the line, adding a weak echo sounding to the last foot, thus accomplishing a soft acoustic effect. More often the ending extra syllable is used to form the feminine rhyme, which is Sidney's contribution to Modern English prosody:

* '/* ' /* ' *

From so ungratefull fancie,

* ' /*'/* ' *

From such a femall franzie, (CS 30)

The feminine rhyme becomes a part of the metrical structure, performing two functions, enriching the musicality of a line on the one hand, interlinking the related lines in a stanza on the other. The variation is also displayed in

* ' / * '/* ' /'

But eyes these beauties see not (CS 23),

The words "see" and "not" are both emphasized in syntactical structure and get their phonetic stresses, which is not common in an English iambic line but not clumsy inside the melody. One solution of the irregular feet / * ' / '/ of this iambic line might be: the word "see" is not emphasized in scansion so that the metrical pattern becomes one / * * '/ foot (anapest), then one of the two weak syllables may be uncounted and the foot may be /(*) * '/ or / * (*) '/, actually being equal to a / * '/ foot. But the rhythmical contour of this line must not be the same as a normal accentual-iambic line. Such an experimental line should draw the researcher's attention, for it is not so rare after Shakespeare and is rather acceptable to a modern reader.

Sidney uses most of his trochaic lines of seven syllables in the songs of *Astrophil and Stella*, a work representing his poetic achievements, and some poems of *The Psalms of David*. "The accentual trochaic" is one of the "greatest" triumphs that Sidney wins in his poetical practice, because he naturalizes "an entirely new rhythm" for the English poetry (Ringler lv). Among these accentual trochaics, the heptasyllabic lines and the octosyllabic lines are the majority and are often woven together into one stanza. It is worth discussing the aesthetic qualities and the poetical characteristics of the accentual trochaic lines. The trochee is not an easy foot to manage in English, but that, when it is managed, it produces a literally extraordinary result (196; Saintsbury, vol. 2). Corresponding to an iambic verse discussed above, a trochaic line of seven syllables shares the similar changes in metrical design:

' * / ' */' * /'

Sleeping, grants a free resort: (AS ii)

This typical line of Sidney's poetical invention might possibly cause the ambiguity in scansion. Although the word "sleeping" projects a very strong shape of falling rhythm, the stressed ending syllable of the line can easily overthrow the contour hovering in the mind of a reader. The distinction made between the iambic and the trochaic becomes difficult and even impossible to common people—the cadence is not echoed in a pure rising rhythm or a pure falling rhythm, but in a mingled one. The discrimination seems meaningless. Who will care that the impure metre if the melody sounds beautiful and charming. The natural combination of the language structure with the accentual-syllabic verse announces that the poet has tamed the metre and been able to fly freely with the wings of Dedalus in the realm of poetical form. Sometimes the initial foot is inverted:

```
x   '  /  '      *  /*    ' /x
This small wind which so sweete is,
'   '  /*  * /'     x  /'
See how it the leaves doth kisse (AS viii),
```

Sidney observes the same principle of the initial foot inversionin his iambic lines. The only licence is that he begins a trochaic line with an iambus or a spondee (or even a pyrrhic):

```
x * /  '     * /  '  * /  '
In a grove most rich of shade (AS viii),
```

It should be explain that a spondee or a pyrrhic used as the initial foot in a trochaic verse is similar to that used in the same position of an iambic line though, for in both cases, such a device serves the same purpose—to alter the monotonous rhythmical contour, the effects it produces in the two kinds of lines are different.

The substitution occurs within a trochaic line as well:

> * ' / ' */* ' / '
> Their eares hungry of each word,
>   ' */' ' / ' */'
> Which the deere tongue would afford (AS viii),

It is hard to scan the feet "of each" and "deere tongue" as trochees unless the practitioner intentionally neglects the natural rhythm of the language. In fact the reader need not worry about the conflicts between the language and the metre, for there is no real discord happening if the idea of prosodic substitution accepted. As is mentioned above, the change that Sidney makes in the unitary metre enriches the aesthetical effect of the line.

The octosyllabic line, which also frequently appears in the English traditional verse, is a major metrical design only next to the decasyllabic line in Sidney's poetical construction, used in all his works from the *Old Arcadia* to *The Psalms of David*. The arrangement of the duple metre seems natural for Sidney to compose a line of even numbered syllables:

> * ' / * ' /* '/* '
> We finde most sweete affection's snare,
>   * ' /* ' / * ' /* '
> That sweete, but sower despairefull care (OA 6).

These lines are regular iambic tetrameter, in which the phonological stresses coincide with the metrical emphases in a roughly harmonious state. Such early lines Sidney writes still bear the brand of the early Elizabethan accentual-syllabic verse, either of the ballad, or of the lyric, as in

* ' / * ' / * ' /* '

to cast me off discurteously (Woudhuysen 193):

and

* ' / * ' / * ' / * '

ther naughty slawnderous offense (387),

of which the exertion of binding together the language and the metre is obvious. The promotion of the last syllable in "discurteously" (discourteously) and "slawnderous" (slanderous) is rather reluctant. The lines look clumsy with polysyllabic words crammed or with a polysyllabic word set among the monosyllabic words. Sidney's lines are better. Later when he masters the art of newly forged English lyrical poetry, Sidney achieves highly in making the flexible verse. One of the notable things is the metrical variation. There are many examples in Sidney's octosyllabic lines:

* ' / * ' / x ' / ' '

(a) And of their wounds make brave lame showes (OA 25):

' '/ * ' / * ' / * '

(b) First let them die, then passe the starres (OA 25),

' * /* ' / * ' / * '

(c) Whiter indeed; more white then snow,

' * /' '/ * ' / ' '

Which on cold winter's face doth grow (OA 62).

' x / ' ' / * ' / * '

(d) Nay like young Calves in leapes are born (PS 29),

* '/ * ' / ' '/ x '

(e) For then my Hill Good God did stay (PS 30);

' * /* '/ * '/ * '

(f) Take me to thee, and thee to me,

' x / ' x / x ' / ' '

"No, no, no, no, my Deare, let be (AS iv)."

Usually an English metrical line allows the changes and substitutions in the first hemistich, but in (a) Sidney overthrows the rule with a pattern / x ' / ' ' / governing the second half-line, altering the basic iambic metre. The example (b) begins the line with an initial inversion—a spondee "First let". Both the two lines in (c) have the initial inversions leading the line, casting a falling shade in the beginning of the rising rhythm; and to avoid the monotonous repetition of the rhythm, Sidney replaces the second iambic foot and the fourth iambic foot with two spondees as their substitutes in the second line. The alteration of the line in (d) happens in the first half-line, where an initial foot inversion and a spondaic substitute are distributed; and contrary to the example (d), the change of the metrical design in (e) occurs in the second hemistich, of which the rhythmical pattern / ' ' / x ' / varies from the mode of the example (a), displaying the richness of Sidney's prosodical art. The basic rhythm of (f) is a falling one, because the lines consist mostly of trochees; however, the variation exists in that the second line provides several possible ways of scansion. These examples have just displayed a miniature of Sidney's large amount of practices in the exploration of constructing an accentual-syllabic verse.

In Sidney's poems, a line with odd number of syllables often has two or more syllables used for rhyming with other lines, known as feminine rhyme (double rhyme) and triple rhyme. The feminine rhyme frequently appears in Sidney's heptasyllabic lines, which is discussed above, and those lines of nine, eleven or thirteen syllables:

(a) For if my place give me great pl*easure*,
Having before me Nature's tr*easure* (CS 29),

(b) Who hath the feet, whose step all sweetnesse pl*anteth*,
Who else for whom Fame worthy trumpets w*anteth* (AS i)?

(c) Then grew my tongue and pen records unto thy gl*ory*:
...
And all eares worse then deafe, that heard not out thy st*orie* (AS v).

The italic part in every line of these three groups of examples contains the syllables for the feminine rhyme. These lines of nine, eleven and thirteen syllables are equivalent to the lines of eight, ten and twelve syllables, for the weak syllable in the end of the line, as a part of the feminine rhyme, is not counted in the metre scansion. Sidney treats these lines as the related parts to the even-numbered lines when designing the metrical variations.

There are some exceptions in Sidney's practice of the enneasyllabic lines. The extreme examples are those in the twenty-fourth poems of his *Certain Sonnets*. Sidney arranges five consecutive lines of the accentual-enneasyllabic verse in a stanza without making them rhyme in feminine rhymes. These enneasyllabic lines of iambus account for Sidney's poetical quest:

'/* '/* ' /* ' /* '

Who hath ever felt the change of love,

* ' / * ' /* * '/* '

And knowne those pangs that the loser prove,

* '/* ' /* ' /' */ '

May paint my face without seeing mee,

* ' /* ' /* * '/* '

And write the state how my fancies bee,

* ' /* ' / ' */ ' * / '

The lothsome buds growne on sorrowe's tree.

The first line brings to the reader a possible combination of the iambic and the trochaic, an amalgamation of the rising rhythm and the falling rhythm—both the beginning syllable and the ending syllable of the line are intensive (the ending syllable sounds stronger than the commencing one, ensuring the overall rising rhythm of the line). It is successful: the cadence of the line is fluid; the phonetic emphases coincide with the metrical stresses. The penultimate foot in each of the even lines contains an extra weak syllable that, as is mentioned above, can be neglected in the scansion though, it renders some soft delay when the line ends. The ending feet in the third and the fifth lines are formed with a trochaic and a monosyllabic foot, altering temporarily the verse rhythm from the rising to the falling through the trochaic but immediately restoring to the current of rising rhythm by the stressed monosyllabic foot at the end of the line. Such a design enhances the beauty of the melody. In fact, all the changes scattered in the lines enrich the charm of the lyric. These delicate contraptions, as the results of Sidney's learning from the classical prosodies, become popular just after Sidney.

Sidney has used the accentual dodecasyllabic lines in several poems as the experiments on the English accentual hexameters. Most of these poems are in his *Astrophil and Stella*. Substitutes in an accentual dodecasyllabic line occur often in the positions of the first, the second and the fourth foot, and sometimes in the positions of the third and the fifth. Sidney's design is related to the Latin hexameter practice. If the replacement of a long syllable to two short ones occurs within a Latin foot, which causes the change of the foot, it is regarded as substitution. Take the metrical pattern of Latin dactylic hexameter for example. The basic unit of movement of such a line is the dactyl; the only admitted substitute for the dactyl is the spondee. ① Substitution of the foot is limited. "The first four feet are variable, i. e. either dactyl or spondee, the fifth is almost always dactyls; and the last a spondee (or trochee ...) (Flewett and Patin xxviii)." Substitution in Sidney's dodecasyllabic line seems not restricted as that in a Latin verse. Either a spondee or a trochee is acceptable to replace an iambus, as is shown by the italicized words in the lines "Of living deaths, *deare wounds*, *faire stormes* and freesing fires (AS 6)" and "*Broadred* with buls and swans, *powdred* with golden raine (AS 6)". The words "deare wounds" and "faire stormes" form two spondees which substitute theoretically two iambus. In the same way, "Broadred" and "powdred" are two trochees replacing two iambus.

The seventh song in *Astrophil and Stella* is written in fourteeners (heptameters). Sidney has composed this only poem with sheer fourteeners. He weds the fourteeners into rhymed couplets which in turn form three stanzas of three couplets. It is interesting that Sidney uses less frequently the substitution in his long lines. Only a few substitutes appear in his eighteen fourteeners. And such a line is rare: "A lesson fit, both sight and skill, *love and firm love* to breede. " For two consequent feet are not iambus. The foot

---

① There is one possible substitute, the trochaic, for the last foot of a Latin dactylic hexameter. Only such substitution is not counted by some metrists.

"love and" is a trochee, while "firm love" a spondee. The phenomenon of Sidney's substitution in the long lines exists in his poulter's measure. The following are only two lines rich in substitutes:

> *What length* of verse can serve *brave Mop*sa's good to show,
> *Whose ver*tues strange, and beauties such, as no *man them* may know
> (OA 3)?

Four italicized parts are the substitutes. The initial inversion is a common practice of Sidney in either of his long or short lines, becoming a prosodical convention of English metrical poems after Sidney. The positions of the last but two and the last but one are also the usual places in his long or short lines for substitution. Sidney devices more substitutes in his iambic pentameters or the lines shorter than ten syllables than in iambic hexameters or heptameters. Because less metrical units within a shorter line might make the deployment of language inconvenient.

The substitutes in Sidney's lines express the idea that in maintaining the natural rhythm of the language, a poet may organize different metrical units in a line, which is not only acceptable but also helpful for him to reach his poetic and aesthetic goal. Sidney displays this idea fully in his decasyllabic line.

4.5 Substitutes in the Iambic Pentameter Verse

The iambic pentameter line, as a decasyllabic verse with "the five-stress alternating pattern", and being a fruit of Chaucer's learning from the Italian *endecasillabo*, was "reconstructed" under the mingled influences of the classical prosodies, the vernacular manners of Italian and French, and the English prosodic tradition during the English Renaissance by the poets from

Wyatt and Surrey to Sidney, Spenser and Shakespeare (Preminger and Brogan 277). Among them, Sidney has composed a large amount of the iambic lines—one hundred and thirty-seven out of his two hundred and ninety-one poems are written in or partly in decasyllabic lines, and almost all of these decasyllabic lines are in iambic (Ringler 569-571).

The metrical norm of an iambic pentameter is / * ' / * ' / * ' / ' * / * ' /, but poets from Sidney on do not insistently abide by it, for they had seen not occasionally that the metrical rhythm clashes with the rhythm of language. It might be a better solution to change the metrical design of a line than to twist the sentence structure. Some conventions for the variation have been established in Sidney's poetical practice, mainly by adding or deleting an extra syllable and by replacing the iambic foot with the trochaic, the spondaic or the pyrrhic. The iambic pentameter may be a line of eleven or nine syllables when one syllable is added to or deleted from it. Although decasyllabic lines form the majority of the iambic pentameter and are the focus of the topic here, it is worthwhile to make a digression in a brief discussion of those irregular iambic pentameter lines.

The practice of the "extra" syllable comes from the classical prosody. Majorie Boulton explains that "In classical prosody a line which has an 'extra' syllable or syllables is called a line with hypermetric syllables and a line which has a syllable short is called catalectic. It is also for a whole foot to be hypermetric" (28). In English verse, the extra syllable added to the line can be used in two ways: the hypermetric which means "beyond the measure" (Preminger and Brogan 546), an extra syllable not counted as part of the regular metrical pattern; and the extrametrical syllable that is at the end of a line, or just before a caesura that is also regarded as a sort of end (note 1; Saintsbury 18). Sidney uses both kinds of extra syllable in his lines. The extra syllable is either stressed, forming an extra monosyllabic foot at the beginning or the ending of the iambic pentameter line, or unstressed, as in the feminine rhymes. So the hendecasyllabic line in Sidney's poems can be treated as the varied iambic or trochaic pentameter. ①

Poets seldom adopt a catalexis (coming to an abrupt end) in iambic pentameter. Sidney is not exceptional. The catalectic often appears in an English trochaic pentameter of many poets, but there is almost none in Sidney's. ② So it is better to catalogue an iambic line of nine syllables in Sidney's composition into the variant of an iambic tetrameter verse.

Most of Sidney's decasyllabic lines are acatalectic. However, most of them deviate from the norm of metre. His iambic pentameter lines are abundant and teemed with metrical substitutes, either as the inversion of the initial foot or as the substitution in other places.

Sidney displays his skills as a master of English metre in contriving the inversion of the initial foot in an iambic pentameter. He uses a trochaic foot to replace an iambic one and lead the line, thus adding the tonal richness to the monotonous rising rhythm:

' */* ' / * '/* '/* '

---

① There are hendecasyllabic lines in accentual trochaic, according to William A. Ringler, Jr., which appear in the twenty-sixth poem in Sidney's *Certain Sonnets*, being the ending lines of the stanza, echoing the first line of the stanza in melody (Ringler 571; 155). The following is cited from the second stanza of the poem,

' */ ' */' * /' / ' */' *
End the way, where all men stay. No, no, no, no.

It answers the initial line of this stanza in metrical design. (The first line is "No, no, no, no, I cannot hate my foe" of which the metre is analyzed in the following part in this section.) The monosyllabic word "stay" which forms a stressed monosyllabic foot is taken as an extrametrical syllable or foot, for it is in the position just before the principal caesura. If this extra monosyllabic foot is neglected in scansion, the line is a trochaic pentameter.

② The statistics in the "Table of Verse Forms" made by William A. Ringler, Jr. show that there is no trochaic pentameter line lacking a syllable at the end (Ringler 571).

(a) Scourge of it selfe, still climing slipprie place (AS 23),

' * / * ' / * ' / * ' / * '

(b) Trust in the shade of pleasing *Orange* tree (AS 30);

The treatment of initial feet in (a) and (b) suggests that Sidney understands the relationship between metre and the prosodic feature of the English language. In a verse, when the sentence begins with a content word, the stressed syllable in this word usually will get an emphasis in the sentence rhythm, forming a prominent position in the metre. Sometimes this emphasis in language rhythm clashes with the normal iambic verse metre. An inversion might be a solution to avoid the clash. Sidney may not necessarily explain clearly the inversion of initial foot in a modern linguistic way; yet, he does choose a correct way in keeping the harmony between language and metre, probably by his intuition or his sense to the phonological features of English. Therefore, once the inverted metrical pattern like those in "scourge of" or "Trust in" is accepted as a principle of the iambic pentameter, a poet may feel freer and more natural in composing his English metrical lines. Sidney has made it a convention: the substitutive foot in the initial inversion is not limited to trochees; a spondee also frequently strikes the listener's ears or the reader's eyes:

' ' / ' ' / ' ' / * ' / * '

(a) Faire eyes, sweet lips, deare heart, that foolish I (AS 43)

' ' / * ' / * ' / * ' / * '

(b) Dear, love me not, that you may love me more (AS 62).

' ' / * ' / ' ' / * ' / * '

(c) Wise silence is best musicke unto blisse (AS 70).

Theses spondees are guaranteed or even strengthened by pause (as in (a)),① or by pause and language rhythm (as in (b)),② or by word stress (as in (c)). The initial spondee opens the line with a double emphasis, slowing down the tempo of the verse melody, making it suitable for the expression of pathos or exclamations. Some scholars points out that Sidney also uses the pyrrhic to replace the initial iambic foot, which may not necessarily true and will not be supported here,③ for it lacks strong evidences from the recent phonological research to the English language.

Sidney has partly made the rigid iambic pentameter flexible and more compatible with the English language through the design of the inversion of the initial foot. The poet can easily begin an accentual-syllabic line either with a content word or with a form word as natural as he delivers his speech among his audience. Yet, it seems that he is not quite satisfied with the only variation in the initial position of a metrical line, for Sidney abundantly adopts

---

① A pause in a line is often regarded as a stop, though not as long as the ending stop of the line, which gives emphasis on the stress just before it. This accords with the ending focus in the English sentence rhythm as well.

② The phonologists have observed a tendency of the binary structures predominating the English rhythmical contour in which the adjacent stresses and a sequence of weak syllables which are three or more are likely to be avoided in the natural speech flow. In (b), the word "love" cannot be weakened although it might be possible in the first foot, for "deare" is projected to the prominent position by the pause after it. Because it is a content word and in the phrase "love me not", it should be given an enough emphasis so as to meet the reader's psychological expectation to the alternation of the strong and weak sound pattern. Noam Chomsky and Morris Halle have summarized in their work *The Sound Pattern of English* the rules of the English phonology at the word-level which contain the rules of the word stress adjustment. Iggy Roca and Wyn Johnson describe "the rhythm rule" at the phrase-level in the book *A Course in Phonology*. Derek Attridge, in his *The Rhythms of English Poetry*, applies Chomsky's generative accounts of phonology into the observation of the English metrical verse and concludes the metrical rules from his research.

③ For example, David Keppel-Jones, in the work *The Strict Metrical Tradition: Variations in the Lterary Iambic Pentameter from Sidney and Spenser to Matthew Arnold*, suggests that Sidney has used the pyrrhic in the leading position of an iambic pentameter. For example, "In thine owne seate (* * / ' ') a forraine state shall sit". But Keppel-Jones says immediately after such a scansion that "one could stress *thine* and retain an essentially iambic reading" as well (Keppel-Jones 10).

substitutes within an iambic pentameter other than the position of the commencement. He makes the substitution occur most frequently in the position of third foot,① with a trochee or a spondee replacing the iamb (the italicized part in the line):

(a) I like this place, *wheare at* the least the darke (OA 39)
(b) In steade of gall, *leaving* to her my hart (CS 22):
(c) This sowre-breath'd mate *tast of* those sugred lips (AS 59).
(d) And in thy feare *knees of* my heart will fold (PS 5)
(e) For reason will, *great sight* of hope blisse (OA 37),
(f) A banisht man, *long bard* from his desire (OA 44)
(g) Their master is *faire warn'd* his will to make (CS 22).
(h) But in Vert field *Mars bare* a golden speare (AS 13),

In the lines from (a) to (d), the tint of falling rhythm is set amid the rising rhythm contour; while in the lines from (e) to (h), a sound peak seems to stand in the middle. All these changes have already broke away from the acoustical monotony of sheer iambic metre.

Interestingly, Sidney often combines the third-foot substitution with a pause just in front of it. When the pause separates the iambic pentameter into two hemistiches, the substituting trochee comes to the beginning of the second half line, reminding the reader of the similar technique of the inversion of the initial foot of the whole line. The repetition of the identical metrical design in the two hemistiches simplifies the metre of iambic pentameter in the endeavour to avoid the monotony. Balance and counterpoint are formed in this repetition as well. The aesthetic symmetry comes into being.

---

① John Thompson has counted the substitutes in a limited way of Sidney's verse practice. His statistic is basically reliable (Thompson 144; 148).

The substitution also occurs in the second and the fourth foot of an iambic pentameter line, such as "Bitter *griefe tastes* me best, *paine is* my ease (OA 41)," or "With sword of wit, giving *wounds of* dispraise (AS 10)". The italicized parts in these two examples are the feet other than the iambic ones. The spondaic feet "griefe tastes" and "paine is" are put in balance in the counterposed positions, altering prominently the melody of the line. The trochaic foot "wounds of", following closely the trochaic "giving", sets a new tone to the second hemistiches, which is mainly not an iambic pattern. Furthermore, The combinatory use of substitutes in one accentual-syllabic line, which frequently strikes the reader's mind for Sidney's abundant practices, shakes profoundly people's idea of an iambic pentameter or a trochaic line with the identical meter from the very beginning to the very end. More examples may explain his metrical design clearer. The line "*Take thou* of me *smooth pil*lowes, sweetest bed (AS 39)" has an initial inversion and a substitutive spondee in the third foot; "*Listen* then Lordings with *good eare* to me (AS 37)" has an initial inversion and a substitutive spondee in the fourth foot; "*Long since forc'd by* thy beames, but stones nor tree (AS 36)" has an initial inversion and a substitutive trochee in the second foot; "*Cease ea*ger muse, *peace pen* for my *sake stay* (AS 70)" has an initial inversion and two substitutive spondees in the third and fifth feet; "Now with *slow words*, now with *dumbe e*loquence (AS 61)" has at least one spondaic substitute in the second foot and one trochaic substitute in the fourth foot. The result of the substitution is that no identically metrical repetitions exist there. The scansion of an iambic pentameter becomes sophisticate. But a decasyllabic line with the mixture of the trochaic and the iambic may be more flexible and more effective in the hands of a poet:

* ' / ' ' /' */' */* '

That her cleare voice lifts thy fame to the skies (AS 12).

It is rather arbitrary to scan the beginning foot "That her" as an iambus, for once the foot is used in a trochaic line, it is natural to be treated as a trochee, and when considered in the phonological layer, both the words "that" and "her" are likely to be read in an unstressed way. Because of the closer position of "her" to the phrase "cleare voice" it modifies, "her" is more likely to be weakened. Considering the phonological rule and the phonetic convention, the word "voice" may be less stressed than adjacent words emphasized. Only one foot, "the skies", is no doubt an iambus in the line. Even if the first two feet of the line are scanned as the iambus in this iambic line, there are still two trochees, the third foot and the fourth one, which cannot be regarded as the iambus. The smoothness of the measure and the musicality of the line are not spoiled by the mixture. The variation tunes well the metre to the natural language rhythm:

' */' */* '/* ' /* '

No, no, no, no, I cannot hate my foe (CS 26), ①

This is an amusing arrangement, though not common in Sidney's lines, for two hemistiches of different measures are seamed naturally with a pause. "No, no, no, no," imitates possibly an anticlimax through the diminuendo pronunciation; then "I cannot hate my foe" reverses the descending tune of the first-half line, creating a crescendo in melody. The contradictory feelings are shown vividly through the onomatopoeic falling and rising rhythm. Such a

① Ringler has classified this line into the accentual trochaic, but actually it is not a pure trochaic line.

line looks mediocre in the eye of a modern reader, but it was bold and innovative in the early Elizabethan era.

From the initial foot inversion and the frequent substitution in different positions of an iambic pentameter, the foreign influences can be traced①. In the Latin hexameter, the foot substitution may occur in any position except the fifth that usually is a dactyl and the sixth (the last foot) that is almost always a spondee②. And because the third foot is often split by a pause, to keep balance, there often has a spondee replacing the dactyl. But there is one strict rule for the substitution, that is, only spondees are admitted to replace the dactyls. Variation of the metrical patterns within a dactylic hexameter line makes it impressive as a vehicle for both epic and lyric poetry:

– ⏑⏑ – ⏑⏑– – – ⏑ ⏑–⏑ ––

(a) Omnia possideat, non possidet aëra Minos (*Metamorphoses*, VIII).

– ⏑⏑ – – – –– – –⏑ ⏑ – –

(b) at lubet innuptis ficto te carpere questu (Catullus 72). ③

(Maidens enjoy attacking you with false complaints.)

The number of syllables in a Latin dactylic hexameter line may vary from thirteen to seventeen, which makes the lines under the same name of dactylic

---

① Because the ancient Greek pronunciation had been Latinized in the history, it seems impossible to reach the original Greek cadence; thus, the classical prosody study in this book is mainly focused on the Latin samples. Besides, there is a very strong similarity between the ancient Greek prosody and its Latin imitation.

② The last foot may be scanned as a trochee because the last syllable can be read either long or short according to the rule of prosody; such a syllable is called *anceps*, meaning "ambivalent" (Raven 91).

③ The English translation is given by Guy Lee (73).

hexameter behave quite differently in conveying the meaning and the feelings. A dactylic hexameter of seventeen syllables, because of the teemed short syllables which are unemphatic, sounds soft and stately. The above epic line (a), shows a similar taint of the standard one, suitable to a serious meditation or soliloquy. A dactylic hexameter of thirteen syllables, because of the long syllables running through, causes some masculinely sonority. The comic effect is achieved in (b) just for such a metrical design. The English iambic pentameter line, though fixed in length—no variation in the number of syllable, different from its Latin counterpart which permits the change of the syllable number—is freer than a Latin dactylic hexameter in the metrical pattern, for its substitution admits the replacement of a trochee or a spondee to an iamb. Therefore it can express what an exalted classical line reaches, fitting for different poetic purposes. The rich variation within the metrical pattern of an iambic pentameter marks the poetical achievements of Sidney from his contemporaries. In this aspect, even Spenser cannot compete him.

Italian *endecasillabo* (hendecasyllable), as one of the most frequently used metrical line by the poets such as Petrarch (Francesco Petrarca), imprints its poetical features directly on the English iambic pentameter. It is a line of eleven syllables with the principal stress falling on the tenth syllable, the penultimate syllable of the line. ① The following is an example of the Italian *endecasillabo* cited from Petrarch' *Il Canzonière*:

' ' ' ''

---

① "The name of the line forms in Italian prosody are established by the place of the principal accent", for "In Italian prosody, any line that has the principal accent on the penultimate syllable, making the line ending paroxytonic; Italian line forms are named on this basis." In the term of the Italian prosody, this is called *verso piano* (verse plan, or verse map) (Preminger and Brogan 515; 1356).

Voi ch' ascoltate in rime sparse il suono (canzoniere 1)①

(You who hear the sound, in scattered rhymes,)

The principal stress is fixed onto the first syllable of "suono", the penultimate syllable of the line, establishing the basic metre for the verse. However, the unfixed subordinate stresses decide the rhythm of an *endecasillabo* line. ② The scansion here is one possible result with the metrical pattern coming regularly as / ˌ * * / ˌ * * * / ˌ * / ˌ * /, or / ¯ ˘ ˘ / ¯ ˘ ˘ ˘ / ¯ ˘ / ¯ ˘ /, in a falling rhythm. The early English imitations of this Italian *endecasillabo* follow the pattern of that one decasyllabic line plus an extra weak syllable, ending the line with a feminine rhyme. Although the poets have made up the equal number of the syllables, they cannot produce different melody within a rigid iambic pentameter. The scansion of the Italian line may draw the attention of an English imitator like Wyatt and Sidney to the foot substitution, for the result of scansion is just an arrangement of different metrical feet.

Similar things are also observed in the English poets's learning from a French Alexandrine. Based on syllable-count rule of composing a line, which is also similar to the Italian and some other languages from the Roman family, the rhythmical contour in an Alexandrine is determined by both its principal stresses and subordinate stresses:

---

① The English translation by A. S. Kline is also cited from the same website. Because of liaison, the last syllable in "ch' ascoltate" is amalgamated with the syllable in "in" and, the last syllable in "sparse" amalgamated with the one in "il", together with the diphthong in "voi" and semi-consonantized /u/ in "suono", the syllables counted in the line is eleven.

② Different *endecasillabo* lines may have different distributions of the subordinate stresses, forming different contour of the rhythmic pattern. But, in one definite *endecasillabo* line, the positions of the subordinate stresses are fixed. So the unfixed subordinate stresses here indicated that these stressed syllables may appear in different positions in different lines, even if these lines are named with the same term of *endecasillabo*.

ˈ ˈˈ ˈ ˈˈ

Direz, chantant mes vers, et vous émerveillant:

(81; "Les Amours d'Hélène", xliii)

(Tell me, singing my verse, and you wonder)

Generally, a principal stress may fall on the last syllable of a French line, while other stresses may be determined either by the syntactic structure or by the rhetorical emphasis. Usually there are two or three principal stresses in an Alexandrine according to the number of caesuras occurring within the line. If there is one caesura happening amid an Alexandrine, like the above example, then there are two principal stresses each falling on the syllable just before the caesura and the syllable which ends the line. The positions of the principal stresses are fixed, which brings the balance and symmetry to the line and sets up the rhythmical shape for the line. Within an Alexandrine of two principal stresses, there often will have two other stresses, each being allocated in one hemistich before or after the caesura. Different Alexandrine lines may have different arrangements for these two non-principal stresses, enabling the flexibility in rhythm within a regular metre. The scansion of the above Alexandrine may be / * * ˈ / * * ˈ || * * ˈ / * * ˈ /, or / ˘ ˘ ˉ / ˘ ˘ ˉ || ˘ ˘ ˉ / ˘ ˘ ˉ /, in a regular anapaestic tetrameter. The other Alexandrine lines may not be scanned in the same way because those two non-principal stresses may fall to different positions of the two hemistiches. The shifting stress position causes the variation of the metrical pattern and the rhythmical contour of the line. The effects of these variations in a French Alexandrine are very similar to those by the substitution in the English iambic pentameter. And, when the English poets began to invent their iambic pentameter, the French Alexandrine had already reached its early maturity and been quite familiar by these English poets. Furthermore, before they constructed their own iambic pentameter lines, these English poets had already done quite enough translations or imitations of the brilliant Alexandrine lines composed by those French of the same trade.

The beauty of Sidney's accentual-syllabic verse also comes from his experiments on some fine adjustment of the cadence of a line. For example, he arranges carefully of a word with two or more syllables in the verse so that the stress pattern of the word may be consistent or in contrast with the rhythmical contour of the line:

' */* ' / * '/* ' /* '

Sicke to the death, still loving my disease. (OA 41)

Here are two disyllable words in the line, "loving" and "disease". The stress pattern of "loving" is / ' * /, forming a falling tone, which contrasts to the line rhythm, while the stress pattern of "disease" is / * ' /, accordant with the cadence of the line. An acute reader may find these delicate musical effects in this arrangement.

It is not surprised that Sidney assiduously works on the English accentual-syllabic verse. The evolution of the English metrical poems has already proved the value of his innovation on the pattern of an English line. The design of pauses and the substitution liberates the metrical lines from rigidity. Sidney's practice has been inherited by English poets as prosodical convention today. His ideas on the rhythmical design of an accentual-syllabic line become the fundamental thought of English prosodic theory.

Chapter 5 Devices in the Design of English Stanzas

The system of English metrical prosody has been mostly established in the Elizabethan Renaissance, or established via this era. New poetical form was accompanied by new organizational rules flushed when Sidney was active in literary activities. Sidney is an assiduous experimenter, having exploited almost all the popular foreign poetical genres brand-new to the English people under the reign of Queen Elizabeth, or the newly emerged forms created by his compatriots. He set up or helped set up some conventions for English lyrics which have been called new poetry in the history of English poetry. The conventions include the techniques of knitting separate lines into a stanza or a poem. Two groups of poetical skills among these techniques have been improved to quite a perfect level in the hands of Sidney. The first group contains the devices of the rhyme and the designs of the enjambment. On the improvement of these skills, Sidney owes much to the foreign prosodies. The second group includes the methods of the rhetorical prosody, concerning Sidney's practice of the musical effects of the English phonological features. In this respect, the English native prosody influences greatly on Sidney. The innovative contribution of Sidney to the design of an English stanza lies in his revival of the feminine rhyme and his abundant use of the enjambment, which deserves careful examination for its inventiveness.

5.1 Feminine Rhyme

Sidney's practice of verse rhyme covers almost all the spectrum the rhyme theory described in the twenty-first century, which may surprise the modern readers. George Puttenham has illustrated people's knowledge of rhyme in poetry in the sixteenth century, which leaves a general impression to the later generations:

> For wanting the currantnesse of the Greeke and Latine feete, in stead therof we make in th' ends of our verses a certaine tunable sound: which anon after with another verse reasonably distant we accord together in the last fall or cadence: the eare taking pleasure to heare the like tune reported, and to feele his returne (Puttenham 76).

And a poet may keep his rhyme at the "end of euery verse, or perchaunce the middle and the end in meetres that be long" (78). But Sidney has done more than that. He may have a better understanding of the rhyme than most of his contemporaries. Sidney regards that "the chiefe life" of "moderne" versification "standeth in that like sounding of the words, which we call Rime" (Feuillerat 44), and that the modern versification

> "with his rime striketh a certaine Musicke to the ear: and in fine, since it dooth delight, though by an other way, it obtaineth the same purpose, there being in either sweetnesse, and wanting in neither, majestie" (44).

Sidney describes the musical effects made through the rhyme, emphasizing the importance of the rhyme in English poetry. In practice, he does not fetter the rhyme to the ending part of the lines, which broadens his experiments on different rhymes: the end rhymes (which include the masculine rhyme and the feminine rhyme), the internal rhyme, or, to borrow an Italian term, the *rimalmezzo*,① and the alliteration, and so on.

The end rhymes in Sidney's poems contains mainly two types, the masculine and the feminine. There are also rhymes covering three or more syllables. But they usually are categorized either as masculine rhymes or the feminine ones. Sidney has displayed his art in arranging the masculine rhymes. His control on the rhymes in a poem, in the number or in the accuracy, is almost unmatchable in the time before Shakespeare. Only the mighty Spenser can equal him in this respect. Sidney may compose a poem with monorhyme (e. g. OA 42 or PS 15), or with just two rhymes (e. g. OA 39 or OA 51), showing both his ability and the capability of English language in forming verse rhyme. The fact that in most of Sidney's sonnets a poem contains no more than five rhymes, which is regarded as the usual number of the rhymes in an Italian sonnet that an English poet feels hard to manage, refutes the allegation that the English sonnet permits seven rhymes just because the language does not provide enough rhyme sources. The exact rhymes across the lines should be identical in phonological formation and in prominence, i. e., the rhyming part of every line should be the same end nucleus, or the same combination of nucleus plus coda, and this nucleus or the combination of nucleus plus coda should be given the same prominence in the rhythm of the lines. Sidney observes the rule strictly. "He almost always rhymed with complete phonetic accuracy (Ringler lvi)."

The internal rhymes can be formed within a line, and be arrayed across

---

① Rhyme in the middle.

lines as well. The former is generally treated as the devices of rhetoric prosody. The latter is thought as complicated linkage of the poetical structure. The Italian *rimalmezzo* belongs to the latter rhyming construction. Sidney has experimented not many lines of internal rhymes. But he has tried out almost the whole panoply of them:

(a) Whose *force* had such *force* so to trans*forme*, nay to re*forme* me (OA 13),

(b) With neighing, bl*aying*, br*aying*, and barking (OA 66),

(c) D*ay* unto d*ay* doth it displ*ay*,

...

And n*ight* to n*ight* succeding r*ight* (PS 19)

(d) For if my pl*ace* give me great pleasure,

...

What in your f*ace* mine eyes do measure (CS 29).

(e) Dep*art*, a word so gentle to my minde,

Weakely did seeme to paint death's ougly d*art* (CS 20).

(f) Which breakess the clowdes and opens forth the l*ight*,

That doth both shine and give us s*ight* to see (CS 32).

The repetition of the word "force" in (a) and "day" and "night" in (c) is called polyptoton, a special kind of internal rhymes. The repetitions of the italicized parts of words "transforme" and "reforme" in (a), of words "blaying" and "braying" in (b) and of words "day" and "display", and "night" and "right" in (c) are the internal rhymes within the lines. The italicized parts of words "place" and "face" in (d) form the usual internal rhymes across lines. The cases in (e) and (f) explain the varied rhymes. The internal rhymes perform the phonological connectors in a poem.

Especially, Sidney's innovative use of rhymes lies in his practice of the feminine ones, which is one of his contributions to English poetical construction.

Sidney has tamed the feminine rhyme in his early works and regularly uses it in his mature compositions in the *Astrophil and Stella*, in the songs of the sonnet sequence. The feminine rhyme was a compensative result to the lines when Wyatt and Surrey and their followers try to imitate the Italian examples, especially those Petrarch used in his *Il Canzoniere*. ① They usually added an extra weak syllable to the English counterpart, the iambic pentameter, for example, to the imitation of Italian *endecasillabo*. English is rich in monosyllabic words; therefore, such a design is easy to achieve. And this extra weak syllable is not counted in scansion for it is extrametrical. But poets before Sidney seldom willingly and normally use the feminine rhyme, so they often avoid such a use and stick to the masculine rhyme, without thinking of naturalizing the device. Sidney's great innovation on the rhyme is "to bring feminine back in to English verse and to make it a formal structural element in the shaping of his stanzas" (Ringler lvi). He displays his arts well in describing the lyric competitions held by those shepherds in his *Old Arcadia*:

> [A.] We love, and have our loves rew<u>arded</u>.
> [B.] We love, and are no whit reg<u>arded</u> (OA 6).

---

① The feminine rhymes used to be common in Middle English poetry, e. g. in Chaucer's poetic works. It is not often adopted in Modern English verse; one reason may be the disappearance of the word inflections. There is a revival of feminine rhymes in Elizabethan lyrics, which lasts for some decades and sharply dwindles in the eighteenth century. Then from the nineteenth century on, the feminine rhymes become frequent again in metrical verses (Schipper 146-147).

The underlined syllables① are used for feminine rhymes. If the whole lines are scanned, each line is an iambic tetrameter plus a weak extrametrical syllable. Yet, "the terminal syllables are pronounced in English, so carry weight even if slight" (Preminger and Brogan 737). Thus the ending syllable effects on the contour of the melody of the line. And the repetition of the identical sound in the identical position in a sequence of lines certainly will shape the cadence of the stanza comprising these lines:

> Such Kala is: but ah, my fancies raysedbe
> In one, whose name to name were high presumption,
> Since vertues all, to make her title, pleased be.
> O happie Gods, which by inward assumption
> Enioy her soule, in bodies faire possession,
> And keep it ioynde, fearing your seates consumption.
> How oft with raine of teares skies make confession,
> Their dwellers rapt with sight of her perfection
> From heau'nly throne to her heau'n vse digression?
> Of best things then what world can yeeld confection
> To liken her? Decke yours with your comparison:
> She is her selfe, of best things the collection (OA 7).

The rhyming scheme of this stanza is: *ababcbcdcded*, and the echoing sounds of /ˈʌmpʃən/, /ˈeʃən/ and /ˈekʃən/ constantly strikes the reader's mind. The weak syllable /ʃən/ almost always comes to the reader's expectation of the ending rhyme with its not so weakened sound, forming a sonorous flow of

① The same underlines will be used to label the end rhymes in the lines of the following citations in this section, as is done here.

speech, vividly presenting the oratorical eloquence that the narrator displays in the pastoral contest. Such an arrangement of feminine rhymes challenges a poet's talent, for it demands very mature skills. Yet, compared with the theme and matter the lines convey, the verse form, decorating with the pleasant feminine rhyme, sounds phonily exaggerating, just like the exercise of the technique in the hands of a learner. Sidney's assiduous exercise of the end rhymes even extends to the trisyllabic ones:

> As for thy wish to my enraged spitefulnesse,
> The lovely blowe with rare reward, my prayer is
> Thou mayest love her that I may see thy sightfulnesse (OA 28).

The phonological segment /ˈaitfulnis/ which covers three syllables in the word "spitefulnesse" at the end of the first line is exactly copied in the ending word "sightfulnesse" of the second line. Possibly Sidney has not considered fully the parallels between verse form and theme. For example, if the salient repetition of /ˈaitfulnis/ is used to emphasize the semantic meaning of the lines, it seems that no signs strong enough to suggest such relationships. But Sidney quickly overcomes the awkwardness by making the form well suitable to the subject it expresses:

> And mournfully bewailing,
> Her throate in tunes expresseth
> What griefe her breast oppresseth,
> For *Thereus*' force on her chaste will prevailing (CS 4).

The tune of these four lines imitates the singing of a nightingale. In the first and the fourth lines rhymed with feminine rhymes, the stressed syllables are linked with unstressed syllables which exceed the stresses in number, slowing down the tempo of the rhythm; and the duration is further extended by the combination of /ˈeiliŋ/ which possesses the lengthening characteristics in pronunciation①. The first and the fourth lines imitate the long spans of the bird song. The fourth is longer than the first, making the verse end in seemingly endless songs. The second and the third lines are both in the metrical pattern of short iambic trimeter plus an extrametrical syllable, rhymed with the hasty /ˈesiz/②(also feminine rhymes), reproducing the short span of the bird song. One slow singing followed by two swift chirms, then followed by a lengthened song, the nightingale's singing is copied in the verse form, both of the language structure and the metrical pattern. And more significantly, the mood spread through the lines exactly suggests the pathetic story connoted in the allusion. ③

This suitableness is developed to a more harmonious state in the songs of Sidney's *Astrophil and Stella*. He integrates the weak syllable into the metres of the lines, making it no more extra, whether it is set in the designs of rising rhythm, or in those of falling rhythm. In the lines of rising rhythm, like the iambic, the feminine ending is amalgamated with the foot substitutions:

---

① The vowel /ei/ is a diphthong which equals in length to the long (pure) vowels, and "the vocalic nature of the nasals is underlined by the fact that they readily perform the syllabic function of vowels" (Cruttenden 195). The velar nasal /ŋ/ often cannot be independent though, it also share the quality of performing the function of a vowel. So when the syllable /iŋ/comes into being as an ending syllable, it is a conjunction de facto of two vowels, pronounced with some length usually longer than one pure short vowel (195).

② Both /e/ and /i/ are short vowels, which determine that the length of the whole combination cannot be very long. Beside, the stressed /e/ is shortened by the voiceless consonant /s/, which makes the combination even shorter when pronounced.

③ The story of the bird nightingale is told in the Book vi of Ovid's *Metamorphoses*, a tragic story of rape and revenge. Greek poets generally made Procne the nightingale, Philomela the swallow; Roman poets usually do it in an opposite way. See E. J. Kenney (Ovid; Melville Trans; xxviii-xxix; 413; 134-142).

Who hath the eyes which marrie state with pl<u>easure</u>,
Who keepes the key of Nature's chiefest tr<u>easure</u>?
To you, to you, all song of praise is due,
Only you the heav'n forgate all m<u>easure</u> (AS i).

There are eleven syllables in each of the first two lines, which are both iambic in metre, thus protruding the weak tag of the extrametrical syllable at the end of each line. However, the initial inversion balances the feminine rhyme with the altered rhythm contour. And the fourth line, feminine rhymed with the first two lines, comprises five disyllabic feet, accepting the feminine ending as a foot substitution in its metrical pattern.

Similarly, in the lines of falling rhythm, the trochaic for instance, the feminine ending is naturally absorbed into the metrical designs, even without making the reader think of the foot substitution:

But ô foole, thinke of the d<u>anger</u>,
Of her just and high disdaine:
Now will I alas refraine,
Love feares nothing else but <u>anger</u> (AS ii).

The feminine ending /ˈæŋgə/ which forms the feminine rhymes between the first and the fourth line is just in tune of the trochaic verse. Of course the metrical designs of these two lines feminine-rhymed are not in rigid trochaic pattern. The scansion of the first line may be / * '/' , '/ * * /' * /. The comma inside the second foot, which is a spondee, causes a pause, separating the line into two hemistiches. Then there rises the contrast of the rhythm contours between the two hemistiches—a rising rhythm of the first hemistiches and the falling rhythm of the second. And, because of the larger proportion the latter occupies and the convention that the ending foot determines the metrical quality, the line can be regarded as a trochaic tetrameter. The fourth line can be scanned as / ' ' / ' * / ' * / ' * /, with the last foot, a trochee, playing the role of feminine rhyme. In this way, the generally extrametrical syllable becomes "a formal structural element in the shaping of" Sidney's stanzas (Ringler lvi).

Further experiments were still carried on in Sidney's later mature poetical practice—some new designs appeared in the arrangement of the feminine rhymes:

For my God Thy sight
Give me my might,
  Why then hast thou left me?
Why walk I in woes
While prevayling foes
  Have of joyes bereft me (PS 43)?

Besides the normal feminine rhymes of the underlined parts in line three and line six, the ending parts underlined with the wave lines are worthy of study, because they display Sidney's new efforts in feminine rhymes. If judged in a standard way, /ˈaisait/ and /ˈaimait/ are not identical; therefore, they are not truly feminine rhymed. So are not /ˈinwəuz/ and /ˈiŋwəuz/. But the sounds are very similar and ostentatiously distributed in the position of end rhymes, performing of the feminine rhymes, and projecting the correspondent semantic meanings. The pseudo feminine rhymes are carefully woven into the metrical forms as well.

Sidney's experiments on feminine rhymes usher in a new trend of the English rhymed verses. The masters of English poetry of his time follow his patterns in a very controlled way, which can be revealed in their limited adoption the feminine rhymes in their successful works:

And raungéd farre abroad in every border,

They would have causéd much confusion and disorder.

(*Edmund Spenser's Poetry* 411)

The two lines written by Edmund Spenser are rhymed in feminine rhymes which, seeming tamed in knitting the lines, serve quite well the cadence, the feelings, and the meanings of the completed stanza. Spenser might have accepted Sidney's idea reluctantly, for he practiced the same arrangements in a small amount in his later works when Sidney was establishing the convention①. However, Spenser did not use the feminine rhymes as ostentatiously as Sidney had done. The conservative attitude of Spenser to the feminine rhymes possibly reveals at least two implications: he doubted the life-span of such a device in English poetical construction; he realized that the sources of feminine rhymes in English language are bare. Sidney also was awared of the limited sources in English, but he is unwilling to abandon the anglicization of the foreign prosody he admires.

There are a few feminine rhymes scattered in Spenser's rhymed poems, including his sonnets.② The following lines are cited from Spenser's "Prothalamion", a focused exhibition of his skill in such designing:

The little Dazie, that at evening closes,

---

① Spenser has used feminine rhymes in his "The Shepherd's Calendar", for instance, the ones in "Thou barren ground, whom winter's wrath hath wasted, / ... / Whilom thy fresh spring flowered, and after hasted / ..." (January). Such practice may not be carried on under the influence of Sir Philip Sidney, since the work is completed before or at the same time that Sidney's composes his feminine rhymed lines.

② In the sonnet sequence *Amoretti* Spenser has used the feminine rhymes in 19 sonnets, about one fourth of the total 88 (or 89 as some scholars acclaimed) poems. Usually he permits only two lines in a sonnet rhymed in this way, with only two extreme exceptions, sonnet 39 which contains four feminine rhymed lines, and sonnet 84 with five such lines. From this intensive group, a researcher cannot find sequence of lines ended with feminine rhymes. But the phenomena are common in Sidney's compositions. Therefore, it might be reasonable to conjecture that Sidney has plunged himself much into the experiments of the feminine rhyme than Spenser.

The virgin Lillie, and the Primrose trew,
With store of vermeil Roses,
To deche their Bridegromes posies (547),

It is surprising that Spenser can skilfully use the feminine rhymes strictly in a continuous way. More surprisingly, he even embeds a similar syllable "rose" near the end of the second line which is not rhymed with other lines, making it echo with the feminine rhymes of the stanza. Though he has the talent, Spenser seems unwilling to devote much energy to the experiment. But greater masters of English poetry after Sidney have applied his inventions into their compositions, freely, smoothly and naturally. Shakespeare composes abundant lines with feminine rhymes,① seemingly without difficulties that Sidney encountered in his invention:

But all these poor forbiddings could not stay him;
He in the worst sense construes their denial:
The door, the wind, the glove, that did delay him,
He takes for accidental things of trial;
Or as those bars which stops the hourly dial,
  Who with a ling' ring stay his course doth let,
  Till every minute pays the hour his debt (Shakespeare 1263).

The whole stanza consists of seven lines, among which five are rhymed uninterruptedly in feminine rhymes, arranged in a fluent way. Unlike Sidney who depends mainly on polysyllabic words in designing the feminine rhymes, Shakespeare turns to the monosyllabic words, the rich vocabulary sources of

① In every kind of Shakespeare's rhymed poems a reader can easily find the lines with feminine rhymes.

English, making the shaping of feminine rhymes become much easier. The skillful manipulation of the feminine rhymes matches Shakespeare's expressive lines. There is a mood of hesitation lingering among the lines, and the feminine rhymes last the mood. Shakespeare does much better than Sidney in making the feminine rhymes convey the feelings and meanings the speaker in the poem expresses. He has developed the poetical technique that Sidney invented, pushing it to a higher level:

> Who is Silvia? what is she,
> That all our swains commend her?
> Holy, fair, and wise is she;
> The heaven such grace did lend her,
> That she might admired be (44).

Some people may argue that the repetition of "is she" in the first two odd lines cannot be treated as a true feminine ending, because the last word "she" gets enough emphasis so it will not be weakened as a normal extrametrical weak syllable. However, it does play the role of a feminine rhyme. The ending parts of these two lines repeat in double identical syllables, so it is possible that the ictus falls on the penultimate syllable of each line. The rhymes of the even lines of the stanza are feminine rhymes, or strictly, similar to mosaic rhymes—of which the norm was popular in the sixteenth century, evolving from the alternative use of masculine rhyme and feminine rhyme. Shakespeare's forming of the feminine rhymes here varies slightly from Sidney's own patterns:

> Gloves as sweet as damask roses;
> Masks for faces and noses;

Bugle-bracelet, necklace amber,
Perfume for a lady's chamber (392);

The lines are closely woven with the adjacent feminine rhymes, overflowing a tint of humour. Shakespeare contrasts different things in the well-weighed identical sounds—"roses" versus "noses", and "amber" versus "chamber"—endowing the feminine rhymes with rich connotations, either sensory or romantic. Together with the paronomasia the writer plays in the lines, the echoing sounds and the imagination of concatenate decorations amusingly reach the reader. A feminine rhyme here serves not merely as a musical ornament, but as a functional device, which enriches Sidney's poetical convention.

John Milton was another great master of English poetry during the Renaissance, who contributed extraordinary contribution to Sidney's conventions. He applied the feminine rhyme in a deliberate way into his rhymed verses, especially his sonnets:

When faith and love, which parted from thee never,
  Had ripened thy just soul to dwell with God,
  Meekly thou didst resign this earthly load
  Of death, called life, which us life doth sever.
Thy works and alms, and all thy good endeavor,
  Stayed not behind nor in the grave were trod,
  But as faith pointed with her golden rod
  Followed the up to joy and bliss forever. (Milton 35)

The feminine rhymes here display the merits of Shakespeare's. Their poetical functions even extend to the construction of the stanza in its structure. They are put in prominent rhyming positions, echoing with each other, upholding the octave of the sonnet. The lasting ending awards the lines stately dignity. And in turn, the structural feminine rhymes enhance the solemnness of the poem. The artistry of Milton and his poetry may dwarf Sidney and his composition. But a careful reader may never forget that Milton, just as Shakespeare, achieves his feminine rhymes on the basis of what Sidney has established. The feminine rhyme, as a poetical convention, has been observed and developed by generations of later English poets. Its modern source should be traced back to Sidney.

5. 2 Enjambment

Just as influential as his practice on the feminine rhymes, Sidney has done a pioneering work in English enjambment. The term "enjambment" or "enjambement" comes from the French "enjambement", referring to the

> non-alignment of (end of) metrical frame and syntactic period at line-end: the overflow into the following poetic line of a syntactic phrase (with its intonational contour) begun in the preceding line without a major juncture or pause" (Preminger and Brogan 359).

The French word "enjamber" means "le franchir en faisant un grand pas", or " stride over" or "go beyond" in English. An enjambment line, which is also called a "run-on" line, can be understood as a line of which the metrical structure is complete, but of which the syntactical structure and most often the phonological structure are incomplete and to be continued in the next. The opposite term of the enjambment is the "end-stopped", referring to a line ending both metrically and syntactically (yet may not necessarily ending with a punctuation mark). The enjambment is not Sidney's invention. Its history in English poetry can be traced back to the works of Chaucer, or even earlier poets. Surrey had wedded the enjambment to the blank verse. He never expected that so soon this ugly duckling growing into a giant swan of dignity under the loving care of Shakespeare and Milton, especially in their blank verse. But most of Surrey's lines of the blank verse are end-stopped. Spenser had used the enjambment in his poems, however, it seems that he prefered the end-stopped rather than the run-on, for he ended the majority of his lines both metrically and syntactically. Only when Shakespeare and Milton practiced the blank verse, did the enjambment become the major connecting method of the lines and stanzas. Sidney's contribution to this technique is that he shows other poets a possible way of maintaining the completeness of language structures, both phonological and syntactical, with expanding the metrical structures across lines, a way of expressing the feelings and meanings in the tension of poetical frames that are not coincident or even conflicting in different layers (Preminger and Brogan 359).

When Sidney firstly set to this device in the eclogues of his *Old Arcadia*, he might feel more or less embarrassed to break away from custom. The enjambment was not popular in Sidney's time. Most of his contemporary poets, including Gascoigne, Puttenham and their advocators, seldom touched the pattern. ① The end-stopped lines dominate the English prosody, and the general appetite of the literary people turns also to a poetical line or stanza which ends both metrically and syntactically. However, a poet may often have to consider an actual difficulty: the lines, including the decasyllabic, one of the most popular English verse form, cannot match a larger syntactical structure which contains a complete meaning that a single line cannot hold

---

① Both Gascoigne and Puttenham have neglected the enjambment in their treatises, "Certyne Notes of Instruction" and "The Arte of English Poesie".

independently. Sidney has to cut a long sentence into pieces so as to conform the metre. A Latin poet may stretches his Latin verse to the length he satisfies without violating the prosodic rules—a line with the number of its syllables varying from thirteen to seventeen is enough to meet an epic writer's demand. Sidney does not have this privilege—a line with the limited number of syllables prevents him. So he turns to the enjambment. Uniting the pieces of a sentence again with this method, Sidney finds a way to enlarge the capacity of the English lines. He does it clumsily in the beginning:

(a) Yet high is my attempt. O Muse historifie
Her praise, whose praise to learne your skill hath framed me (OA 7).

(b) Is he a manlike man, that doth not know man
Hath power that Sex with bridle to withhold (OA 9)?

The lines are cut wherever a group of feet are counted. Therefore, the run-on occurs unnaturally when the grammatical structures are severed suddenly as if torn broken abruptly by the outside force. "Historifie" is a transitive verb in (a), should be followed by an object. Yet its object "her praise" is put at the initiation of the second line. It is certain that "Her praise" and "whose praise" in the second line has a close relationship because of the repetition. But the incompleteness of the latter hemistich of the first line is obvious, both in syntax and in semantics. The meaning covers from the first line to the second, accompanied with the grammatical structure, but it does not overflow. In (b), the stressed end-syllable weakens the tension caused by the grammatical pattern, although Sidney counteracts the emphasis on "man" with another stressed word "know" within the same foot. This explains why the masculinely rhymed lines are not easy to run-on. ①

Then Sidney realizes the clumsiness of the lines where he considers too much in observing metres while ignores the syntactical structure of the language. He tries to balance the both sides:

> Thou purest stone, whose purenesse doth present
> My purest minde; whose temper hard doth showe
> My tempred hart; by thee my promise sent
> Unto my selfe let after-livers know (OA 18).

Sidney arranges the grammatical units of different layers rather appropriately in the run-on lines. A repetition of the relative clauses covers three metrical lines, together with the enjambment, ensuring the meaning of the sentence flows from one part to the other among the syntactical structures. The enjambments occur properly between the syntactical segments within the relative clauses. In this way, the integrity of the sub-clause units is preserved, or seems preserved, and at the same time, the clauses are severed reasonably to observe the poet's design in metre. Sidney keeps preliminarily the harmony in the balance.

If Sidney had only achieved these in his enjambment practice, he may not worth much attention. He can make the run-on more flexible:

> One Echo to another Echo cast
> Sounde of my griefes, and let it never ende (OA 75),

---

① According to T. V. F. Brogan and Clive Scott, "rhyme itself, by enhancing closure, will diminish this effect" of enjambment. In fact, the masculine rhyme, because of its ending emphasis, may diminish tension of the run-on more strongly (Preminger and Brogan 359).

The word " cast" plays an interesting role. On the one hand, it gives completeness to the first line—the echoes cast; on the other hand, it helps to extend the grammatical structure into the second line with its status of a transitive verb. Sidney even tries to make the metrical pattern run on in order to naturalize the enjambment:

> But so confusde, that neither any eye
> Can count them just, nor reason reason trye (CS 22),

The language structures cover the two lines, seamed by the enjambment. The metre tends to accompany the language structures. The normal iambic foot in the leading position of the second line shows the possible connection of the second line to the first in a smooth rhythmical cadence. So Sidney tries to make the enjambment performing some functional roles in the stanza—to balance the metrical structure and the language structures, to adjust differently layers of the language structures (phonological, syntactical and semantical) and to ensure the flow of the feelings of the speaker in the poem and the meaning expressed naturally running on from one line to the next. Thus, Sidney organizes the short lines into a large metrical pattern, conforming to a long and complicated sentence in the conveyance of the rich feelings and meanings more effectively. At the same time, he preserves the merits of the strict accentual-syllabic metre.

It is just for convenience here to explicate of Sidney's poetical techniques separately. In fact, Sidney prefers to combine the devices in his poetical construction. All skills, the pauses, the substitutes, the rhymes, the enjambments, and the devices of rhetoric prosody, are distributed to the adjustment of the melody of a poem with the accentual-syllabic rhythm. For example:

    ' ' * ' * ' * ' * '

No Patience, if thou wilt my good, then make

    ' ' * ' * ' * ' * '

Her come, and heare with patience my desire (AS56),

These two lines are connected by the enjambment, and at the same time, formed a contrast through the enjambment. The connection ensures the extension of the syntactical structure from the first line to the second so that the flows of meaning and feelings run on fluently. The contrast comes from the different designs of the pauses in the two lines, which is enhanced with the enjambment. The pauses divide the first line into three parts, tearing down the unities of syntactical structure and metrical structure, and resulting in three different rhythmical contours within the whole line as well. On the contrary, the pause in the second line does not alter much the frame and features of the line. The second line does not appear as fragmentarily as the first one. Such a pattern agrees with the mood it conveys. The rhetoric devices, like the alliterations, the assonances and the polyptoton, add the musical effects to the lines, linking the units of the movement in lines with acoustic repetitions.

In the poetry of later generations, the reader will find much more brilliant use of enjambment. However, the basic principles these poets observe is just the same Sidney adheres to: to conform the metrical design to the language structure so as to make the lines more effective in the conveyance of feelings and meanings. Only the poets like Shakespeare and Milton in the past and J.

H. Prynne① at the present time have more insightful understanding than Sidney on this point.

Shakespeare uses the enjambment in his rhymed verses. However, his lines are no better than Sidney's:

> Who is so faint that dares not be so bold
> To touch the fire, the weather being cold (Shakespeare 1249)?

The enjambment occurs unnaturally among the lines, because "To touch the fire" does not follow very closely the "bold" it modifies. The incompleteness of a line demands the "run on" in structure, but the "run on" does not mean the line abruptly broken unless the poet deliberately does it:

> For thou betraying me, I do betray
> My nobler part to my gross body's treason (1304),

The beauty of the lines may come mainly from the melody of rhythm contour and the phonological decorations. The enjambment is only enough to maintain the unity of the syntactical structure that covers two lines. What Shakespeare surpasses Sidney much in enjambment is his practice in the lines of blank verse:

---

① J. H. Prynne is one of the leading poets of the English world today. He has dwarfed almost all his contemporary poets since the 1960s with his astounding poetical art, his profound poetic wisdom and his amazing knowledge of occidental and oriental cultures which they dare not compete against. Just because of the difficulty in reading his poems, not many consumers of vogue doggerels can appreciate the greatness of this great master. But poetry cannot be vulgarized. It is not novel or story, the popular form for the consuming society. The highest aesthetic issues should be revealed in poetry. J. H. Prynne does catch the subtle beauty in his best poems. To understand more of J. H. Prynne, an intelligent and erudite reader may challenge him or her self in Mr. Prynne's *Poems*.

Had I been any god of power, I would
Have sunk the sea within the earth or ere
It should the good ship so have swallow'd and
The fraughting souls within her (2).

The lines run on fluently with the language as natural as an elegant conversation while the metrical pattern of iambic pentameter is almost intangible though it does exist and dominate the rhythm contour. The enjambment happens most often between the subordinate grammatical units when the principal structure is separated to meet the form of the metrical pattern, between the conjunction ("ere" and "and") and the clause or phrase ("It should the good ship so have swallow'd" and "The fraughting souls within her") for example.

Sidney did not compose a poem in blank verse. It is supposed that he was influenced by the idea people in his time held—that the unrhymed verse is only suitable to epic or other narrative poems, but not appropriate to the musical lyrics. Yet, it is suspicious to allege that his exercise on the enjambment has worked no effect on the growth of the English blank verse.

Milton practiced the enjambment in his rhymed verse much better than Sidney and Shakespeare, for he not only tamed the run-on lines to their natural language state, but also endowed them functional roles in expression:

Or if the earlier season lead
To the tann'd Haycock in the mead (Milton 54),

The word "lead" causes the ambiguity of understanding the line. According to its literal meaning, it is "guide". Then syntactically the enjambment happens between a verb and its complement of prepositional phrase. The scene of the autumn is presented with warm colour. But the connotation of the word "lead" is rather rich; therefore, different interpretations of the lines may be raised. Suppose the word means a black metal, it must be treated as an attributive after the word it modifies. The feelings, even the melody, of the lines will change with the changing meaning. It is possible although not very reasonable in grammar. Milton put the similar devices extensively in his sonnets:

> Avenge, O lord, thy slaughtered Saints, whose bones
> Lie scattered on the Alpine mountains cold—
> Ev'n them who kept thy truth so pure of old,
> When all our fathers worshipped stocks and stones!
> Forget not! In Thy book record their groans,
> Who were Thy sheep and in their ancient fold
> Slain by the bloody Piemontese that rolled
> Mother with infant down the rocks. Their moans
> The vales redoubled to the hills, and they
> To Heav'n. Their martyred blood and ashes sow
> O're all th' Italian fields where still doth sway
> The triple tyrant: that from these may grow
> A hundred-fold, who having learnt Thy way
> Early may fly the Babylonian woe (38).

Nothing is new in technique when the enjambment covers the first two lines. However, it is amazing when the enjambment covers continuously from line six to the end in a sonnet. ① Milton brings his epic eloquence into the short lyric form, matching it well with the fervent feelings rushing through the lines. The stressed end-rhymes have not affected the lines' running on, proving the misjudgment of some modern criticism on the enjambment.

Milton forges his mighty sonnet form with enjambment. He applies the technique skillfully in his blank verse too. His epic lines are evidential:

> His fair large front and eye sublime declared
> Absolute rule; and hyacinthine Locks
> Round from his parted forelock manly hung
> Clust'ring, but not beneath his shoulders broad.
> She as a veil down to the slender waist
> Her unadornèd golden tresses wore
> Disshevelled, but in wanton ringlets waved
> As the vine curls her tendrils, which impli'd
> Subjection, but required with gentle sway (Milton 248),

The gracefulness and dignity of Adam and Eve are displayed with two long balanced sentences. Each sentence covers several lines which are knitted up with the enjambments. The syntactical structures of these two sentences spread clearly and leisurely, illustrating the gentleness and beauty of human beings in their natural and innocent state. With the help of enjambments, the iambic pentameters are seamed into an eloquent metrical pattern in which the metrical movement is almost intangible. The natural rhythm that English possesses is expressed through Milton's careful manipulation of the linguistic structures. Language and metre cooperate well in Milton's hands.

---

① Some editions of Milton's sonnet 18 may have a comma attached to the end of thirteenth line, but that does not change much the effect of constant enjambment.

The intentional practice of the enjambment in this way might be germinated in Sidney's composition. The device becomes maturer in the hands of poets from the twentieth century on. The enjambments, together with other devices, in the following piece of free verse explicate the development of the functional roles of the poetical form:

You spin with erotic doubt, ah then,
hysteric tenderness, is this
the mount of our youth
or his body? He must
be eaten slowly, by autolysis of face
thus forced to riot, claimed
by soft hands in his shirt: not a beast of virtue (Prynne 219).

The lines account a kind of emotional experience—the thrillingness caused by the impulsion from the inside of the body. Prynne captures the momentary feeling and presents it directly. The arrangement of the lines and the language structures visualizes the abstract activity of psychology through imitating the flows of streams down from the hillside under the melting snow. Separate pieces are linked up weakly by the enjambments functioning differently from those in Sidney's poems or Shakespeare's. In most cases of the traditional composition, the enjambment is used to keep the unity and completeness of language structures across the lines. But in Prynne's lines, the enjambments maintain barely the continuity of the syntactical structure of the language. The coincidence between the syntactical structure and the phonological structure is not always preserved by the enjambments. The line "the mount of our youth" is linked closely with the line before it but not with the line after it. There is a clear boundary in phonological structure at its end. It is similar to the enjambments before and after the line "be eaten slowly, by autolysis of face".

In a free verse, the enjambment occurs even if there is a punctuation attached to the end of the line, like the connection between the following second and third lines:

> In his youth he walked much.
> Tears streamed down his unlined face,
> damping his shirt. Sleep glows
> in its beads, staring the wing blind (159).

The phrase "damping his shirt" cannot be independent in grammar, nor can it be closely connected with the beginning part of the next sentence, "Sleep glows" in the same line through the syntactical structure because of the period. The comma in the second line does not affect the enjambment of the two lines. This arrangement seems rare in Sidney's verses, nor is it common in Shakespeare's or Milton's. But the tension caused by the contrast between the rhythmical contour and the language structure exists, even stronger than a usual one caused by the enjambment of the metrical lines. For there is an obvious pause at the end of the line "Tears streamed down his unlined face", completing the meaning with a closed grammatical structure. But the comma breaks the completeness of the line, both in grammatical structure and in the flow of meaning, thus arousing reader's new expectation. The enjambment in Prynne's poems explains the inheritance and development of the poetical device exercised by Sidney and poets during the English Renaissance.

The techniques of the feminine rhyme and the enjambment have been spread widely after Sidney's exertion. His inventive use of these metrical designs enriched not only his poetical construction but also the English prosodic theory and practice.

Chapter 6 Sidney's Anglicization of Foreign Poetical Genres

It would be an excessive ambition to exhibit the whole panoply of Sidney's verse stanzas—being a treasure of the English poetry, they are in a very large number, though most of them have not spread widely①. But those influential poetical experiments among them are worthy of careful examination. These experiments have displayed Sidney's efforts in anglicizing foreign stanzas, in exploring the potential capability of the native stanzas in lyrics, and in forging new poetical forms on the basis of the first two.

With regard to the anglicization of foreign stanzaic forms, Sidney explores the compatibility of the foreign poetical construction to the English language and the English prosodic custom, in William Webbe's words, for "the meetnesse of our speeche to receiue the best forme of Poetry" (Smith 256). The norm he observes is the harmonious organization of the lines. The aim he pursuits is the musicality of the natural sounds, an ideal of poetic

---

① William A. Ringler, Jr. has done an exact statistical work on the verse forms Sidney uses. The statistic shows that Sidney's "286 poems contain 143 different lines and stanza patterns, 109 of which he used only once" (Ringler lviii; 569-572).

aesthetics of Elizabethan poets.① Sidney intends to achieve the aesthetical symmetry of both the language structures and the metrical patterns. Some of his experiments have directly set up the examples for the English poets; some have bridged the foreign prototypes and the established English genres.

Sidney had tried to anglicize almost all important foreign stanzaic forms he knew. The elegiacs, the Sapphic stanza, the madrigal-poem and the sonnet (and the sonnet sequence), being the influential poetical forms, have entered the English poetry through the efforts of many poets, among whom Sidney is one of the decisive contributors.

6.1 Elegiacs

Before the discussion of Sidney's English elegiac couplet, it is neccessary

---

① This may be shown in the criticism of that time. Sidney himself emphasizes the importance of musical beauty, regarding that the perfection poetry achieves is "fit for Musick" or "striketh a certaine Musicke to the eare" (Feuillerat 44). Gacoigne concretizes it as "to place euery worde in his natural Emphasis or sound", that is, "to place all wordes in their naturall or most common and vsuall pronuciation" (Smith 49; 53). Gabriel Harvey echoes Gascoigne with his dispute of the pronunciations of "Carpenter" and "Heauenli Virginals" (117; 95). William Webbe thinks that poets (Vates) should be "tuning them to the stroake of some of the pleasantest kind of Musicke", that the poetry "being framed in such sweete measure of sentences and pleasant harmonie called 'Ρυθμός' (rhythmos, rhythm, symmetry)", and "indued with great gyfts of wysedome and knowledge in Musicke aboue the rest", the poet's "wytt" (talent) is used "to make goodly verse, measured according to the sweetest notes of Musicke" so that there is not "the sence hendered" (230; 268). George Puttenham points out that "Poesie is a skill to speake & write harmonically: and verse or rime be akind of Musicall vtterance, by reason of a certaine congruitie in sounds pleasing the eare" (64). The voices of these people are representative, forming the general view on the purpose of the poet's poetical efforts. For more detailed information of the above cited ideas, the readers may consult the related parts in the following books: (1) Albert Feuillerat. ed. *Complete Works of Sir Philip Sidney*, vol. iii. Cambridge: Cambridge University Press. 1923. (2) G. Gregory Smith. ed. *Elizabethan Critical Essays*. Oxford: Clarendon Press. 1904. (3) George Puttenham. *The Arte of English Poesie*. Gladys Doidge Willcock. ed. Cambridge: Cambridge University Press. 1936.

to describe briefly the structure of classical elegiacs. The classical elegiacs is also called elegiac couplet, or elegiac distich, comprising the alternating dactylic hexameters and pentameters in couples, very popular for a variety of subjects since the seventh century B. C. in the ancient Greco-Roman literary world (Preminger and Brogan 321). The basic metrical pattern consists of a strict dactylic hexameter and a pentameter formed through the repetition of the first hemistich of a usual dactylic hexameter:

˘˘ ˘˘ ˘˘ ˘˘
– – – – – || – – – – ˘˘ – –

˘˘ ˘˘
– – – – –||– ˘˘ – ˘˘ –(Raven 104)

Latin elegiacs has some features. A Latin poet would strictly observe the rules of the central caesura, the line ending and the texture (105). In a Latin elegiacs, the caesura occurs after the first syllable of the third foot in the hexameter and amid the two hemistiches in the pentameter; the end word of the line is a disyllabic one; and the elision should be avoided. Besides, the substitution is generally rare in the second part of the second line. However, violation of these rules appears rather common in the works of Roman poets. The post-Augustan poets seldom observed the rule of the line ending (108). As for the linguistic structures,

> Elegiac couplets are mainly self contained entities: the sense frequently runs on from hexameter to pentameter ... but the sentence, or at least the clause, normally ends with the couplet, and it is very rare for couplets to be closely linked in sense (104).

Poets at the time of Catullus did not have the strict metrical pattern to observe. They followed closer the fashion of Greek metre (Catullus 193):

Cum puero bello praeconem qui uidet *esse*,
quid credat nisi se uendere *discupere* (Catullus 140)?
(Seeing an auctioneer with a pretty boy
One can't but think he wants to sell himself (141).)

The obvious difference between Catullus's elegiacs and the basic Latin pattern is that both lines do not end with disyllabic words. But in cope with the sense of language he had followed the rule mentioned above. Both the two lines are end-stopped; and the syntactic structure is complete within the couplet. In this respect Catullus behaved almost no compared difference with the later Latin poets. Catullus is one of the classical models Sidney imitates.

When Sidney comes to the metrical pattern, it has already had its form changed in some aspects, and its topics narrowed to the epigrams of love and death. But he decides to turn directly to the classical type, especially the Latin type, like most of his contemporaries do. The thirteenth poem in *Certain Sonnets* is his translation, or adaptation, of Catullus' Elegiacs:

Nulli se dicit mulier mea nubere malle,
Quam mih no si se Iupter ipse petat,
Dicit sed mulier Cupido quœ dicit amanti,
In vento aut rapida scribere oportet aqua. ①

---

① The Latin text is cited from Ringler's edition of Sidney's poems, together with Sidney's translation. There is a slight difference between Ringler's edition and the others. For example, the word "quœ" in the third line is spelled as "quod" (meaning "because" or "the fact that") in Guy Lee's edition (122).

Unto no body my woman saith she had rather a wife be,
  Then to my selfe, not though Jove grew a suter of hers.
These be her words, but a woman's words to a love that is eager,
  In wind or water streame do require to be writ.

Sidney reproduces in his English version most of the essence of Catullus's elegiacs: the quantitative metre, the line ending, and the familiar or conversational style. Following Catullus's example, Sidney's elegiac couplets have no end rhymes too. ① Yet, Sidney does not follow Catullus's treatment of the central caesuras. The stops in his lines behave more freely as the English pauses. Sidney's long line in the elegiac couplet seems not to belong to the English verse. It appears clumsy when too many words (especially many monosyllabic words) are lined up. A common English reader might not possibly accept his imitation of Catullus's quantitative metre. And when he composes his own elegiacs in English, Sidney adopts the skills he practiced in his translation. In the eleventh poem of his *Old Arcadia*, Sidney follows the metrical pattern as " – – – – – ∪ ∪ – ∪ ∪ – ∪ ∪ – – // – – – ∪ ∪ – – – ∪ ∪ – ∪ ∪ – ", with lines unrhymed, neither within the couplets, nor between the couplets:

Fortune, Nature, Love, Long have contended about me,
  Which should most miseries, cast on a worme that I am.
Fortune thus gan say; 'misery and misfortune is all one,
  And of misfortune, fortune hath only the gift.
With strong foes on land, on seas with contrary tempests
  Still doo I crosse this wretch, what so he taketh in hand'.

---

① It is strange that Sidney even turns the originally rhymed Latin elegiac couplet into the unrhymed English one when he translates or paraphrases Seneca's *Oedipus*, line 705-706, which is the fourteenth poem in his *Certain Sonnets* (see also Ringler 428).

This is an archaistic arrangement—the couplet, being a self-contained entity, consists of a dactylic hexameter and a dactylic pentameter, permitting only the sense running on within the couplet (Raven 104). Like Catullus, Sidney observes the rule of central caesura this time. Unlike Catullus, he adds several pauses cutting one line into several pieces. Sidney does not follow the rule of disyllabic ending. In the clash between the natural English pronunciation and the classical metre, the language wins the advantage. For a common English reader who does not have the special knowledge of Latin prosody may have an amusing feeling of the lines when he reads them in his normal way. The Latin metre almost does not affect him. The self-contained feature of the couplet has been preserved. And the English pauses, the English schemes, and the English monosyllabic words have been successfully syncretized into the Latinate style.

The subject Sidney chooses for his elegiacs appearing closer to the classical tradition, reflecting the serious meditation. The eleventh poem from his *Old Arcadia* is a lament of Dorus (Musidorus in disguise) about his torturous adventure. The seventy-fourth poem from the same book is a story told by Philisides. ①

Sidney's poems explicate that the Latin metre cannot be rigidly borrowed. The unrhymed quantitative couple of dactylic hexameter and pentameter, though elegant in Latin and suitable for eulogizing the heroic deeds or conveying the sublime lament, is almost impossible to be copied in English poetry writing. However, Sidney's quantitative verse is

> an extended attempt to introduce into English poetry those features of

---

① The elegiac couplet was also used by the classical poets as a vehicle for story telling.

> classical verse so highly admired by the Elizabethans, without losing too much of the rhythmical quality of traditional English verse (Attridge 187).

This ensures his quantitative lines, when read in English stressed rhythm, sounds not harsh to the ear in most occasions. The other English poets have benefited from Sidney on at least three aspects: his treatment of the subjects, his style of language and his careful coping with the natural rhythm of English in his Latinate experiments. When composing his "Astrophel", Spenser turns directly to the iambic pentameter, and makes the lines rhymed. He designs a stanza of six lines, rhyming *ababcc*:

> The Gods, which all things see, this same beheld,
> And, pitying this pair of Lovers true,
> Transforméd them, there lying on the field,
> Into one flower that is both red and blue;
> It first grows red, and then to blue doth fade,
> Like Astrophel, which thereinto was made.
>
> (*The Shepherd's Calendar and Other Poems* 275)

Some features that Sidney displays in his elegiac distiches are also shown here in Spenser's stanza: the self-contained couplet in which the flows of the feelings and the meaning that the speaker in the poem expresses run on; the end-rhyming which is only a tendency in Sidney's poems but is realized in Spenser's verses; and the English prosodic elements that Sidney integrates into the lines are also revealed here. Equipped with the iambic pentameter, Spenser's elegiac stanza is lighter and smoother than Sidney's, closer to the classical poetical design in essence.

John Donne also wrote the elegiac couplets in iambic pentameter, but he did nothing in developing a fixed elegiac stanza. Milton established the elegiac poem as a definite genre to the limited subjects, yet he, as Donne, did not contribute much to the poetical form. It seems that both of them had neglected Sidney's endeavour.

Only when Thomas Gray had composed his "Elegy Written in a Country Churchyard" in the middle of the eighteenth century did the settled English elegiac stanza come into being at last. It is a quatrain of iambic pentameters rhyming *abab*, renamed as elegy after the name of his poem:

> Full many a gem of purest ray serene,
>   The dark unfathomed caves of ocean bear:
> Full many a flower is born to blush unseen,
>   And waste its sweetness on the desert air (Abrams 2460).

It looks like that Spenser's six-line stanza being cut off the rhymed couplet. Still, the self-contained couplets are inherited, and the familiar style. Gray organized his distiches in the same way Sidney had done after from the Latin examples. He shared with Sidney the elegant oral English and the Latinate sentence style as well. Gray's elegy stanzas is extraordinary, for

> it speakes to our common humanity through an art so subtle that one can know the poem for many years before becoming aware of its scores that echoes from other poems, its complex organization, and its balance of Latinate phrases with living speech (2454).

Gray is in the shade of Sidney's influence. And from Gray, the coming poets have enjoyed the heritage that Sidney bequeathed them.

6. 2 Sapphic Stanza①

Just as the elegiac couplet, the Sapphic stanza had come through a long history of evolution from the 7th-6th B. C. to the 20th century in the western world. The term is named after the Aeolian poetess Sappho who had frequently used the stanza. Roman poets had added some variations and strict rules to improve the poetical genre, but the basic metrical pattern remains as:

- ˘ - + - ˘ ˘ - ˘ - -
- ˘ - + - ˘ ˘ - ˘ - -
- ˘ - + - ˘ ˘ - ˘ - -
- ˘ ˘ - - (Raven 143)

The stanza comprises four unrhymed lines. The first three lines repeat the same metrical pattern—a hendecasyllabic line consists of a trochee, a spondee or trochee, a dactyl, a trochee and a spondee (or a trochee), with a strong caesura falling after the first syllable of the third foot (dactyl). The fourth line consists of a dactyl and a spondee (or a trochee). The whole stanzaic structure gives prominence to the quantitative rhythm and the relationship between poetry and music in the proportion of time division. For example,

nec meum respectet, ut ante, amorem,
qui illius culpa cecidit uelut prati
ultimi flos, praetereunte postquam
tactus aratro est. (Catullus 11)

---

① This section is derived from Dr. Shenjie's one unpublished paper "The Acceptance of Sapphic Stanza by English Poets" in Chinese version.

(And let her not as before expect my love,
Which by her fault has fallen like a flower
On the meadow's margin after a passing
Ploughshare has touched it.)①

The stanza shows some poetical features of the classical style: quantitative dactylic verse, the third line and the fourth line being closely connected, and no ending rhymes. Catullus had followed strictly the Greek conventions when he introduced the Sapphic stanza into the Roman world. The contour of the cadence of every line and the whole stanza appears in a falling rhythm in general, and are adjusted through the counter-balance of the spondees in some parts, thus enriching the melody with variation. In the first three lines, the stress and the long syllable coincide only in the beginning and ending feet but not in the middle, making the beginning and ending of the line acoustically distinct with both the emphasis in pronunciation and the correspondence of the emphasized positions, and distributing the prominent sounds of either stress or quantity in a well-proportionate arrangement in achieving the rhythmical beauty of symmetry of the whole line.

Catullus's pattern was further Latinized with two more added restrictions by Horace, "who provided the Sapphic models for subsequent Roman and European poets" (Preminger and Brogan 1113):

integer vitae scelerisque purus
non eget Mauris iaculis neque arcu
nec venenatis gravida sagittis,
Fusce, pharetra (qtd. in Raven 144).

① The English translation is cited from Lee's copy (Catullus 12-13).

(The upright life that is free from evil
need not to have Moorish spears nor a bow
Nor the arrows heavy and poisonous
Quivering, Fuscus)

In Horace's Sapphic stanzas, "the fourth syllable of the longer line is always long", and "in the longer line, there is always a caesura after *either* the fifth syllable" "*or* the sixth syllable" (Raven 144). In this stanza, the caesura happens after the fifth syllable in the longer line. The purpose of Horace's restriction is certainly for a more regulated stanzaic form. It might also suggest that he wants to diminish the effect of the stress of a Latin syllable, purifying the musical effect of a sheer quantitative rhythm.

Ironically, the Latin stress toughly survived, even in a Sapphic stanza. The Middle Ages witnessed two important transformations of Sapphic stanza. The lines were rhymed and the quantitative metre gradually gave way to the accentual metre. The changes influenced profoundly the metrical development in the rising vernaculars of the Modern era.

Therefore, Sidney has two models before him when he decided to anglicize the Sapphic stanza. And he experimented on both, the quantitative and the accentual, with his own designs. The twelfth poem in the *Old Arcadia* is an imitation of the classical examples:

But if eyes can speake to doo harty errande,
Or mine eyes' language she doo hap to judge of,
So that eyes' message be of her receaved,
        Hope we doo live yet.

Sidney arranges the stanza in quantitative metre, observing the rules that

Sappho and Catullus established. However, his innate sense of the rhythm of the English language ensures him laying out, maybe unconsciously, a set of accentual rhythm which is roughly regular within the stanza. Therefore, the stanza may not sound beautiful when recited in quantitative metre① but not ugly when read in the accentual rhythm. And there exists the differences which betray the deviation of Sidney from the classical—He cannot keep the contour of a falling rhythm that a Sapphic stanza usually possesses, and he does not make the fourth line closely connecting to the third, which a Latin poet would do.

But Sidney exerts himself to grasp the essence of a classical Sapphic stanza and represents it in his composition. The fifth poem in Sidney's *Certain Sonnets* is rhymed in feminine rhymes. This is not common in Latin or Greek models.

O my thoughtes' sweete foode, my onely owner,
O my heavens for taste by thie heavenly pleasure,
O that faryre Nymphe borne to doo woemen honor,
Lady my Treasure.

Sidney re-creates the effects of the falling rhythm with the feminine rhyme. Some readers who are familiar with the Middle English lyrics may be clear of Sidney's returning to the feminine-rhyme tradition which was almost ignored by the Renaissance poets before and in Sidney's time. He applies the revived feminine rhymes (actually he revived) to the classical lyric form. As a new tradition, it is accepted by the later generations of poets when they compose the Sapphic stanza in English.

---

① It must sound beautiful when it is set to music and sung in quantitative metre. In fact the poem in the *Old Arcadia* is just composed for singing (*Old Arcadia* 72).

However, Sidney does not stop his experiments thereafter. He wants to reform the stanza. He wants it to be an English stanza, not a foreign one. He tries to compose the Sapphic stanza in accentual metre, which results in two poems, the fifty-ninth in the *Old Arcadia* and the sixth in *The Psalms of David*, in which the typical English iambic pentameter dominates the rhythmical contour of the lines:

> But thou, sure Hope, tickle my leaping heart.
> Comfort, step thou in place of wonted sadnes.
> Fore-felt Desire, begin to savour parte
> of comming gladnes (OA 59).

It is more or less an anglicized Sapphic stanza. The features of an English quatrain are distinct: the accentual-syllabic, not the quantitative, determines the shape of the cadence; the freely distributed pauses replace the strict central caesura; and the lines are mostly decasyllabic and rhymed alternatively—the even lines are even rhymed in Sidney's favorite feminine rhymes. Of course they remain certain foreign tints—the endeavour of keeping the hendecasyllabic verse, the dependent half-line state of the fourth line and the enjambment of the third and fourth lines—telling an Elizabethan reader that the stanza is brand-new to him and to his contemporary English poetry.

> The Sapphics are touchier; for the abundance and persistent recurrence of dactylic rhythm introduce difficulty, and you cannot, owing to the strong trochaic beginning, get anapaestic twist on the ball. It is beautiful, but a professed experiments, a *soteltie* in the old culinary sense (Saintsbury II: 423).

There is another anglicized Sapphic stanza by Sidney:

Mercy, O Mercy lord, for Mercy's sake,
For death doth kill the witness of thy glory;
Can of thy prayse the tongues entombed make
A heavnly story (PS 6)?

The accentual-syllabic rhythm becomes more distinct. And besides the above-mentioned English features, the closed couplet formed by the first two lines can be regarded as one native element in the poem composition as well.

Not a few English poets have written in the Sapphic stanza. The similarities between Sidney and the coming poets in their compositions may suggest the heritage. Richard Stanyhurst concentrates on imitating the Latinate accentual rhythm (Attridge 213). Thomas Campion composes the Sapphic stanzas in quantitative metre for his vocal music, but revises them into accentual trochaic rhythm (214-215). *The Phoenix Nest* (1593) contains four English poems written in Sapphic stanza, including the fifty-ninth poem in the *Old Arcadia*. The metrical pattern, "though it approaches that of the classical sapphic, is basically an accentual iambic pentameter, with frequent inversions, and with a short fourth line" (216). Most English Sapphic stanzas composed after Sidney are in the accentual-syllabic metre (or accentual metre) if they are metrical verses, or freely in the accentual rhythms if they are *vers libre*. The following example is cited from a poem "The Day of Judgement" written by Isaac Watts:

When the fierce North wind with his airy forces,
Rears up the Baltic to a foaming fury;
And the red lightning, with a storm of hail, comes

Rushing amain down (Warren and Erskine 298) ;

The subtitle of the poem "An Ode, Attempted in English Sapphic", tells the reader the poetical aim the poet intends to achieve is the anglicized verse form, the same aim that Sidney has mostly achieved. It seems that Watts wants to keep more classical colours in his accentual-syllabic stanza, for he has tried to observe the convention of three hendecasyllabic lines plus a pentasyllabic half-line. Following the classical custom, he makes all lines unrhymed, and the fourth line closely attached to the third. To compose the hendecasyllabic lines, he adopts the feminine ending once popular in the Middle English poetry and revived temporarily by the Elizabethan poets like Sidney. But Watt's attempt is less successful than Sidney. Watts does not repeat the same metrical pattern in the first three lines, which causes the disorder in metre. Nor can he constantly keep all the three lines ending in feminine endings—the third line ends with a monosyllabic word which is stressed—thus there appears the disharmony in the ending parts of these lines.

What Watts inherits from Sidney in composing the Sapphic stanza, to be conjectural, is the accentual metre. That is the Englishness of their stanzas. And that Englishness is repeatedly confirmed by Alexander Pope, Thomas Hardy, and Ezra Pound, to name a few. Pope designs his metrical pattern in a flexible way:

Sound Sleep by night; study and ease,
Together mixed; sweet recreation;
And innocence, which most does please
With meditation (Abrams 2252).

He shortens the first three lines into octosyllabic lines but keeps the fourth a pentasyllabic half-line, shaping the first and third lines into a rising rhythm (iambic) while the second and the fourth a falling one (trochaic), rhyming the odd lines with masculine rhymes and the even lines with the feminine rhymes, thus rendering the stanza with terseness in line length and richness in melody. The only two foreign features Pope preserves to remind the reader what he uses is an ancient Greek poetical form from Sappho are the dependent half-line after the third line and the close connection of these third and fourth lines (or one and a half line).

Between Pope and Hardy, William Cowper, Robert Southey and Algernon Charles Swinburne have bridged up the evolution of English Sapphic stanza. Cowper learns the flexible lines from Pope but returns to Sidney's earliest models in stanzaic design, e. g. in his "Lines Written During A Period Of Insanity". Southey fabricates his story, "The Widow", with the Sapphic stanzas successfully used for narration in a poem. Swinburne composes his "Sapphics" with a pure aesthetic taste.

Hardy mixes the accentual lines of decasyllabic, enneasyllabic and octosyllabic in his Sapphic stanzas:

Snow-bound in woodland, a mournful word,   9
Dropt now and then from the bill of a bird,   10
Reached me on wind-wafts; and thus I heard,   10
  Wearily waiting:

"I planned her a nest in a leafless tree,   10
But the passers eyed and twitted me,   9
And said: 'How reckless a bird is he,   9
  Cheerily mating!'

"Fear-filled, I stayed me till summer-tide, 9
In lewth of leaves to throne her bride; 8
But alas! her love for me waned and died, 10
Wearily waiting.

"Ah, had I been like some I see, 8
Born to an evergreen nesting-tree, 9
None had eyed and twitted me, 7
Cheerily mating! ('Postponement')"①

The rhyming scheme of the poem is *aaab*, *cccb*, *dddb*, *eeeb*. In the first three lines of each stanza, two shapes of rhythm are amalgamated in the same line. And the fourth half-lines "Wearily waiting" and "Cheerily mating" repeat alternatively through the whole poem, ending the stanzas with a lasting falling rhythm (the feminine rhymes enforce the tune). The stanzas are arranged according to the length of the lines, as is labeled in the example. With these designs, Hardy makes the poetical pattern imitate the birdsong, integrating the form with the feelings and meanings it loads. His poem is extraordinary among the English Sapphic stanzas.

Pound endows the Sapphic stanza with a spirit of free verse, although he abandons the rhymed ending and counts exactly the number of syllables in every first three lines to eleven so as to observe the ancient rules descending from the Greco-Roman world:

Golden rose the house, in the portal I saw
thee, a marvel, carven in subtle stuff, a
portent. Life died down in the lamp and flickered,
caught at the wonder ("Apparuit").

---

① The figures after the lines show the number of syllables in them.

Pound shatters the general completeness of a line. Instead, he makes the lines closely linked together through the enjambment. Thus, a line as "thee, a marvel, carven in subtle stuff, a", like messy pieces of phrases when read separately, becomes expressive while it is organized into the larger syntactical structure. Compared the tightness of the first three lines, a lesser connection between the third line and the fourth half-line appears notable. Different from the usual treatment of the ending part of a Sapphic stanza, Pound space out the third line and the fourth half-line with a comma, leaving the incomplete "caught at the wonder" to an independent position, challenging the reader of his reading habit. The techniques of *vers libre* are applied into the metrical Sapphic stanza, making Pound's poem extraordinary.

There is a clear trace of the evolution of the English Sapphic stanza from Sidney to Pound—the emphasis to the phonological and syntactical structures of their native language has been constantly strengthened. The accentual rhythm, the rhyming convention, the pause distribution and the syllable count of a line, etc., all are used to reconstruct a foreign poetical form. And Sidney's accentual-syllabic Sapphic stanza becomes the model in the history of the evolution.

6.3 Madrigal-Poem

Encouraged by the development of lyrical poetry and the trend of music in England in the sixteenth-century, Sidney experimented on the madrigal-poems and invented a new form ruled by strict metre. He stirred up people's ardour for madrigals; however, Sidney's new form of madrigal-poem received neither the acceptation from the poets, nor the response from the musicians. Nevertheless, considering the significance of literary construction, Sidney's experiment on madrigal-poems attracts people attention to the value of his experiments.

The origin of madrigal can be traced back to the Italian folk song in the fourteenth century. It was secular vocal music which was developed into polyphony, circulated in the upper-class meetings. The name itself may suggest the vernacular colour, for one hypothesis says that the word "madrigal" derives from "matricalis" referring to a song in the mother tongue (Apel 461). ("matricalis" means "of the mother" or "of the womb"). The early Italian madrigal poems "were constructed in two or three three-line stanzas with an additional two-line *ritornello* (refrain) (Stolba 130)". "The subject matter is amatory, idyllic, or pastoral; sometimes the tone is satirical (130)." After a short bloom, the madrigal declined in the fifteenth century. The revival of madrigal in Italy come in the sixteenth century, but there was "no connection between the 14th- and the 16th-chentury madrigal other than that of name" (Apel 461). The latter became the popular form of polyphony (voices sing the same text but not always sing the words simultaneously) from the second half of the century on and spread from Italian to most Renaissance countries, including the Great Britain.

The bloom of the Italian madrigal in the sixteenth century was linked with a rich poetry tradition. This becomes the distinction between the Italian madrigal and the English madrigal. The Italian musicians often set to music of those well-known poems written by great poets, Petrarch for example (Grout and Palisca 162). Therefore, the forms of the Italian madrigal-poems varied differently. The English musicians did not have the brilliant treasure of poetry to resort to. They had to turn to the Italians for help. That is the reason why the first English madrigals had the translated Petrarch set to their music. However, there does exist a madrigal form which arouses Sidney's interest to compete with, a lyric poem "composed of from eight to eleven lines (usually of eleven syllables or a mixture of eleven syllables and seven syllables)"

("Madrigal"). Sidney admired this elegant poetic genre and decided to devise the English form. The madrigal-poems in England before Sidney are translated works from the Italian. It is Sidney who writes the first two English madrigal-poems (Apel 478).

The form of Sidney's madrigal-poems shares the similarities with the Italian models but more difficult to complete. It consists of fifteen lines, rhyming in *aabccbbddeedeff*, with the hexasyllabic lines and the decasyllabic lines used alternatively in the first nine lines and the decasyllabic lines mostly in the last six lines but the twelfth which is hexasyllabic, causing the reader to remember the Italian *terzine* and its combination with the popular rhyme schemes in the madrigal-poem. The fifty-second poem from the *Old Arcadia* is one example of this device, regarded by Ringler as a sonnet variant (571):

Why doost thou haste away
O Titan faire the giver of the daie?
Is it to carry newes
To Westerne wightes, what starres in East appeares?
Or doost thou thinke that heare
Is left a Sunne, whose beames thy place may use?
Yet stay and well peruse,
What be her giftes, that make her equall thee,
Bend all thy light to see
In earthly clothes enclosde a heavenly spark.
Thy running course cannot such beawties marke:
No, no, thy motions bee
Hastened from us with barre of shadow darke,
Because that thou, the author of our sight,
Disdainst we see thee staind with other's light (OA 52).

There is no obvious stanzaic division in this poem, and the rhyme scheme is very strict, quite different from its Italian example. ① But the foreign tints displays strongly. The gracefulness of the Italian poems is preserved. And, following the Italian example in rhyme schemes, Sidney extends it to a more sophisticated level. The combination of long and short lines in the lyric also shows Sidney's inheritance from the Italian madrigal-poem:

> Cantate Ninfe, leggiadrette e belle
> I mici novelli ardori,
> E scherzate e ridete insieme Amori
> Con la mia Filli in queste part' e in quelle.
> Cantate e di piacer gioite tutti,
> Cho d' armor colto i desiati fritti (Machlis and Forney 118).②
>
> (Sing, graceful and lovely Nymphs,
> Of my new ardors,
> And Cupids, joke and laugh together
> With my Phyllis, everywhere in the countryside,
> Sing and be joyous everyone,
> For I have reaped the desired fruits of love.)

The endecasyllabic line and the heptasyllabic line are two common metrical patterns in the Italian lyrics, often used in an alternative or combined way which increases the varieties of the metrical movement. In a madrigal, the

① The Italian model is generally divided into *terzine* (tercet), with rather free choices of rhyme schemes. Among the most popular rhyme schemes the Italian madrigal employs are the following arrangements: (1) abc abc dd; (2) aba bcb cc; (3) abb acc dd; (4) abb cdd ee; (5) abb acc cdd; (6) aba cbc de; (7) abb cdd ee ff; and (8) abb cdd eff gg ("Madrigal").

② The English translation also is cited from the same page of the book.

variation makes the melody of music easily match the words. In the Italian practice of madrigal in the sixteenth century, a musician chooses the words from the famous poems first and then composes his music according to the chosen words. The musician usually does not change the poem, but he has the privilege to select a lyric proper to meet his demand.

Actually, the extensive use of the lines of eleven syllables and seven syllables can be seen in many kinds of Italian lyrics, even in metrically strict sonnet, like "et ragion temean poco, // ché 'ncontra 'l ciel non val difesa humana; ('L'arme tue furon gli occhi, onde l'accese')" (with little fear of reason, // that gives no human defence against heaven;) ("Your weapons were those eyes, where burning"). Sidney transplants the combination of long and short lines form Italian madrigal-poems into his English counterparts. And, like his predecessors, he uses the English decasyllabic lines and hexasyllabic lines to replace the Italian designs of the endecasyllabic and the heptasyllabic.

The above-mentioned fifty-second poem from Sidney's *Old Arcadia* and the fifty-fifth poem from the same romance are all madrigal-poems designed on the basis of the popular Italian forms introduced into the Tudor kingdom. Both poems share the identical verse pattern, following the same strict metre. In the first madrigal-poem, the fictitious Basilius sings his admiration to his love Cleophila. In the second poem, the same Basilius continues his praise to Cleophila:

> "No' saies faire moone, 'my lighte
> Shall barr that wrong, and though it not prevaile
> Like to my brother's raies, yet those I sende
> Hurte not the face, which nothing can amende".

With vivid images, Basilius compares Cleophila with the beautiful moon, and suggests the purgative effect of Cleophila's eyes. The long and short lines bring the direct feeling of the rhythmical changes to the reader. The poem sounds charming: the tender expression from Cleophila's eyes is conveyed with lines of clear rhythm contour.

But the form of Sidney's madrigal-poem challenges the musicians as well as the poets who intend to follow his examples. It is difficult to set his poems to music. The vocal music requires a song poem not very long and not very complicated in metrical devices, especially when the music is polyphonic. In fact, neither the Italian nor the English madrigal-poems circulated in the sixteenth century are complicated as Sidney's samples. And because the English practice on madrigal is different from the Italian habit that the musicians in England compose their madrigal music first and then make the words written according to the need of music, the musicians are not possible to pick up what Sidney offers them. With regard to the writing of a Sidneian madrigal-poem, it is not easy for an ordinary poet to imagine the rolling forward structure of tercets ending with a perplexing rhyme scheme which suggests the distant parallelism.

Then why does Sidney invent such a design of English madrigal-poem? There are possibly two reasons: the rapid development of English lyrical poetry and the spread of madrigal music in Elizabethan England.

From the mid-sixteenth century on, the trend of inventing new poetry opened by Wyatt and Surrey in the earlier time has been resumed. The publication of Tottle's *Songs and Sonnets* (*Tottel's Miscellany*) in 1557 promoted the development of new lyrical poetry. The Elizabethan new poetry is founded mainly on the basis of introduction and digestion of the foreign genres. Learning and imitating the foreign poetry and inventing new poetry by the eager poets were prevailing in the 1570s and 1580s. Major poets like

Sidney, Spenser, Fulke Greville and Edward Dyer are all enthusiastic in exploring the art of poetry (Buxton, John, 102, 112):

> A favourable literary situation developed in the 1570s, when Spenser, Sidney and other ' new poets ' undertook a comprehensive reform of native poetry along Italian lines. The English madrigal development was an accurate reflection of an important literary movement (Apel 478).

Sidney has formed his theoretical ideas in his practice, which makes it possible for him to explore new poetical forms. His literary taste and judgment ensured his experiment on inventing English madrigal-poem. The demand of high quality in composing a madrigal-poem inspires Sidney's desire.

The madrigal is one of the most important genres of Renaissance music in the sixteenth century. In England, the madrigal became popular with the social elites's adoration of Italian Renaissance culture. Queen Elizabeth had promoted the bloom of madrigal by inviting the Italian madrigalist to live in the court (478). However, before Sidney decided to write the English madrigal-poem, there were almost no successful poetry of this genre produced in England. The achievement of English madrigal was chiefly in music before Sidney.

> ... the composition of madrigals in the vernacular was unthinkable until poets could conceive of English verse at least approximately comparable in form and content to Italian madrigal poetry. One could not write madrigals to the lyrics in *Tottel's Miscellany* (1557) or *The Paradise of Daynty Devises* (1576), which are for the most part stiff, stanzaic, alliterative and still "courtly" in the late medieval tradition (Apel 478).

Sidney wrote the English madrigal-poem, probably in order to change the barren state of the genre in England. The English madrigal-poem could not compete with the Italian one, nor could it compete with the English sonnet and blank verse. Of course it could not meet the demand of the development of English madrigal music. When the Italian Renaissance spread quickly in Elizabethan England, the English court had showed its favour to this alien music. It was natural for Sidney, the courtier who had visited Italy during his grand tour on the European continent and was familiar with Italian culture, invented a new design for English madrigal-poem.

Sidney's madrigal-poems are of high value both in the expression of the meanings and feelings and in the construction of the poetical form. But, as is mentioned above, it is not easy to set to music. In this respect, Sidney's experiment might be a failure.

Maybe Sidney just wants to try more poetical forms in his *Old Arcadia*, for he has many new designs in this romance. Many of these new designs appear in the English literature for the first time. And Sidney may feel unconfident in popularizing his madrigal-poem (and many other new poetical forms), for he deletes his two madrigal-poems in his revision of the Arcadian romance. Some authoritative collections of Elizabethan literary works, especially the collections of Elizabethan poetry, do not included Sidneian madrigal-poems. The reader cannot find such poems in a book like *The Oxford Book of English Madrigals* too, in which the sixty madrigals of both music and poem have shown a comparatively complete view of the genre from its rise in the sixteenth century to the fall in the seventeenth century. The facts have explained Sidney's failure too:

> The English madrigals differs, then, from its Italian prototype basically in the greater attention it gives to the overall musical structure, in

its "preoccupation with purely musical devices, a reluctance to follow the Italians in splitting up compositions mercurially at the whim of the text. The English madrigalist is first of all a musician; his Italian colleague is often more of a dramatist. (Grout and Palisca 177)"

Because English musicians pay more attention to the overall music structure, they will not allow that the words become the obstacles of musical expression. In the actual practice, a musician often chooses those poems simple in structure. That will be easy for him to control three or more voices in a madrigal music:

MY Love in her attire doth show her wit,
   It doth so well become her:
For every season she hath dressings fit,
   For Winter, Spring, and Summer.
No beauty she doth miss
   When all her robes are on:
But Beauty's self she is
   When all her robes are gone (Chambers, E. K. 891).

This is an anonymous madrigal-poem of the sixteenth century. It is divided into two quatrain stanzas, much simpler in structure than Sidney's pattern. The rhymes are arranged orderly and with repetition, i. e. , in *abab cdcd.* In the first stanza, the decasyllabic lines and the heptasyllabic lines alternate. In the second stanza, two pairs of hexasyllabic lines form the parallel structure. The simplicity of the poetical form provides a madrigalist much freedom in his composition of music. The parallel structure of the poem is not difficult to be woven into the repetition of the musical melody. The madrigal is often a vocal music of polyphony. Lines like "But Beauty's self she is // When all her robes are gone" will not appear sluggish when the decorated sounds scatter among the words. The rhythm of the poem and the melody of the music will not easily be affected. The lines are more suitable to sing than Sidney's "yet those I sende // Hurte not the face, which nothing can amende". Besides, the quatrain stanza is the tradition of English poetry, which mingles the foreign madrigal-poem with a native colour.

Thomas Weelkes's madrigal "O Care, thou will despatch me" is one popular song in the sixteenth century. The poem set to it is representative among the English madrigal-poems. Its first part is:

O care, thou wilt despatch me,
If music does not match thee.
So deadly dost thou sting me,
Mirth only help can bring me.

The form of the poem assimilated the metrical pattern of the English ballett. Donald Jay Grout praises the poem that particularly "notable is the opening, with its learned imitations in both direct and contrary motion and the chain of suspensions to convey the poet's complaint" (177). Musical melody advances through the partial repetition of each line in the stanza, and reaches its climax.

> The expressive and pictorial traits in the music of the madrigals are combined with accurate, nimble declamation of the English texts. The accents of the words are maintained independently in each voice, so that the ensembles produce sparkling counterpoints of endless rhythmic vitality. More over, with all the sharpness of details, the long line of the music is never obscured (178-179).

Compared with these simple madrigal-poems, Sidney's lyric seems more graceful but less easy to be set to music. His elegant lines display his talent and taste, which are noble and mannerly. The euphuistic style is harmonious with that in the *Old Arcadia*. But, as is mentioned above, the complicated form makes it difficult to be set to music. If the beginning part of the alternation of the decasyllabic lines and the hexasyllabic lines causes no difficulty for musicians, the dense and irregular arrangement of the following decasyllabic lines will thoroughly change the situation and daunt the musicians. The repetition of a single sound or a simple phrase can be sent out clearly in the chorus or in the overlapping or interlocking voices. A short line with a complete grammatical structure is easily adopted. In addition, one line from a poem is usually repeated in several musical phrases, which means the music that Sidney's madrigal-poem set would be very long.

The bloom of English madrigal lasted not very long and was replaced by opera. Many Elizabethan poets were even not ready to complete their apprenticeship in exercising the madrigal-poem when both the musical and the literary trend changed. Sidney has the capability of trying new and difficult poetical forms, most of his contemporaries do not.

Sidney's madrigal-poem expresses the native sense and native colour. It is English lyric. But his madrigal-poem also shows that he has not amalgamated poetry and music in this genre. Anyway, his effort in designing the English madrigal-poem is valuable to the cultural construction of the English nation, no matter what result his efforts lead to.

6.4 Sonnet and Sonnet Sequence

Before Sidney, Wyatt and Surrey had already introduced the Italian sonnets into England in the mid-sixteenth century. But there was a temporary neglect of this poetical form by English poets in the following two decades except Gascoigne and a few people. The flourish of Elizabethan sonnet writing came just with the production by Sidney and his contemporaries. Sidney's experiments appears important to the maturing of the form at the beginning of the English sonnet history—indeed it is necessary and urgent to establish the form of the English sonnet at the beginning.

Sidney has both the foreign and domestic models in his writing. On the one hand, the Italian and French sonnets had been flooding into the Elizabethan England. The brilliant lyrical form attracted both talented and mediocre poets. On the other hand, the astounding Wyatt and Sweet Surrey were admired as sonnet pioneers on the island. Their works were eagerly imitated. Among the foreign sonneteers, Petrarch influences the English poets profoundly. The translations of his poems into English are in the number far larger than his Italian compatriots and most poets of vernaculars from other countries (May and Ringler 2320-2336). Sidney is certainly influenced by Petrarch, which is shown in his treatment of the poetical form and partly the theme of poetry. Petrarch's sonnets are personal, eulogizing some kind of secular and even sensual love to a definite woman Laura. Sidney's sonnets are dramatic, chanting a spiritual love of Platonism to an imagined lady Stella. It is perilous to think that *Astrophil and Stella* is but a confession of Sidney to a lady Rich he might have met once or twice. In treating the theme, Sidney may have the poems of Wyatt and Surrey as his models. Wyatt's sonnets are personal, but they sing no secular love. Surrey's sonnets are dramatic, dealing with the love theme in an uncertain way. Wyatt and Surrey had already done most works in establishing not only the form of English sonnet but also its subject. For example, in the form of an English sonnet, the whole poem is woven with iambic pentameter lines. It consists of three quatrains and a rhymed couplet. In the subject and the treatment of the subject, the more or less Platonic love is presented in a dramatic way in which the poet keeps a distance with the speaker in the poem. Sidney seldom violated the rule of iambic pentameter except in four poems of Hexameters and three poems of hendecasyllabic lines. ① He combined the foreign and domestic sonnet forms and, after experiments, invented an amalgamation of the Italian octave with a *cdcdee* sestet. In the choice and treatment of the subject, Sidney follows the English custom and intensifies the dramatic effect of his sonnets.

Some early sonnets Sidney composes in the *Old Arcadia* and *Certain Sonnets* are constructed by following Surrey's example, arranged in the pattern consisting of three quatrains plus a rhymed couplet:

> Loved I am, and yet complaine of Love:
> As loving not, accus'd, in Love I die.
> When pittie most I crave, I cruell prove:
> Still seeking Love, love found as much I flie.
> Burnt in my selfe, I muse at other's fire:
> What I call wrong, I doo the same, and more:
> Bard of my will, I have beyond desire:
> I waile for want, and yet am chokte with store.
> This is thy worke, thou God for ever blinde:
> Though thousands old, a Boy entit' led still.
> Thus children doo the silly birds they finde,
> With stroking hurt, and too much cramming kill.
> Yet thus much Love, O Love, I crave of thee:
> Let me be lov'd, or els not loved be (OA 20).

---

① Comparing with the total of his 157 sonnets, these seven poems are only a few. But they are important for that they show one direction of Sidney's exploration of sonnet forms. The Hexameter shows the influence of the French Alexandrine on Sidney's sonnets as well.

The four-line stanza is one of the most popular poetical forms in English prosodic tradition. Sidney uses the structure of three quatrains with a couplet in the sonnet to replace the Italian structure of octave plus sestet. The design itself is in accordance with the English prosodic convention, making the feelings and the meaning the poem conveys expressed in different progression from the Italian mode. In an Italian sonnet, the thought ascends to a climax through the octave and descends to a conclusion in the sestet (Courthope 91); the transition from octave to sestet generally is realized through a *volta* (turn), paralleling the mood or argument of the poem. ① There is a division or a turning point between the first eight lines and the last six lines, both in form and in meaning:

Amor, che nel penser mio vive et regna
e 'l suo seggio maggior nel mio cor tene,
talor armato ne la fronte vène,
ivi si loca, et ivi pon sua insegna.
Quella ch'amare et sofferir ne 'nsegna
e vòl che 'l gran desio, l'accesa spene,
ragion, vergogna et reverenza affrene,
di nostro ardir fra se stessa si sdegna.
Onde Amor paventoso fugge al core,
lasciando ogni sua impresa, et piange, et trema;
ivi s'asconde, et non appar piú fore.
Che poss'io far, temendo il mio signore,
se non star seco infin a l'ora extrema?

① T. V. F. Brogan thinks that "the volta is significant because both the particular rhymes unifying the two quatrains of the octave and also the envelope scheme are abandoned simultaneously, regardless of whether this break is further reinforced syntactically by a full stop at the end of the octave (though usually it is), creating a decisive 'turn in thought'" (Preminger and Brogan1367).

Ché bel fin fa chi ben amando more (Petrarca 140).①

The poet offers in the lines of octave the evidences for the poetical syllogism, pushing the argument to its climax. Love enters the speaker's mind, and settles there, and then dominates the speaker, enslaving the speaker. Then the poet turns to account how love is tamed by the lady whom the speaker loves, drawing the conclusion in the sestet unhurriedly. The passion is accumulated to the climax in the end of octave, and then it calms down in an enough space of the sestet. Thus, a balance reaches in the dramatic expression.

Sidney's sonnet coincides with the Elizabethan poets' understanding:

> Sonnets which are of fouretene lynes, euery line conteyning tenne syllables. The firste twelue do ryme in staues of foure lines by crosse meetre, and the last two ryming togeither do conclude the whole (Smith, i 55).

---

① Wyatt and Surrey translated this poem into English respectively. Wyatt's translation is an unsuccessful imitation of the Italian mode: "The long love that in my thought doth harbour/ And in mine heart doth keep his residence, / Into my face presseth with bold pretence, / And therein campeth, spreading his banner. / She that me learneth to love and suffer/ And will that my trust and lust's negligence/ Be reined by reason, shame and reverence, / With his hardness taketh displeasure. / Wherewithal unto the heart's forest he fleeth, / Leaving his enterprise with pain and cry, / And there him hideth, and not appeareth. / What may I do, when my master feareth, / But in the field with him to live and die? / For good is the life ending faithfully." (Wyatt 5) Surrey turns the structure of Petrarch's poem into his three quatrains of alternate rhymes and a rhyming couplet: "Love, that doth reign and live within my thought, / And built his seat within my captive breast, / Clad in the arms wherein with me he fought, / Oft in my face he doth his banner rest. / But she that taught me love and suffer pain, / My doubtful hope and eke my hot desire/With shamefast look to shadow and refrain, / Her smiling grace converteth straight to ire. / And coward Love, then, to the heart apace/ Taketh his flight, where he doth lurk and plain, / His purpose lost, and dare not show his face. / For my lord's guilt thus faultless bide I pain, / Yet from my lord shall not my foot remove: / Sweet is the death that taketh end by love." (Hollander and Kermode 124-125.)

Such a design suggests that the first idea Sidney accepts about sonnet is from the native poets, from Gascoigne's summary of Surrey. The example of the twentieth poem from the *Old Arcadia* shows that he does not well control the English mode. The accumulation of the expression of both the meaning and feelings should be constantly kept in the three quatrains, reaching its climax just before the forceful ending couplet. In his early experiments, Sidney often cannot solve the problem well. The accumulation does not continue with enough tension and the ending couplet appears weak.

Anyway, Sidney's endeavour to improve the English sonnet never ceases. The most frequently used sonnet pattern in Sidney's *Astrophil and Stella*, the sequence of his later and mature sonnets, is an amalgamation of the Italian octave and the English remaining part, or rather, is an English sonnet mingled with a very strong Italian design:

Alas, whence came this change of lookes? If I
  Have chang'd desert, let mine owne conscience be
  A still felt plague, to selfe condemning me:
Let wo gripe on my heart, shame loade mine eye.
But if all faith, like spotlesse Ermine ly
  Safe in my soule, which only doth to thee
  (As his sole object of felicitie)
With wings of *Love* in air of wonder flie,
  O ease your hand, treate not so hard your slave:
In justice paines come not till faults do call;
Or if I needs (sweet Judge) must torments have,
Use something else to chast'n me withall,
  Then those blest eyes, where all my hopes do dwell,
  No doome should make one's heav'n become his hell (AS 86).

The first eight lines are constructed in an Italian octave. It is a narration and explanation of the speaker's pathos, developing accumulatively in the intensity. The structure of sestet is different from the Italian mode in form but similar in function. It consists of a quatrain with the alternate rhymes and a rhymed couplet, sharing the structural similarity with the last six lines of the English sonnet mode. But the progression is in the Italian style— the speaker's mood calms down after he pours out his feelings to Stella. The ending couplet serves as both an extension of the sestet progression in the expression and a relatively independent conclusion of the poem, differentiating the design from the sheer Italian pattern. It is strange for Sidney to employ such a hybrid pattern. Although it is difficult to accomplish, it is not so forceful as the English sonnet improved in the hand of Shakespeare. One of the extraordinary features in the structure of Shakespeare's sonnet is the impressiveness of the rhymed ending couplet. Sidney did not reach Shakespeare's epigrammatism. But his experiments attract the later English poets like Milton seeking inspiration directly from Petrarch the Italian master. The wavering between the Italian mode and the English structure reflects that Sidney does not fully make clear the merits of the two designs. Neither Wyatt and Surrey, nor Gascoigne has a thorough insightful comprehension as Shakespeare or Milton does. And Spenser is no better than Sidney on this aspect. The transplantation of Italian sonnet into the English poetry, with their efforts, is not focused on the structure of logical progression, but on the arrangement of the end rhymes. This focus is misleading. Many people thus believe that the difference between the Italian sonnet and the English sonnet is the different stanzaic arrangement caused by the different scheme of end rhymes. The importance of the scheme of end rhymes in Sidney's conception of sonnet is the musicality it produces.

Sidney has used as many as thirty-nine schemes of end rhymes in his sonnet writing, many of which were used only once, showing the assiduity of

Sidney's practice (Ringler 570-571). Some of his early sonnets have five rhymes, as most of Petrarch's poems do in the *Il Canzoniere*; some have even less. Sidney might intentionly refute the canard that English poets avoid the Italian form because of the difficulty of finding thymes (lviii), for he believes that English is capable of any excellent exercise. The schemes Sidney uses most frequently, which, in his early sonnets, is the English sonnet pattern *ababcdcd efefgg*, in the later works, are the patterns *abbaabba cdcdee* and *abababab cdcdee*. All these three schemes are based on the arrangement of three quatrains plus one rhymed couplet, indicating that Sidney always insists on forging the English sonnet patterns. The third kind of rhyming scheme is only a difficult variation of the common English sonnet mode:

> When Nature made chiefe worke, Stella's eyes,
> In colour black, why wrapt she beames so bright?
> Would she in beamie blacke, like painter wise,
> Frame daintiest lustre, mix of shades and light?
>   Or did she else that sober hue devise,
> In object best to knit and strength our sight,
> Least if no vaile those brave gleames did disguise,
> They sun-like should more dazle then delight?
>   Or would she her miraculous power show,
> That whereas blacke seems Beautie's contrary,
> She even in blacke doth make all beauties flow?
> Both so and thus, she minding *Love* should be
>   Placed ever there, gave him this mourning weed,
>   To honor all their deaths, who for her bleed (AS 7).

The poem has five rhymes, with three in the sestet, like the usual design of the English sonnet; however, with only two in the octave, it has the difficulty of composition by reducing the number of rhymes. The alternative rhyming is not the Italian mode, but a salient English rhyming tradition, at least in sonnets. It is interesting that the combined effect of both the syntactic structure mark "or" and the rhyming scheme affirms the English tint of the sonnet though, the enjambment in the twelveth line and the thirteenth violates its English identity. The experimental characteristics are still obvious in Sidney's mature sonnets.

The Foreign influence on Sidney's sonnet writing is also revealed in Sidney's experiments on the hendecasyllabic line and the Alexandrine. There is one sonnet in the *Old Arcadia* (OA 69), written in the hendecasyllabic lines, which explains the learning of Sidney from Petrarch. As is shown in the example of one hundred and fortieth poem from *Il Canzoniere*, most of Petrarch's sonnets are written in the hendecasyllabic lines (*endecasillabo*) with feminine rhymes, utilizing the abundant vowels of Italian. The sixty-ninth poem in Sidney's the *Old Arcadia* is composed according to the sheer Petrarchian pattern of Italian sonnet. All the fourteen lines are of hendecasyllables, forming the octave with the first eight lines and the sestet with the last six lines, rhyming *abbaabba cdecde* with feminine rhymes. And there are two other poems, the eleventh poem in Sidney's *Certain Sonnets* and the fifty-seventh poem in the *Old Arcadia*, containing the hendecasyllabic lines. Two hendecasyllabic lines with feminine rhymes form the ending couplet of the former, slowing down a bit of the rhythmical tempo of the poem, leaving the reader a lasting echo of the melody and of the speaker's lamentation. The even lines, except the last one, of the latter poem are hendecasyllabic. They are woven alternatively with the decasyllabic lines, which are at the odd positions in the poem, into an English sonnet design:

Beautie hath force to catch the humane sight.
Sight doth bewitch, the fancie evill awaked.
Fancie we feele, encludes all passion's mighte,
Fancie rebelde, oft reason's stregth hath shaked (OA 57).

It is an amusing weaving of the two kinds of lines. The odd lines are decasyllabic; the even lines are hendecasyllabic. ① The odd lines rhyme in masculine rhymes and the even lines in feminine rhymes. The contrastive qualities appear alternatively in the poetical melody, serving well the speaker's (Pyrocles disguising in Cleophila) two thoughts toward Basilius and Gynecia at the same time. The rhyming scheme of the poem is in the pattern of the English sonnet. The decasyllabic lines with masculine rhymes produce a stiff tune, suggesting an attitude of refusal. The hendecasyllabic lines with feminine rhymes produce a soft melody, implying tender passion of love. Such a design is just suitable to Sidney's story. It is also an innovative exploration.

Sidney composes six sonnets with the Alexandrine lines in his *Astrophil and Stella*. Two of them (AS 1 and AS 77) are rhymed in the English sonnet mode. One (AS 6) is in *ababbaba ccdeed*, a combined form of the Italian rhyme pattern and the English one. One (AS 102) is in the Italian pattern. And two (AS 8 and AS 76) are in *abbaabba cdcdee*, Sidney's favorite arrangement in his mature sonnets. The variation of the rhyme patterns is rich enough to compete the sonnets by his contemporary French poets. And the Alexandrine lines Sidney writes in English do not lack the gracefulness of the French counterparts. The first poem in *Astrophil and Stella* is often praised by the readers. For example,

---

① The ending syllable of the word "fancie" and the first syllable of "evill" in the second line are coalesced by liaison.

> Loving in truth, and faine in verse my love to show,
> That the deare She might take some pleasure of my pain:
> Pleasure might cause her reade, reading might make her know,
> Knowledge might pitie winne, and pitie grace obtaine (AS 1).

The symmetrical balance of the French Alexandrine is presented in these English lines. The method for realizing this merit in Sidney's lines is similar to that in the French verse: the design of the English pause is based on the French principle. As for the stress pattern of the French Alexandrine, Sidney replaces it with the English accentual-syllabic metre, here, the iambic hexameter, which is more effective in giving the prominence of the balanced stress pattern. The paralleled linguistic structures are kept through the pauses, exhibiting the aesthetic symmetry. The smooth and meditative melody spreads itself in the lengthy and fluid metrical design of the lines.

Sidney has used the Italian *endecasillabo* and the French Alexandrine in his sonnets. But his usual sonnet line is the iambic pentameter one. The techniques Sidney uses to construct his decasyllabic lines and his stanzaic structures, like the designs of substitutes, pauses and enjambmentdiscussed in Chapter Four, are also noteworthy in his sonnet experiments. Besides, he explores to enlarge the structure of sonnet through adding lines to more than fourteen (e. g. OA 38, OA 49 and OA 50 etc.). A further experiment Sidney carries on uniquely is that he tries to relate the sonnets "to one another to produce larger and more complex unities" (Ringler lix). The extraordinary example is that

> In *Astrophil and Stella*, instead of collecting a mere aggregate of sonnets and songs, he arranged them to provide a narrative and

psychological progression, and so produced a sequence that is more dramatic and highly ordered than any other in the renaissance (lix).

The *Astrophil and Stella* is just like a long poem recording the progress of meditation on love of Astrophil, an imagined speaker, to his admired lady, Stella. ① The sonnets and songs are the stanzaic parts in it. A thread of mood presentation records the courtship from the hopeful commencement to the unsuccessful but still hopeful denouement. The first sonnet announces the purpose of writing like a prologue. And from the second sonnet on there is a retrospective recounting of Astrophil's psychological experience of love: the reluctance to be subdued by the attraction from Stella (AS 2-12), the lovesickness to Stella (AS 13-51), the attempt to win the love of Stella (AS 52-viii), and the reaction to the refusal of Stella (AS ix-108), etc. Accompanied with the change of feelings, Sidney designs different poetical forms to match it. For instance, the one hundred and first sonnet is written with iambic hexameters. The lines of twelve syllables appear lengthy when it is arranged in a regular accentual iambic metre:

Where be those Roses gone, which sweetned so our eyes?
  Where those red cheeks, wich oft with faire encrease did frame
  The height of honor in the kindly badge of shame?
Who has the crimson weeds stolne from my morning skies?

They are suitable to set forth Astrophil's feeling after the failed love. The

① The scholars of Sidney studies, like Sherod M. Cooper, disagree that there exist a complete love story in *Astrophil and Stella*. It is true. But they all acknowledge the integrity of the sonnet sequence. Of course Sidney did not always keep this integrity satisfactorily, which causes the suspicion of some scholars to his organizational plan.

structure of this sonnet is arranged in the Italian mode. The wail of Astrophil echoes through the octave in the description of the sad scenes, in the accumulation of the piled metaphors. Then in the sestet, the description turns to Astrophil's imagination of Stella's love. It is love makes Stella beautiful, giving colors to the scenes before Astrophil himself. The pathetic meditation is conveyed with the smooth and slow lines of iambic hexameters.

The sonnet form Sidney invented through the combination of the Italian octave and the structure of the last six lines of English sonnet is abundantly used in illustrating Astrophil's speculation of love. The lines of this Sidneian sonnet are usually in the iambic pentameters. A debate or an argument can be fully developed in the first eight lines, and then the resolution is given in the next six lines. Such arrangement reminds the reader of the structure of an Italian sonnet. But the rhymed ending couplet of English sonnet is preserved and effective in this construction. The fifty-second sonnet displays such a structure. "*Love*" and "*Vertue*" dispute the possession of Stella. "*Love*" declares the body of Stella, while "*Vertue*" holds her soul. The strife is spread in the octave through a contrastive arrangement. Then the argument continues in the first four lines of the latter part of the poem with an analysis. The ending rhymed couplet gives Astrophil's conclusion.

The match of mood and poetical form is revealed through the arrangements of the songs in the *Astrophil and Stella* as well. All the songs are distributed near but before the climax of the passion presentation, like the songs sung by the chorus in the equivalent position in a play. These songs together show the intensity of Astrophil's feelings. At the same time they are used individually to convey emotion of the speaker in a specific condition:

> Night hath closd all in her cloke,
> Twinckling starres Love-thoughts provoke:

Dange hence good care doth keepe,
Jealousie it selfe doth sleepe:
Take me to thee, and thee to me.
"No, no, no, no, my Deare, let be (AS iv)."

The fine night, the starry sky and the peaceful darkness are described in the falling rhythm, depicting a light surrounding. The short lines add the airy atmosphere with their briefness. The rising rhythm of the last two lines vividly imitates the hurried whispering of the frivolous suitor and the firm refusal of the lady. The structure of this stanza is repeated throughout the song, which describes a hasty and whispering mood.

Sidney's contribution to the English sonnet is that he helps in fixing the form with possible metrical arrangements and that he probes into the extended sonnet form and sonnet sequence which are organic through his design. He has explored more than thirty-nine rhyming schemes and thirty-three varieties in sonnet structures both of the Italian and English types (Ringler lviii; 570-571). Such an assiduous work is rare even among those of the most diligent Elizabethan sonneteers. Sidney is not the first who introduces the sonnet from Italy into England, but he is among the pioneers who are important in improving the English genre.

Sidney also had experimented other foreign forms of poetry, such as the epithalamium and the hymn, anglicizing them to a great advantage. But his poems of these genres are inferior to the some of his contemporaries. For example, Spenser had composed two epithalamia which are among the best of the English wedding songs and have influenced the later generations more greatly than Sidney's poems. Therefore, the exploration in Sidney's uninfluential poetical experiments has to be limited.

Conclusion

The contribution of Sidney to English poetry may not be mainly reflected in what he expressed in his poems but in how he expressed. He had formed some theoretical ideas on poetry, though he did not set up a complete theory system. These ideas seem summaries of those from his predecessors, containing his innovative thoughts which deserve thorough studies. They are not only opinions raised firstly in the history of English literary criticism; probably more important, the valuable poetical remarks in the development of Elizabethan lyrics. Sidney emphasized the specific approach for a poet to reach his poetic aim—designing an appropriate form. Therefore, he proposes theoretically the task of poetical construction, which is essential for the newly born modern English lyrics. The chorus of Elizabethan criticism sings highly of poetical construction, but few persons have an insight that Sidney possesses on this issue. Sidney highlights the poeticality of English language of his time, which makes him extraordinary not just among the Elizabethans, but also among the celebrities in the whole history of English literature. Considering the swift changes caused by the rapid growth of English, his opinion arises preciously. ① Sidney's analysis of the merits of his mother

---

① Sidney's consideration of the poeticality of English language of his time is worth mentioning when people turn their sight onto the construction of Chinese New Poetry after the New Cultural Movement launched at the beginning of the twentieth century. One important reason hidden under the sharp contrast between the achievement that the Elizabethan poetry (to be continued)

tongue in his "Defence of Poesie", exaggerated a bit though, does promote the "forging a poetical language" that the Tudor poets are struggling for (Ringler lii). Sidney's explanation of the relationship between poetry and music leads him to the exploration of the musical effects that the metrical pattern loads. The poetical construction of Sidney is based on the concept of "delightfulness", which includes the musicality that a poem conveys. Such a pursuit urges Sidney to apply his ideas into his practice.

One principal rule in Sidney's composition is that language determines the metrical design. The rule, together with Sidney's practice, ushers in a view of poetical construction different from what Gascoigne and his followers have adhered to. New conventions of metrical poems are established under the principle of predominance of language. The accentual-syllabic verse became the metrical basis of the poetical design in English poetry; and some devices were invented within the frame of the new metre. The feet substitution, the pauses, the enjambment are used to adjust the rhythmical contour of a line so as to avoid the conflict between language and metre and to enhance the effects of expression. Sidney might not be the inventor of these devices, but he has set up examples for other English poets in using them to form a flexible

---

(continued) reached in the past and the languishment the Chinese poetry expresses today might be that people from these two different countries and different times have different realization of the poeticality of the languages they used. Sidney, at the beginning of Elizabethan new poetry movement, drew the attention of his compatriots to study the poeticality of English when the language grew up fast, resulted in the heated debates on its subject and its application of the new poetry the Tudor poets were inventing. On the contrary, the study of the poeticality of Modern Chinese has just commenced till the end of the twentieth century when poets of Chinese New Poetry have groped blindly for almost a whole century. Even today, there are still many Chinese people who are not aware that the Chinese language they are using for poetry is not the same that their ancestors used in their poetry in the *Tang* dynasty. To make clear of the poeticality of Modern Chinese is an urgent cultural task to the Chinese people today, just as the poeticality of Modern English to Sidney and his contemporaries.

metrical line. The maturity of the accentual-syllabic verse resulted from the exertion of the Elizabethan poets in amalgamation of foreign prosodies and the English metrical tradition. Sidney had played a decisive role in the progress. He adopted Latin prosodical rules in his English composition and transplanted the classical quantitative verse into his design of English verse. Though Sidney's experiments were not successful, they made him be aware of the quantitative elements existing in the English syllables and their effects on the melody of English verse. These elements cannot be determinate in the rhythmical movement; however, they can work on the musicality of a line. Sidney's "delightful" poems have benefited from his experiments on English quantitative verse.

Sidney also assiduously constructed his stanzaic forms by imitating the established patterns or by devising his own. He made the enjambment and the rhymes as his tools in connecting the separate lines into stanzas. The enjambment maintains the completeness of language structures across the lines while the rhymes enhance the musicality of the metrical design and at the same time influence the rhythmical contour of a stanza. Sidney innovatively revived the feminine rhyme and made it "a formal structural element in shaping his stanza" (lvi). He anglicized foreign poetry genres and tamed them in his writing.

> His critical preoccupation is shown by his being the first to introduce into English many of the terms which today are part of our basic vocabulary when talking about poetry—"couplet", "lyric", "madrigal", "masculine rhyme", "octave", "stanza", etc. He was also the first Englishman to give formal list of the traditional classical kinds—pastoral, elegiac, iambic, satiric, comic, tragic, lyric, and heroic. ... No previous English poet, from Old English to Tudor times, even approached Sidney

in the variety and complexity of metrical forms that he used (lviii).

In addition, the elegiacs, the Sapphic stanza, the sonnet and sonnet sequence become influential after Sidney's practice. The bloom of English madrigal at the turn of the sixteenth and seventeenth centuries bore the impact of Sidney's exertion. Sidney's poetical construction helped to invigorate the songbird's nest of Elizabethan dynasty.

It is noticeable that Sidney was not only a literary practitioner but also a disseminator of new ideas. He advocated the exploration of Latin metre through "Areopagus", a literary salon set up by him, and launched the "quantitative movement" (Attridge 129-135) in England in the latter part of the sixteenth century. His sonnet sequence has been imitated by many English poets, including Spenser and Shakespeare. His patronage also helped to spread the new established conventions via his practice.

Sidney's endeavours in his poetical construction answered the demand of the growth of English civilization. What he wanted to do in learning the foreign prosodies and poetical genres was to anglicize them, to assimilate their useful elements to enrich the English poetry. The need of his own civilization decides his thoughts and activities. Sidney had his sense of nativeness when he encountered the alien poetical ideas and products. Sidney's insightful ideas and successful poetical practice were mostly inspired by the urgency of the poetical construction, which in fact was part of his national culture construction of his time. Some of these ideas are still gaining people's admiration and usher them to reexamine the significance of these ideas to their own cultures.

Works Cited

Abrams, M. H. Ed. *The Norton Anthology of English Literature*, 6th edition, volume i. New York & London: W. W. Norton & Company, Inc., 1993.

Adams, Hazard and Leroy Searle. Ed. *Critical Theory Since Plato*, 3rd edition. Boston: Thomson Wadsworth, 2005.

Apel, Willi. *Harvard Dictionary of Music*, 2nd edition, revised and enlarged. Cambridge: The Belknap Press of Harvard University Press, 1979.

Aristotle. *Metaphysics*. W. D. Ross. Trans. *English Classics* 3000. CD-ROM. Beijing: Peking University Press, 2009.

Armstrong, David. *Horace*. New Haven & London: Yale University Press, 1989.

Aronoff, Mark and Kirsten Fudeman. *What Is Morphology*? Malden: Blackwell Publishing, 2005.

Attridge, Derek. *Well-weighed syllables: Elizabethan verse in classical metres*. London and New York: Cambridge University Press, 1974.

Attridge, Derek. *Poetic Rhythm: An Introduction*. Cambridge: Cambridge University Press, 1995.

Ault, Norman. Ed. *Elizabethan Lyrics: from the Original Texts*. London: Faber and Faber Ltd., 1986.

Baldick, Chris. *Oxford Concise Dictionary of Literary Terms*. Shanghai:

Shanghai Foreign Language Education Press, 2000.

Barber, Charles. *Early Modern English.* London: André Deutsch Limited, 1976.

Baudelaire, Charles. "Les Fleurs du mal," LXXXIX, "Le Cygne". *Six French Poets of the Nineteenth Century.* E. H. and A. M. Blackmore. Ed. Oxford: Oxford University Press, 2000.

Baugh, Albert C. and Thomas Cable. *A History of the English Language*, 5th edition. London & New York: Routledge & Kegan Paul, 2002.

Bec, Christian. *Précis de littérature italienne.* Paris: Presses Universitaires de France, 1982.

Blake, Norman. Ed. *The Cambridge History of the English Language*, Volume II. Beijing: Peking University Press, 2002.

Boulton, Majorie. *The Anatomy of Poetry.* London: Routledge & Kegan Paul Limited, 1953.

Bridges, Robert. *Milton's Prosody.* Oxford: Oxford University Press, 1921.

Britannica Encyclopaedia. http://www.britannica.com/eb/article-9110446/poetry, 09/13/2006.

Buxton, John. *Sir Philip Sidney and the English Renaissance.* London: Macmillan & Co. Ltd., 1964.

Bysshe, Edward. *The Art of English Poetry* (1702). Electronic Text Center, University of Virginia Library. (2000) http://etext.lib.virginia.edu/etcbin/toccer-new2?id=BysEngl.sgm&images=images/modeng&data=/texts/english/modeng/parsed&tag=public&part=all, 07/27/2006.

Catullus, Gaius Valerius. *The Poems of Catullus.* Ed. and Trans. Guy Lee. Oxford: Oxford University Press, 1998.

Chambers, E. K. Chosen. *The Oxford Book of Sixteenth Century Verse.* London: Oxford University Press, 1976.

Chaucer, Geoffrey. "Troilus and Criseyde". *The Riverside Chaucer*, 3rd edition. Ed. Larry D. Benson. Oxford: Oxford University Press, 1988.

Chaucer, Geoffrey. "The Complaint of Chaucer to His Empty Purse." *Six Centuries Great Poetry.* Robert Penn Warren and Albert Erskine. Ed. Now York: Random House, Inc., 1992.

Chiappelli, Fredi. "Madrigal". *Dictionary of Italian Literature.* Ed. Bondanella, Peter and Julia Conaway Bondanella. Westport: Greenwood Press, 1979.

Corbett, Edward P. J. *Rhetoric for the Modern Students*, 3rd edition, 1998.

Courthope, W. J. *A History of English Poetry*, vol. ii. London: Macmillan and Co., Limited, 1935.

Cruttenden, Alan. *Gimson's Pronunciation of English*, 6th edition. Beijing: Foreign Language Teaching and Research Press, 2001.

Crystal, David. *The Cambridge Encyclopedia of Language*, 2nd edition. Beijing: Foreign Language Teaching and Research Press, 2002.

Cuddon, J. A. *A Dictionary of Literary Terms*, revised edition. London: Andre Deutsch, 1979.

Dickens, Charles. *A Tale of Two Cities.* New York: Bantam, 1981.

Du Bellay, Joachim. *Les regrets.* http://dillenschneider.net/Poesie/DuBellay/Sileslarmesservaientderemedeaumalheur.html, 08/17/2006.

Duncan-Jones, Katherine. *Sir Philip Sidney: Courtier Poet.* London: Hamish Hanmilton Ltd., 1991.

Feuillerat, Albert. Ed. *The Complete Works of Sir Philip Sidney*, vol. iii. Cambridge: Cambridge University Press, 1923.

Flewett, H. W. and W. E. P. Pantin. *A First Book of Latin Poetry.* London: Macmillan & Co. Ltd., 1958.

Garrett, Martin. "The Introduction". *Sidney: The Critical Heritage.* Martin Garrett. Ed. London: Routledge, 1996.

Gascoigne, George. "Up the theme: Magnum vectigal parcimonia." *The*

Penguin Book of Renaissance Verse. H. R. Woudhuysen. Ed. London: Penguin Books Ltd., 2005.

Gascoigne, George. "The Looks of a Lover Enamoured." *Elizabethan Lyrics: from the Original Texts*. Norman Ault. Ed. London: Faber and Faber Limited, 1986.

Gebert, Clara. Ed. *An Anthology of Elizabethan Dedications & Prefaces*. Philadelphia: University of Pennsylvania Press, 1933.

Grimald, Nicholas. "A Truelove." *Elizabethan Lyrics: from the Original Texts*. Norman Ault. Ed. London: Faber and Faber Limited, 1986.

Grout, Donald Jay and Claude V. Palisca. *A History of Western Music*, 4th edition shorter. New York: W. W. Norton and Campany, Inc., 1988.

Gussenhoven, Carlos and Haike Jacobs. *Understanding Phonology*. Beijing: Foreign Language Teaching and Research Press, 2001.

Hardison, O. B. Jr. *Prosody and Purpose in the English Renaissance*. Baltimore and London: The Johns Hopkins University Press, 1989.

Hardy, Thomas. "Postponement." *Wessex Poems and Other Verses*. Project Gutenberg Etext. http://www.gutenberg.org/dirs/etext02/wsxpm10.txt, 09/03/2006.

Hegel, Georg Wilhelm Friedrich. *Āsthetik* (*Aesthetics*). ZHU Guangqian. Trans. (Chinese version). Beijing: The Commercial Press, 1981.

Hollander, John and Frank Kermode. Ed. *The Literature of Renaissance England*. New York: Oxford University Press, 1973.

Howaston, M. C. and Ian Chilvers. Ed. *Oxford Dictionary of Classical Literature*. Shanghai: Shanghai Foreign Language Education Press, 2000.

Jensen, De Lamar. *Renaissance Europe: Age of Recovery and Reconciliation*. Lexington: D. C. Heath and Company, 1981.

Keppel-Jones, David. *The Strict Metrical Tradition: Variations in the Lterary*

Iambic Pentameter from Sidney and Spenser to Matthew Arnold. Montreal & Kingston: McGill-Queen's University Press, 2001.

Kuiper, Koenraad and W. Scott Allan. *An Introduction to English Language: Word, Sound and Sentence*, second edition. New York: Palgrave Macmillan, 1996.

La Chanson de Roland. LXXI, http://www.fh-augsburg.de/~harsch/gallica/Chronologie/11siecle/Roland/rol_ch01.html; http://www.fh-augsburg.de/~harsch/gallica/Chronologie/11siecle/Roland/rol_ch02.html, 10/02/2006.

Lass, Roger. Ed. *The Cambridge History of the English Language*, Vol. III. Beijing: Peking University Press, 2002.

Law, Vivien. *The History of Linguistics in Europe from Plato to 1600.* Cambridge: Cambridge University Press, 2003.

Leitch, Vincent B. *The Norton Anthology of Theory and Criticism.* New York & London: W. W. Norton & Company, Inc., 2001.

Lewis, C. S. *English Literature in the Sixteenth Century, excluding drama.* Oxford: Oxford University Press, 1954.

Li Funing. Ed. *Ouzhou Wenxue Shi* (*History of European Literature*), vol. I. Beijing: Commercial Press, 1999.

Li Funing. *Yingyu Shi* (*History of English*). Beijing: Commercial Press, 1991.

Longeon, Claude. *Premiers combats pour la langue française.* Paris: Librairie Générale Française, 1989.

Machlis, Joseph and Kristine Forney. *The Enjoyment of Music: An Introduction to Perceptive Listening*, 7th edition. New York: W. W. Norton & Company, 1995.

Mallarmé, Stephane. "Plusieurs Sonnets". *Six French Poets of the Nineteenth Century*. E. H. and A. M. Blackmore. Ed. Oxford: Oxford University

Press, 2000: 286.

May, Steven W. and William A. Ringler, Jr. Ed. *Elizabethan Poetry: A Bibliography and First-line Index of English Verse*, 1559-1603. London & New York: Thoemmes Continuum, 2004.

Milton, John. *The Annotated Milton: Complete English Poems.* Burton Raffel. Ed. New York: Bantam Books, 1999.

Ou Hong. "Foreign Literature and the Sense of Nativeness." *Dangdai Wentan Bao (Contemporary Literary World)*, 1988.

Ovid. *Metaporphoses*, VIII. qtd. in. H. W. Flewett and W. E. P. Pantin. A First Book of Latin Poetry. London: Macmillan & Co. Ltd., 1958.

Partridge, A. C. *The Language of Renaissance Poetry.* London: Andre Deutsch, 1971.

Petrarca, Francesco. "L'arme tue furon gli occhi, onde l'accese." *Il Canzoniere.* http://petrarch.petersadlon.com/canzoniere.html, 10/05/2006.

Petrarca, Francesco. "Your weapons were those eyes, where burning." http://petrarch.petersadlon.com/canzoniere/the_canzoniere.txt, 09/01/2006.

Pound, Ezra. "Apparuit." *Ezra Pound: Poems and Translations.* New York: The Library of America, 2003

Preminger, Alex and T. V. F. Brogan. Ed. *The New Princeton Encyclopedia of Poetry and Poetics.* Princeton: Princeton University Press, 1993.

Prynne, J. H. *Poems.* Fremantle: Fremantle Arts Centre Press; Highgreen and Tarset: Bloodaxe Books Ltd., 2005.

Puttenham, George. *The Arte of English Posie.* Ed. Gladys Doidge Willcock and Alice Walker. Cambridge: The University Press, 1936.

Quirk, Randolph et al. *A Comprehensive Grammar of the English Language.* Beijing: World Publishing Corporation, 1989.

Raven, D. S. *Latin Metre.* London: Faber and Faber Limited, 1965.

Ringler, William A. Jr. Ed. *The Poems of Sir Philip Sidney.* Oxford: Clarendon Press, 1962.

Ramzani, Jahan et al. Ed. *The Norton Anthology of Modern and Contemporary Poetry*, 3rd edition, Volume 1. New York and London: W. W. Norton & Company, Inc., 2003.

Roca, Iggy and Wyn Johnson. *A Course in Phonology.* Oxford: Blackwell Publishers Ltd., 1999.

Roe, John. "Theories of Literary Kinds." *A Companion to English Renaissance Literature and Culture.* Michael Harttaway. Ed. Oxford: Blackwell Publishers Ltd., 2000. 287.

Ronsard, Pierre de. "Les Amours d'Hélène." *Anthologie de la littérature française*, Troisième édition, Tome I. Robert Leggewie. Ed. New York & Oxford: Oxford University Press, 1990.

Rudenstine, Neil L. *Sidney's Poetic Development.* Cambridge & Massachusetts: Harvard University Press, 1967.

Sabatier, Robert. *La Poésie du XVIe siècle.* Paris: Albin Michel, 1975.

Saintsbury, George. *A History of English Prosody*, Volume I. London: Macmillan and Co. Limited, 1923.

Saintsbury, George. *A History of English Prosody*, Volume II. London: Macmillan and Co. Limited, 1923.

Saintsbury, George. *Historical Manual of English Prosody.* New York: Schocken Book Inc., 1966.

Schipper, Jakob. *A History of English Versification.* Oxford: Clarendon Press, 1910.

Shakespeare, William. *The Complete Works of William Shakespeare.* W. J. Craig. Ed. Oxford: Oxford university Press, 1924.

Sidney, Sir Philip. *Sir Philip Sidney: The Major Works.* Ed. Katherine

Duncan-Jones. Oxford: University Press, 1989.

Sidney, Sir Philip. *The Countess of Pembroke's Arcadia* (*Old Acadia*). Ed. Katherine Duncan-Jones. Oxford: Oxford University Press, 1999.

Smith, G. Gregory. Ed. *Elizabethan Critical Essays* (two volume). Oxford: Clarendon Press, 1904.

Sorley, W. R. *A History of British Philosophy to* 1900. Westport: Greenwood Press, Inc., 1973.

Spenser, Edmund. *The Shepherd's Calendar and Other Poems*. Ed. Philip Henderson. London: J. M. Dent & Sons Ltd., 1978.

Spenser, Edmund. *Edmund Spenser's Poetry*. Ed. Hugh Maclean. W. W. Norton & Company, Inc., 1982.

Stolba, K. Marie. *The Development of Western Music*: *A History*, 2nd edition. Boston: Wm. C. Brown Communications, Inc., 1994.

Stumpf, Samuel Enoch. *Socrates to Sartre*: *A History of Philosophy*, 5th edition. New York: MacGraw-Hill, Inc., 1993.

Tasso, Torquato. *Gerusalemme Liberata*, CXLIV. http://www.liberliber.it/biblioteca/t/tasso/gerusalemmeliberata/html/completo.htm, 08/31/2006.

Thompson, John. *The Founding of English Metre*. London: Routledge & Kegan Paul, 1961.

Townsend, Dabey. *An Introduction to Aesthetics*. Malden: Blackwell Publishers Inc., 1997.

Trumble, W. R. and A. Stevenson. Ed. *Shorter Oxford English Dictionary*: *On Historical Principles*, 5th edition. Oxford: Oxford University Press, 2002.

Verlaine, Paul. "Sagesse I," XIX. *Six French Poets of the Nineteenth Century*. E. H. and A. M. Blackmore. Ed. Oxford: Oxford University Press, 2000.

Verlaine, Paul. "Sagesse III," X. *Six French Poets of the Nineteenth*

Century. E. H. and A. M. Blackmore. Ed. Oxford: Oxford University Press, 2000.

Verlaine, Paul. "Mon Rêve familier." *Six French Poets of the Nineteenth Century*. E. H. and A. M. Blackmore. Ed. Oxford: Oxford University Press, 2000.

Virgil. *Aeneid*. http://vergil.classics.upenn.edu/workspace/display_frame.html, 10/19/2006.

Ward, A. W. and A. R. Waller. Ed. *The Cambridge History of English Literature*, Vol. III. Cambridge: Cambridge University Press, 1949.

Warren, Robert Penn and Albert Erskine. Ed. *Six Centuries of Great Poetry*. New York: Random House, Inc., 1955.

Whitman, Walt. *Complete Poetry and Collected Prose*. New York: The Library of America, 1982.

Woudhuysen, H. R. Ed. *The Penguin Book of Renaissance Verse*. London: Penguin Books Ltd., 2005.

Wyatt, Sir Thomas. *Collected Poems*. Joost Daalder. Ed. London, Oxford, New York: Oxford University Press, 1975.

Selected Bibliography

Alexander, Gavin. Ed. *Sidney's 'The Defence of Poetry' and Selected Renaissance Literary Criticism.* London: The Penguin Groups, 2004.

Bailey, Cyril. Ed. *The Legacy of Rome.* Oxford: The Clarendon Press, 1968.

Baum, Paul Franklin. *The Principles of English Versification.* Cambridge: Harvard University Press, 1929.

Beardsley, Monroe C. *Aesthetics from Classical Greece to the Present: A Short History.* New York: The Macmillan Company, 1966.

Bec, Christian. *Précis de littérature italienne.* Paris: Presses Universitaires de France, 1982.

Berley, Mare. *After the Heavenly Tune: English Poetry and the Aspiration to Song.* Pittsburgh: Duquesne University Press, 2000.

Berry, Francis. *Poets' Grammar: Person, Time and Mood in Poetry.* London: Routledge and Kegan Paul Ltd., 1958.

Binns, J. W. *Intellectual Culture in Elizabethan and Jacobean England: The Latin Writings of the Age.* Leeds: Francis Cairns (Publications) Ltd., 1990.

Boitani, Piero. and Jill Mann. Ed. *The Cambridge Chaucer Companion.* Shanghai: Shanghai Foreign Language Education Press, 2000.

Bolgar, R. R. *The Classical Heritage and Its Beneficiaries.* Cambridge: Cambridge University Press, 1977.

Bondanella, Peter and Julia Conaway Bondanella. *Dictionary of Italian Literature*. Westport: Greenwood Press, 1979.

Braden, Gordon. *The Classics and English Renaissance Poetry: Three Case Studies*. New Haven and London: Yale University Press, 1978.

Bradford, Richard. *The Look of It: A Theory of Visual Form in English Poetry*. Cork: Cork University Press, 1993.

Bradford, Richard. *A Linguistic History of English Poetry*. London and New York: Routledge, 1993.

Brogan, T. V. F. *English Versification*, 1570-1980: *A Reference Guide with a Global Appendix*. Baltimore and London: The Johns Hopkins University Press, 1981.

Castiglione, Baldassare. *The Book of the Courtier*. Sir Thomas Hoby. Trans. London: J. M. Dent & Sons Ltd., 1974.

Cockcroft, Robert. *Rhetorical Affect in Early Modern Writing: Renaissance Passions Reconsidered*. New York: Palgrave Macmillan, 2003.

Conrad, Carl W. *From Epic to Lyric: A Study in the History of Traditional Word-Order in Greek and Latin Poetry*. New York and London: Garland Publishing, 1990.

Conrad, Peter. *The History of English Literature; One Indivisible, Unending Book*. Philadelphia: University of Pennsylvania Press, 1985.

Cooper, Sherod M. Jr. *The Sonnets of Astrophil and Stella: A Stylistic Study*. Paris: Mounton & Co., N. V., Publishers, The Hague, 1968.

Coup, W. A. et. al. *The Continental Renaissance*: 1500-1600. Harmondsworth: Penguin Books Ltd., 1971.

Courthope, W. J. *A History of English Poetry* (six volumes). London: Macmillan and Co., Limited, 1922-1935.

Delumeau, Jean & Thierry Wanegffelen. *Naissance et Affirmations de la Réforme*. Paris: Presses Unversitaires de France, 2003.

Duby, Georges. *Histoire de la France des origines à nos jours.* Paris: Larousse, 2003.

Duncan-Jones, Katherine. *Sir Philip Sidney: Courtier Poet.* London: Hamish Hamilton Ltd., 1991.

Erskine, John. *The Elizabethan Lyric: A Study.* Now York: Colombia University Press, 1903.

Evans, Maurice. Ed. *Elizabethan Sonnets.* London: J. M. Dent & Son Ltd., 1977.

Fabb, Nigel. *Language and Literary Structure: The Linguistic Analysis of Form in Verse and Narrative.* Cambridge: Cambridge University Press, 2002.

Fabb, Nigel. *Linguistic and Literature.* Oxford: Blackwell Publishers Ltd., 1997.

Feuillerat, Albert. Ed. *The Complete Works of Sir Philip Sidney* (four volumes). Cambridge: Cambridge University Press, 1923.

Fox, Alistair. *The English Renaissance: Identity and Representation in Elizabethan England.* Oxford: Blackwell Publishers Ltd., 1997.

Fox, Barbara A. *Discourse Structure and Anaphora: Written and Conversational English.* Cambridge: Cambridge University Press, 1987.

Freeborn, Dennis. *From Old English to Standard English*, second edition. Beijing: Foreign Language Teaching and Research Press, 2000.

Gayley, Charles Mills and Clement C. Young. *English poetry: Its Principles and Progress.* New York: The Macmillan Company, 1906.

Gilbert, A. J. *Literary Language from Chaucer to Johnson.* London: The Macmillan Press Ltd., 1979.

Grazia, Margreta de. et al. Ed. *Subject and Object in Renaissance Culture.* Cambridge: Cambridge University Press, 1996.

Greville, Fulke. *Life of Sir Philip Sidney.* Oxford: The Clarendon Press,

1906.

Gross, Harvey. *Sound and Form in Modern Poetry: A Study of Prosody from Thomas Hardy to Robert Lowell.* Ann Arbor: The University of Michigan Press, 1965.

Hall, John. *The Sociology of Literature.* London and New York: Longman Group Limited, 1979.

Harttaway, Michael. Ed. *A Companion to English Renaissance Literature and Culture.* Oxford: Blackwell Publishers Ltd., 2000.

Hogg, Richard M. general Ed. *The Cambridge History of The English Language.* (Hogg, Richard M. Ed. vol. i; Blake, Norman. Ed. vol. ii; Lass, Roger. Ed. vol. iii; Romaine, Suzanne. Ed. vol. iv; Burchfield, Robert. Ed. vol. v; Algeo, John. Ed. vol. vi). Bejing: Peking University Press, 2002.

Hollander, John. *Melodious Guile: Fictive Pattern in Poetic Language.* New Haven and London: Yale University Press, 1988.

Hollander, John. *Rhyme's Reason: A Guide to English Verse* (new, enlarged edition). New Haven and London: Yale University Press, 1979.

Holt, Mack P. Ed. *Renaissance and Reformation France*: 1500-1648. Oxford: Oxford University Press, 2002.

Horne, Merle. *Prosody: Theory and Experiment.* Dordrecht: Kluwer Academic Publishers, 2000.

Kallendorf, Craig. Ed. *Landmark Essays on Rhetoric and Literature.* Mahwah: Lawrance Erlbaum Associates, Inc., Publishers, 1999.

Kalstine, David. *Sidney's Poetry: Contexts and Interpretations.* Cambridge: Harvard University Press, 1965.

Keen, Ralph. *The Christian Tradition.* Upper Saddle River: Prentice Hall, Inc., 2004.

Kennedy, George A. *A New History of Classical Rhetoric.* Princeton:

Princeton University Press, 1994.

Kennedy, George A. *The Cambridge History of Literary Criticism*, volume 1. Cambridge: Cambridge University Press, 1993.

Ker, William Paton. *The Art of Poetry: Seven Lectures*. Oxford: The Clarendon Press, 1925.

Klein, Lisa M. *The Exemplary Sidney and the Elizabethan Sonneteer*. Newark: University of Delaware Press, 1998.

Knecht, R. J. *The Rise and Fall of the Renaissance France: 1483-1610*, 2nd edition. Oxford: Blackwell Publishers Ltd. , 2001.

Kristeller, Paul Oskar. *Renaissance Thought and the Arts, Collected Essays*. Princeton: Princeton University Press, 1990.

Ledger, Philip. Ed. *The Oxford Book of English Madrigals*. London: Oxford University Press, 1978.

Lee, Sidney. Ed. *Elizabethan Sonnets*, newly arranged and indexed. New York: E. P. Dutton and Co. , 1905.

Leech, Geoffrey N. *A Linguistic Guide to English Poetry*. Bejing: Foreign Language Teaching and Research Press, 2001.

Leggewie, Robert. ed. *Anthologie de la littérature française*, troisième édition, tome i. New York & Oxford: Oxford University Press, 1990.

Lemon, Lee T. and Marion J. Reis. trans. *Russian Formalist Criticism: Four Essays*. Lincoln and London: University of Nebraska Press, 1965.

Levinson, Jerrold. *The Oxford Handbook of Aesthetics*. Oxford: Oxford University Press, 2003.

Lowes, John Livingston. *Conventions and Revolt in Poetry*. London: Constable & Co Ltd. , 1930.

Lyas, Colin. *Aesthetics*. London: UCL Press Limited, 1997.

MacEachern, Claire. *The Poetics of English Nationhood*, 1590-1612. Cambridge: Cambridge University Press, 1996.

Martinnich, A. P. *The Philosophy of Language*, fourth edition. New York & Oxford: Oxford University Press, 2001.

Matz, Robert. *Defending Literature in Early Modern England: Renaissance Literary Theory in Social Context.* Cambridge: Cambridge University Press, 2000.

Maynard, Winfred. *Elizabethan Lyric Poetry and Its Music.* Oxford: The Clarendon Press, 1986.

Miles, Josephine. *Major Adjectives in English Poetry: From Wyatt to Auden.* Berkeley and Los Angeles: University of California Press, 1946.

Morgan, Kenneth O. Ed. *The Oxford History of Britain*, revised edition. Oxford & New York: Oxford University Press, 1999.

Murray, Gilbert. *The Classical Tradition in Poetry.* Cambridge: Harvard University Press, 1927.

Myrick, Kenneth Orne. *Sir Philip Sidney as a Literary Craftsman.* Cambridge: Harvard University Press, 1935.

Nicoll, Allardyce. *The Elizabethans.* Cambridge: Cambridge University Press. 1957.

Norton, Glyn P. ed. *The Cambridge History of Literary Criticism*, volume 3. Cambridge: Cambridge University Press, 1999.

Page, Norman. Ed. *The Language of Literature: A Casebook.* London: The Macmillan Press Ltd., 1984.

Palliser, D. M. *The Age of Elizabeth: England Under the Later Tudors* 1547-1603, 2nd edition. London and New York: Longman Group UK Limited, 1992.

Partridge, A. C. *English Biblical Translation.* London: André Deutsch Limited, 1973.

Pask, Kevin. *The Emergence of the English Author: Scripting the Life of the*

Poet in Early Modern England. Cambridge: Cambridge University Press, 1996.

Payen, Jean Charles et Henri Weber. *Manuel D' histoire Littéraire de la France*, tome I. Paris: Editions Sociales, 1971.

Perloff, Marjorie. *Poetic License: Essays on Modernist and Postmodernist Lyric.* Evanston: Northwestern University Press, 1990.

Perrine, Laurence. *Sound and Sense: An Introduction to Poetry.* San Diego: Harcourt Brace Jovanovich, Inc. , 1982.

Porter, Simon. *Changing English*, 2nd edition. London: Andre Deutsch Limited, 1975.

Prynne, J. H. *Stars, Tigers and the Shape of Words.* London: The William Matthews Lectures Delivered at Birbeck College, London, 1992.

Ratcliffe, Stephen. *Campion: On Song.* Boston: Routledge & Kegan Paul Ltd. , 1981.

Raven, D. S. *Greek Metre: An Introduction.* London: Faber and Faber Limited, 1962.

Richards, I. A. *Practical Criticism: A Study of Literary Judgement.* New York: Harcourt, Brace and Company, 1929.

Rowse, A. L. *The England of Elizabeth: The Structure of Society.* London: Macmillan & Co. Ltd. , 1951.

Saintsbury, George. *A History of English Prosody* (three volumes). London: Macmillan and Co. Limited, 1923.

Saintsbury, George. *A History of Elizabethan Literature.* London: Macmillan and Co. Limited, 1920.

Shapiro, Michael. *Asymmetry: An Inquiry into the Linguistic Structure of Poetry.* Amsterdam: North-Holland Publishing Company, 1976.

Smith, G. Gregory. Ed. *Elizabethan Critical Essays* (two volumes).

Oxford: Clarendon Press, 1904.

Smith, Hallett. *Elizabethan Poetry: A Study in Conventions, Meaning, and Expression.* Cambridge: Harvard University Press, 1952.

Spearing, A. C. *Readings in Medieval Poetry.* Cambridge: Cambridge University Press, 1987.

Stevens, John. *Music & Poetry in the Early Tudor Court.* Cambridge: Cambridge University Press, 1979.

Stravinsky, Igor. *Poetics of Music: in the Form of Six Lessons.* Arthur Knodel and Ingolf Dahl. Trans. Cambridge: Harvard University Press, 1970.

Symonds, John Addington. *Blank Verse.* London: John C. Nimmo, 1894.

Symonds, John Addington. *Sir Philip Sidney.* London: Macmillan and Co. Limited, 1909.

Turco, Lewis. *The New Book of Forms: A Handbook of Poetics.* Hanover & London: University Press of New England, 1986.

Underhill, John Garrett. *Spanish Literature in the England of the Tudors.* New York: The Columbia University Press by the Macmillan Company, 1899.

Vickers, Brian. Ed. *English Renaissance Literary Criticism.* Oxford: Clarendon Press, 1999.

Ward, A. W. and A. R. Waller. Ed. *The Cambridge History of English Literature* (fifteen volumes). Cambridge: Cambridge University Press, 1949.

Wallace, Malcolm William. *The Life of Sir Philip Sidney.* New York: Octagon Books, Inc., 1967.

Wellek, René and Austin Warren. *Theory of Literature.* Harmondsworth: Penguin Books Ltd., 1986.

Wilson, Mona. *Sir Philip Sidney*. London: Duckworth, 1931.

Wilson, Norman J. *World Eras*, vol. i. Farmington Hills: Gale Group, 2001.

Wimsatt, William K. Jr. & Cleanth Brooks. *Literary Criticism: A Short History*. New York: Alfred A. Knopf, Inc. , 1957.